THE LOST NOTEBOOK

LOUISE DOUGLAS

Boldwood

First published in Great Britain in 2022 by Boldwood Books Ltd.

Copyright © Louise Douglas, 2022

Cover Design by Becky Glibbery

Cover Imagery: Shutterstock

The moral right of Louise Douglas to be identified as the author of this work has been asserted in accordance with the Copyright, Designs and Patents Act 1988.

All rights reserved. No part of this book may be reproduced in any form or by any electronic or mechanical means, including information storage and retrieval systems, without written permission from the author, except for the use of brief quotations in a book review.

This book is a work of fiction and, except in the case of historical fact, any resemblance to actual persons, living or dead, is purely coincidental.

Every effort has been made to obtain the necessary permissions with reference to copyright material, both illustrative and quoted. We apologise for any omissions in this respect and will be pleased to make the appropriate acknowledgements in any future edition.

A CIP catalogue record for this book is available from the British Library.

Paperback ISBN 978-1-83889-292-0

Large Print ISBN 978-1-80483-390-2

Hardback ISBN 978-1-80483-391-9

Ebook ISBN 978-1-83889-293-7

Kindle ISBN 978-1-83889-294-4

Audio CD ISBN 978-1-83889-290-6

MP3 CD ISBN 978-1-80483-389-6

Digital audio download ISBN 978-1-83889-291-3

Boldwood Books Ltd
23 Bowerdean Street
London SW6 3TN
www.boldwoodbooks.com

PROLOGUE
MORANNEZ, BRITTANY

I have found him, the old woman wrote, *the last of the seven.*

She dragged the pen beneath the sentence, scoring an underline. She felt no satisfaction; no sense of victory; only sorrow.

And she was tired.

The light was fading and her eyes were hurting. She had done enough for now.

She picked up her phone and took a photograph of what she'd written. Then she lay the pen in the gulley between the open pages and put the book carefully on the ground beside her.

She leaned back in her chair beside the smoky little fire, and closed her eyes, rubbing at the pain in her knuckles. Somewhere in the woodland, an owl hooted.

When she started this quest the woman had been driven by passion and a desire for revenge. Now she only wanted it to be over, so she could go home.

It wouldn't be long. Soon, she would pass the book into the hands of the authorities. Justice would be served. Lessons would be learned.

The woman pulled the shawl tighter around her shoulders. The chair was padded with cushions, the fire was company of a kind and she was comfortable. She wasn't yet ready to climb into the old horsebox that she currently called home. She dreaded its dark interior; the loneliness; the struggle to sleep; the nightmares that assaulted her when she did.

She closed her eyes and recalled the red-tiled roofs of the houses in the town where she used to live, and beyond, the snowy peaks of the mountains. She remembered the café she and her family used to visit on Saturday mornings, her husband folding his newspaper and laying it down on the table with his spectacles on top. She recalled him catching her eye, taking her hand, raising it to his gentle lips. And their son, their only child, looking out across the square, waving to a schoolfriend. The waiter, a young man with blonde curly hair, bringing their coffee, saying: 'Isn't it a beautiful day?' The petrol smell of that aftershave all the boys used to wear in the eighties; the young man's confident, wide smile.

No, she wouldn't think of him.

The old woman sat by the fire, beside her rickety old van in the middle of the countryside and she sifted through her favourite memories, pulling them out like cards from a pack. Singing to her baby son in the dappled shade of the birch tree. The dimples on his fingers; the softness of his skin. Holding him on her lap as he fell asleep, kissing the dark hair. His first day at school; the pictures he used to bring home. A card for Mother's Day: a flower made of red tissue paper glued to a piece of cardboard.

She still had the card, but she no longer had the boy.

That was why she was here.

Because she loved him with all her heart and every atom of her being.

Because of love.

Because of him.

Story on the front page of Bretagne Today, the newspaper for English-speaking residents of north-west France

Could Morannez dig reveal the grave of the French Tutankhamun?

A six-month project being hailed as the most important archaeological excavation in decades began this week outside the seaside town of Morannez in southern Finistère.

A specialist team, including students from the University of Rennes, has been given the green light to excavate privately owned land close to the spot where the 'Morannez Hind' was discovered earlier this year.

The twenty centimetre whalebone statuette of an antelope was found in a cornfield, close to the famous Kyern dolmen. Tests have shown that it was carved more than 10,000 years ago.

The dig's director and lead archaeologist, Professor Timor Perry, said: 'Even in a region blessed with more than its fair share of standing stones, ancient burial tombs, and other Mesolithic and Megalithic remains, this discovery is exceptional and is generating an enormous amount of excitement amongst archaeologists, anthropologists and social historians worldwide.'

Professor Perry, 49, of Cambridge University, is one of Europe's leading authorities into the Mesolithic or Middle Stone Age, the period which lasted between 10,000 and 8,000 BC.

Preliminary ground works for the construction of a new restaurant on the site have been halted for six months to give the archaeology team the chance to investigate thoroughly.

A spokesperson for the dig sponsor, the World Archaeological Society, said: 'The Middle Stone Age was a time when our ancestors honed their creative and artistic skills. The rise of agriculture meant they were becoming settled, rather than nomadic, people. This gave them the time and space to paint, sculpt and decorate their utensils.'

In a paper submitted to the World Archaeological Society Magazine, Professor Perry heralded the find of the statuette as 'one of the most exciting ever to be discovered in Northern Europe'.

Project spokesperson and educational co-ordinator Alban Hugo, a teacher at Morannez International School, added: 'We're hoping the Hind is the first of many treasures to be uncovered. This site could be Europe's answer to the tomb of Tutankhamun!'

Pictured below are Professor Perry, holding a replica of the Hind, with Monsieur Hugo and Rennes University student volunteers beside the Kyern dolmen. The dolmen will remain open to visitors throughout the duration of the dig. Visit www.kyerndolmen.fr for more information.

THURSDAY, 28 JULY

It was nine o'clock in the evening, and still Ani was not home. Her aunt, Mila, pulled the two sides of her cardigan tight over her chest and walked to the gate at the end of the garden. The light was fading fast and Ani had promised she'd be back an hour ago.

Mila took her phone from the pocket of her shorts and checked for messages or missed calls. Nothing.

Where was Ani? *Where was she?*

Mila went out of the gate and walked fifty paces along the track beyond. There was no sign of Ani. No creaking of her bike chain, no dark shadow moving between the hedgerows that might be her, coming home.

It's probably fine, Mila told herself.

Ani is almost certainly perfectly fine.

It was highly unlikely that she'd been abducted or assaulted or raped or run over or got into a car driven by a teenage junkie.

Unlikely but not impossible.

Earlier, a long time earlier, at breakfast that morning, Ani had told Mila she was going to her friend, Pernille Sohar's house after school. 'I'll be back before eight,' she'd said.

Pernille's family lived in a luxurious modern villa up on the hill overlooking the coast. The girls were planning to celebrate the end of term by swimming in the Sohar family's pool and then having supper together.

Cecille Toussaint, Ani's grandmother and Mila's stepmother, had a suspicion Pernille's brother, JP, was the reason why Ani was suddenly keen on spending so much time at the Sohars'. Mila wasn't so sure. She hadn't observed Ani showing any of that kind of interest in boys yet.

Now she wondered if Ceci might be right. If she was, then wasn't it possible that Ani had gone for a walk with JP, that the two of them were in the woods that surrounded the Sohars' villa, perhaps, alone in the dusk? With alcohol? Was it appropriate for a fourteen-year-old girl to be on her own with a fifteen-year-old boy and a bottle of pastis?

What do you think, Sophie? Mila wondered.

She didn't need a response. If Ani's mother, Sophie, was still alive, she would have been happy for Ani to be with JP because Sophie assumed things would turn out well even when they blatantly wouldn't. She was always doing stupid things, like, for example, going sailing with her husband, Charlie, in their ridiculously small and flimsy boat when a storm was forecast.

Like drowning in the ensuing, utterly predictable accident – something that Mila, no matter how long she lived, would never be able to forgive.

It should be Sophie standing here, worrying about Ani, not Mila. It wasn't fair that the responsibility had ended up on Mila's shoulders; so much responsibility that she felt consumed by it.

She checked the phone again, *nothing*, crossed her arms, and paced the length of the garden.

Fourteen-year-old girls were often late home; it didn't mean anything awful had happened. It wasn't as if the town of Morannez was a crime capital. Although there *were* a great many strangers around – holidaymakers and seasonal workers and others who'd come because of the archaeological dig.

Mila felt literally sick with worry.

What if something terrible was happening to Ani at this exact moment and she, Mila, was doing nothing?

Well do something then, Sophie said.

What should I do?

Go and find her, Sophie answered. *Find our girl!*

Mila decided she'd cycle the route that Ani would take returning home from Pernille's and if she hadn't met her niece by the time she reached the Sohars' villa, then she'd raise the alarm that the girl was missing.

She went back inside, scrawled a quick note to Ani telling her to call and then wait at the sea house if they missed one another. She slipped on her tennis shoes, picked up Sophie's old bicycle – switched on the lamp and pushed it out into the lane. She mounted it and pedalled, wobbling at first then speeding up as she found her balance, along the track that led to the lane that ran parallel with the sea. A few kilometres away she could see the bright lights of Morannez town. People would be milling on the busy streets, perusing the menus outside the restaurants, enjoying their evening meals.

She remembered herself and Sophie, aged about eleven, walking behind Cecille and her second husband – Mila's father, Patrick – through the town, the girls giggling at some joke of Sophie's. It could have been difficult for the two of them, almost identical in age but so different in personality and life experience, being thrown together as stepsisters, but it never was. Shy, awkward Mila had been grateful that someone like Sophie would even think of being her friend, and was overwhelmed when Sophie began to refer to Mila as 'my sister'. It was lucky neither of them had any premonition of the trouble that lay ahead.

The bike lurched to the left. Mila put a foot down to prevent herself from falling. She shook away the image that had come unbidden into her mind: Sophie's body being carried to the shore, brought in by the tide after the accident, face down, her arms spread wide, fingers trailing in the water as if she was playing the piano and her hair floating around her like weed, lifting and falling as the water moved beneath it.

It was awful but it wasn't real. Mila had never seen Sophie's body. She didn't know why her subconscious tormented her with this false memory, ambushing her at the most unlikely times – not only hurting her emotionally but triggering a visceral fear.

An aeroplane cut through the sky high above. Mila looked up and saw how the sky had darkened; she saw the silver glow of a fragile moon, swathed in clouds. The Sophie image came again; this time she saw the detail of the Gallic triple spiral symbol, the triskele, tattooed on Sophie's wrist and she touched her own bare wrist and felt a clutch of grief. She wished she knew how to get through this sadness; this obsession with the past. She wished there was some plan she could follow; some routemap back to happiness.

Ani, she reminded herself. *You need to find Ani. She's all that matters now.*

She pushed the bike forward and set off again cycling through the gloaming, concentrating on the route until, after about a kilometre, she neared the T-junction at the end of the lane. To the right was a scrubby patch of land where teenagers came to ride their bikes; they had created ramps and jumps to make a circuit amongst the natural hills and dips. On the other side was a wide verge over-

hung with trees. This was where Mila saw a large black shadow –
an old van, and beside it a small fire was burning.

She recognised the van, a converted Renault horsebox that
looked to be on its last legs; she'd cycled past it several times
without paying much attention. It belonged to an old woman, a
'traveller', people said, who lived in the van and who had, for the
past few days, been making fires and drying her laundry on the
bushes. Depending on your point of view, the old woman was
either a charming eccentric, an object of pity or someone feral, who
would deter the tourists and ought to be chased out of town.

Mila slowed as she approached and saw that two people were
beside the fire: the squat, broad form of the old woman, and a slight
figure she knew very well – Ani.

Mila's heart leapt in relief at seeing her niece safe and well, and
almost at once the relief was chased away by its companion, anger.
Why hadn't Ani texted to say where she was? Why hadn't she come
straight home? Why did she insist on putting Mila through all this
stress? Why was she so selfish?

The girl was sitting on a camping chair, with her elbows on her
knees, leaning towards the flames. As Mila watched, the woman
stood up and crossed to the van where a collection of wood was
neatly stacked beneath a plastic sheet. She took a log from the stack
and put it onto the flames.

Mila let the bike roll to a stop, and laid it on the grass. She
called out: 'Hello!' so that the pair would not be alarmed by her
approach. She could see Ani clearly now in the light of the fire. One
of her knees was bandaged. A shawl was wrapped around her
shoulders and she was holding a mug between the palms of her
hands. Her face was lit by the flickering flames and she'd been
crying. Mila nodded to the old woman and went to the girl. She put
her arm awkwardly around her, feeling as if she was acting a role.

'What happened, Ani?' she asked. 'Are you all right?'

'I hit a pothole at the crossroads and fell off my bike,' Ani said. 'Gosia helped me.'

'Gosia?'

'Me,' the woman croaked. 'I'm Gosia.'

Close up she was like a caricature of someone aged; her face was so hoary and lined, hairs growing from a wart on her chin. She was wearing mismatched clothes: old trousers fastened with a piece of baling twine, a flowery shirt, a knitted cardigan, fingerless gloves and several shawls. Her body was toadlike.

'Thank you for looking after my niece,' Mila said stiffly.

The woman spat into the grass at the side of her chair.

Even though the smell of woodsmoke was pervasive, Mila could smell the woman: a musty, peaty smell. Beside her chair was an enormous book, like a ledger, too full of pictures and pieces of paper to close, with a pen lying in the gulley of its spine. One side of the open book was covered in lines of small, neat, handwriting. Clipped to the other page was a newspaper cutting. In the light of the fire, Mila could pick out a picture of the archaeology team at the Kyern dig with the famous prehistoric dolmen tomb behind. The face of one of the men in the foreground of the image had been circled with a marker pen.

Mila turned back to her niece.

Ani's face was small, her eyes swollen.

'You should have called me,' Mila said, more gently. 'I was so worried about you.'

'I broke my phone when I fell.' Ani scowled in a combative way as if challenging Mila to scold her for this. But the anger and fear were draining from Mila now, replaced with relief and sympathy for the child. She hadn't been selfish. She hadn't been losing track of time in the woods with JP. She'd fallen off her bike and injured herself, poor thing.

'How badly hurt are you?' she asked.

'It's mainly my knee.'

'Will you be able to walk home?'

'That's what I was going to do,' Ani said defensively, 'but Gosia said I should wait for you.'

'You were bound to come this way looking for her sooner or later,' said the old woman. She spoke English but slowly, with a thick accent that Mila could not place. Russian, perhaps?

'Waiting was the best idea,' said Mila. She turned to Gosia. 'Perhaps you'd like to come back with us, tonight. We have a spare room and you'd be most welcome to it.'

'I always sleep in my van,' the woman replied.

'Yes,' said Mila, 'but you're quite isolated here and...'

The old woman glanced at the book beside her. In the flickering of the fire, with her grey-white hair wisping wildly about her face, she seemed otherworldly, like a creature of mythology. She looked back towards Mila, and her eyes were bright and intelligent.

'I need to be here,' she said.

Why on earth would anyone need to be here, out by the woods, on their own? Mila wondered. But there was an adamance to the woman's tone that meant she did not try to persuade her to come. In her heart, she hadn't wanted her to accept the offer anyway. Now she knew Ani was safe, she was looking forward to a glass of wine and a quiet evening, once her niece was in bed, by herself.

* * *

They left Ani's bike with its buckled front wheel where it was, off the track at the edge of the woods, and walked back to the sea house together, Mila pushing Sophie's bicycle and carrying Ani's rucksack. Ani was still wearing the shawl Gosia had put around her shoulders. She was limping.

Neither Mila nor Ani spoke until they were out of the old woman's earshot.

Then Mila said: 'That was kind of Gosia to look after you.'

'Yes.'

'She was okay with you, was she?'

'What do you mean?'

'Only that she's a bit odd. I hope she didn't frighten you.'

'She was kind.'

'Oh. Good.'

They went a little further. The air was cooling. Insects were singing in the hedgerows.

'Did she tell you anything about herself?' Mila asked.

'No.'

'Nothing?'

'*No.*'

'What about the book? The one with all the writing?'

'Why do you have to ask me questions all the time?'

'I'm not asking about *you*, I'm asking about *her*.'

Ani sniffed. 'She said the book was her work.'

'Maybe she's a writer, then.' Mila didn't add: *Like me*, because Ani didn't know about the novel she was trying to finish. She hadn't wanted Ani to feel that Mila resented being in France or that she regarded her responsibilities here as a burden, even if, more often than not, she did.

She tried again. 'Does Gosia have friends in Morannez? Is that why she came here, perhaps?'

'She knows Jenny.'

'Jenny in the café?'

'Yeah. Jenny lets her charge her phone there.'

'Oh. Well, that's good.'

They walked on in silence for a little longer before Ani added, 'And she has a son.'

'A son?'

'She showed me some pictures. His name is Tomas. When he was my age, he wanted to be a vet.'

'Oh,' said Mila. 'That's nice. Did he get to be a vet?'

'Dunno,' said Ani.

And that was the end of that.

3

FRIDAY, 29 JULY

The next morning, Mila woke as dawn was breaking. A gold rim stretched across the lower part of the sky, beyond the branches of the trees that were catching the first rays in their uppermost branches. There was a haze hanging over the woodland to the north, which Mila took to be an early mist.

She dressed, came downstairs and made the instant coffee that she preferred to the rich 'proper' coffee that the French drank. After the first hit of caffeine, she examined Ani's phone, and concluded that it was broken beyond repair.

She took another drink and opened her laptop to see if any work emails had come in overnight.

Since Sophie's death, as well as looking after Ani, Mila had been helping Ceci with her business, Toussaint's Agency. In her heyday, Ceci had been a lawyer, representing people who worked in the film industry; that was how she had met Mila's father, the actor, Patrick Shepherd. A side-line to that work, and one that Cecille Toussaint had enjoyed, had been tracking down family members with whom her clients had lost contact over the years. In some cases, this was to bestow upon long-lost relatives some portion of an inheritance; in others, it was to settle a dispute, to arrange a divorce or simply a reunion.

After Sophie's addiction troubles, when Ceci realised it would be impossible for her to maintain her own high-flying career *and* take care of her daughter, she'd packed in the lawyering and set up her own agency, with Sophie established as her business partner. As well as searching for the missing, the agency also carried out minor investigative work. Sophie had confided in Mila that she was sure the job, indeed the business, had been created specifically to keep her busy and stop her thinking about *stuff*, but even if that was true, Toussaint's Agency was successful, with more than enough work to occupy both Sophie and Ceci. By the time of the boating accident, the agency was making a good profit each year and was regularly employing freelance private investigators and heir hunters to supplement their capacity.

When she first arrived in France, after Charlie and Sophie didn't come home from their sailing trip, Mila had been as anxious as Ceci and Ani. The coastguard told them that the couple had almost certainly encountered some kind of accident and that they should prepare themselves for the worst.

And then Sophie's body turned up on the shore, found by a dog walker early one morning – being found, ironically, being the incontrovertible evidence that she was lost. Telling Ani that her mother was dead had been the most difficult thing Mila had ever had to do. She did not consider abandoning the girl, a decision that, although it had felt right at the time, she had subsequently come to question on many occasions.

Charlie's body had never been found. Although they never talked about it, Ani still hoped he'd come back one day and Mila, although she didn't believe he would, hoped so too.

All Mila could think about, during those early, dreadful days, was making things better for Ani, even when it seemed things could never be made better. She had assumed, without really thinking it through, that sometime soon she'd be able to go home and return to her fledgling writing career. Her partner, Luke, was waiting in Bristol, their relationship now reduced to WhatsApp calls and text messages – sometimes a single emoji when Mila was too tired to talk. Looking after Ani, being strong for her, and finding the energy to buoy her through each day was exhausting, and it was enough. Mila had never intended to become involved at the agency; she'd never wanted to.

But then, on top of everything the little family was already dealing with, Ceci had had a heart attack. Mila was convinced that her stepmother's heart had actually broken, so devastated was she by the loss of Sophie, even though Ceci never spoke of her own grief. Whatever, she was nearly lost too; she had only been saved because of the quick reactions of the woman who worked in the patisserie shop beneath the agency offices who'd heard the thump on the floor above when Ceci had fallen.

The following day, Mila had gone to visit her stepmother in hospital and found her in a private room, propped against the pillows, with her glasses on her nose, her phone by her bed and her laptop rested on her knees.

'Ceci, what on earth are you doing?'

'Darling, don't look at me like that; I promised dear Anthony that I'd have the contact details he requested by the end of this week. I can't let the poor man down; he's always been so good to me.'

'This is crazy!' Mila had said. 'You need to *rest*, Ceci. You need to get better!'

'It won't take five minutes and then I've just got the London work to finish...'

'You're going to kill yourself!'

'No, I'm not. I'm strong as an ox.'

'You had a heart attack literally twenty-four hours ago!'

'Oh that, it was a scare, nothing to worry about.'

'The doctors told me it was "a severe myocardial infarction". *"Severe!"* They said it was amazing you survived.'

'Sweetheart, everyone knows how doctors exaggerate.'

'Ceci!'

What about me? Mila wanted to cry. *What's going to happen to me if you die? I'll never get back to my life! I'll be stuck here forever!*

She didn't say another word. She calculated that her only hope of ever returning to the UK was to get Ceci back on track as quickly as possible, and that meant Ceci resting. So, she'd perched on the bed beside her stepmother and peered over her shoulder at the computer screen.

'Explain what you're doing,' she'd said. 'Show me what has to be done. I can take over for a few days, until you're better.'

'Darling, I wouldn't put on you like that.'

'Ceci, I'm really tired and I haven't the energy to argue. Please just show me.'

So Ceci had shown her and Mila had picked the work up quickly; her previous experience in communications stood her in good stead. Her French wasn't brilliant, but around half of Ceci's clients were English-speaking anyway, so, when Ceci returned to full-time work, the two of them divided the cases between them according to language.

Mila had only ever intended to work at the agency for a few weeks, but the weeks had turned into months, months into almost a year. Every now and then, she would open the Word file that contained her novel on her laptop and read the first few chapters and the characters were like strangers to her. They had conversations she could not remember writing. She had forgotten some of their names.

Who's Evaline? she wondered. *What's Bathsheba doing in bed with William?*

She realised she could not dip in and out of writing any more than she could dip in and out of caring for Ani; it was either a full-blown commitment or nothing.

But at last things were resolving. In six weeks' time, Ani would be going away to boarding school and Mila would be free to go home. Ceci had been interviewing full-time replacements for Sophie at the agency and had narrowed them down to a shortlist of one – and he was due to take up his position any time now. Mila had promised the amendments to the novel requested by the publisher would be made by the end of November. Once she was back in Bristol, in her own home, with nobody besides Luke making demands on her time and energy – and Luke was so tied up in his own work with the police that he could never be described as 'demanding' – then she could see no reason why she shouldn't have the changes made in time. Her life, at last, would be back on track.

That morning, curled in one corner of the sofa in the living room of the sea house, with sunlight streaming through the window, and the feel of high summer in the air, Mila felt a kind of contentment that came with knowing this part of her life would soon be over. She almost enjoyed responding to the queries that had come into Toussaint's Agency because she knew she wouldn't have to answer such emails for much longer. She worked quickly and by the time she had finished, it was almost eight o'clock. Not too early to wake Ani.

She went into the kitchen, poured milk into a pan and detected a faint smell of burning. She checked the cooker and the toaster: nothing was accidentally switched on. It must, she thought, be coming from outside. Berthaud, the cat, was sleeping in a patch of sunlight on the wooden table. Mila leaned over and sniffed her fur. It was definitely smoky. A farm fire, then. Manure heaps sometimes combusted spontaneously, especially during spells of warm weather.

When the hot chocolate was made, Mila carried it upstairs, knocked lightly on the door to Ani's bedroom, and went in. The smell of smoke was stronger here. Mila put the cup on the shelf at the side of Ani's bed. The girl was curled up, her face tucked under the patchwork top cover, only her dark hair spread about the pillow. Mila put a hand gently on her shoulder and said, 'Wake up, sleepy-head.' Then she went to the window and pushed back the curtain.

A cloud of thick smoke was hanging, not above the farm, but rather the woods where Gosia's van was parked.

4

The old woman had been camped by the woods for some time and Mila had never noticed smoke during daylight hours before. She knew Gosia was careful because the previous evening's fire had been safely contained in a small pit. This was something altogether different.

Perhaps Gosia had lit a fire to heat water for coffee for her breakfast, and the fire had run through the grass at the edge of the woods and ignited the fallen pine needles and cones that lay at the feet of the trees. These were tinder-dry and would burn hot and fast.

'Ani, I'm going to go back to where we were last night to make sure Gosia's all right,' Mila called across the room. 'I won't be long.'

"Kay,' Ani said, turning over beneath the bedclothes. She added: 'I need a new phone.'

'I know.'

* * *

Mila cycled the same route she'd travelled the previous evening, only this time the darkness had been replaced with brightness, the gloom with glorious colour. White laceflower frothed amongst the greenery at each side of the lane, and pink dots of wild geranium blooms brightened the hedgerows. Birdsong filled the trees and occasionally the artificial chimes and bongs of the music that was blasted through the speakers at Morannez's AquaSplash water park drifted over from a distance. Mila stood on the pedals, her chest heaving with the exertion, occasionally cycling into a patch of smoke.

As she approached the spot where the old van was parked, the air thickened and her eyes began to sting. She narrowed them, laid down the bike and went forward.

The smoke was wreathed around the horsebox like a scarf; the morning air was still and it moved slowly, circling the vehicle with malevolence.

'Gosia!' Mila called. 'Hello!'

There was no sign of the old woman but she heard laughter and scuffling from behind the van.

On this side, nothing moved, apart from the prowling smoke. But shadows were breaking up the bright daylight falling onto the ground on the other side. Mila crouched down and looked underneath. She could see the bottom half of several pairs of legs.

Kids.

'Who's there?' she called again in a fiercer voice.

The scuffling intensified and there was some nervous giggling.

Feeling more confident, she stepped around the side of the van and saw four teenage boys running into the woods, where they picked up bikes and cycled off. The source of the smoke was now obvious. The boys had made a fire, using the wood that Gosia had collected for her own use and they'd used her furniture, the chair on which she'd been sitting the previous evening and the collapsible camping chair that Ani had used, to sit upon. Cushions and shawls were draped on the ground.

From the scraps of food that lay around, Mila surmised the boys had been cooking sausages and making hot dogs. They'd probably brought the food to cook in the woods, but seen the chairs outside the van, and the neatly stacked wood, and taken advantage of it.

They'd thrown green wood onto the fire, which accounted for the quantity of smoke. Mila stamped on the ashes until the fire was extinguished. She picked up the shawls and folded them over the back of the chair and placed the cushions back on their seat.

She looked around. Still no sign of Gosia.

The old woman might have risen early and walked into town; she might be eating breakfast at Jenny's café while she waited for her phone to charge.

Or she might still be inside the van. She might have decided to stay there while the kids were outside, fearing they might taunt her, although that seemed unlikely. Mila hadn't spent much time with Gosia, but she didn't seem the kind of woman to be easily intimidated.

What if she'd had an accident, or been taken sick during the night?

In daylight, the van looked worse than it had done at dusk. It was battered, dented and dirty, as old and careworn as the woman who owned it. Weeds had begun to grow up around the tyres and the grass beneath the chassis was yellowing and dry. Now the boys were gone, the only sound was birdsong in the trees.

How lonely, Mila thought, *to wake to this each morning.*

She walked around the vehicle. There were two small windows on one side, at a height where, if the van had been carrying horses, they could have looked out. The windows were too high for Mila to look in.

She stood next to it, with the side of her head pressed against it, but couldn't hear anything inside.

For fuck's sake, Sophie whispered in her ear. *Just knock on the door and if there's no answer, open it.*

Mila took a deep breath, went to the back, knocked gently, and called: 'Hello! Gosia? It's Mila from last night!'

When there was no response, she knocked again, her heart thumping. 'I'm opening the door,' she called. 'Don't be alarmed; I only want to make sure you're okay.'

The handle was within easy reach. Mila pressed down on it, half-expecting it to be locked from the inside, but it wasn't. She opened the door a fraction. The air that squeezed out from inside the van was colder than that on the outside. It had a strange, sour odour.

'Hello?'

The door swung wide. Mila narrowed her eyes to accustom them to the gloom of the interior. A small ladder lay on the floor. She pulled it out, hooked it in place and climbed up, the van rocking with her weight as she did so.

It was a cramped space: cluttered, but not untidy. There was a bed of sorts, a mattress on a wooden shelf attached to the back of the driving cab, which took up about half of the available room. In front of this was a storage area. Pans, plastic washing bowls, a large cool box and a tatty shopping trolley on wheels; a huge old raincoat and books, dozens of books in boxes. Mila peered at the spines but her eyes hadn't completely adjusted to the dark and the titles were in a language she couldn't understand.

More urgently, she could tell from the hump beneath the covers on the bed that Gosia was still in it.

She stepped cautiously, the floor of the van creaking beneath her feet, noting the transistor radio, the bucket, a roll of toilet paper, a tube of hand cream. Only three steps to the bed, where the smell was worse. She stood on a drawing pin and it pierced the thin sole of her tennis shoe and bit into the flesh of her foot. She resisted the urge to cry out, stood on one leg to pull the drawing pin out, and placed it on the shelf. Through all this, there was no movement from the bed.

'Gosia?' she whispered.

The old woman was lying with her back to Mila, the cover pulled right up to her ears.

'Gosia?'

As Mila's eyes became used to the gloom, she studied the bedding. She couldn't see any of the lift and fall that she would expect to see if the person beneath it was breathing. The wispy grey hair that sprouted from a waxy skull was motionless on the pillow. There was no sound at all.

This was how Mila knew, even before she put a gentle hand on the old woman's forehead, that Gosia was dead.

5

Mila was afraid of death. All her life, she'd done her best to avoid it, turning her head from the corpses of deer at the side of the road, steering clear of the meat on the shelves in the supermarkets. She had had pets which had died, but she'd never had to deal with the aftermath directly, herself. And although she could have gone with Ceci to identify Sophie's body, she had chosen not to. She didn't want the memory of her dead stepsister to be imprinted in her subconscious forever – ironic given how she was plagued by fake flashbacks.

Even though Gosia was someone she hadn't known well, even though the situation was peaceful, her death was still a shock to Mila. It was also discomfiting to realise that she was going to have to deal with the consequences of being the person who'd found the body. As far as she was aware, the traveller woman had nobody in Morannez, no family who cared for her. It was Mila's responsibility to make sure that Gosia was treated with dignity and respect.

She left the body where it was, went the few steps to the open door at the back of the van, and jumped down onto the hard ground outside, too eager to escape to bother with the ladder. She dusted herself down, took the phone out of her pocket and reported the death to the doctor.

The doctor said that she would come at once and the operator at the gendarmerie also said her colleagues would get there as quickly as they could. Still, Mila estimated she had a good ten minutes to wait. At this time in the morning, the town would be teeming with tourist traffic which was bound to delay the official vehicles.

Mila's mouth was dry as ash. She looked around and located the container that held Gosia's supply of water. She lifted it up, raised the tap and drank from the nozzle. The water was lukewarm and tasted of plastic.

She didn't want to go back inside the van, but now was the only opportunity to look around before the police and doctor arrived. Mila didn't think there was anything suspicious about Gosia's death, but her sense of responsibility towards the other woman made her feel she ought to take another look.

Luke would be sure to ask if she had done so when she told him about this over the phone later. Luke was a detective with the Avon and Somerset police and during the course of their relationship, almost ten years now, he had instilled in Mila a good understanding of the dos and don'ts of potential crime scene etiquette, the most important of which was not to do anything that might contaminate a scene, *any* scene, no matter how mundane. Sometimes when it didn't look as if any crime had taken place, that was when the worst crimes had been committed.

Mila returned to the back of the van, and climbed the ladder, being careful only to touch things she had already touched. She turned on the torch on her phone and worked backwards, starting where the old woman's body lay on the bed. The skin on Gosia's face was yellowish in colour, and the mouth was open. Gosia only had three teeth. There was a hollowness to the cheeks and a sunken-ness to the eyes and the stillness was disconcerting. Living people, even when they were asleep, made miniscule movements of the eyes and lips; their blood pulsed beneath the skin. Gosia was bone-still.

Mila used the tip of her little finger to pull back the covers a little. There was no obvious sign of injury to Gosia's neck, no bruising that Mila could see, no sign of a fight. She replaced the cover and looked around the makeshift bed. There was a small triangular ledge in the corner next to the pillow. On this were several pillboxes, a book, face down, and a small, battery-operated lamp. Mila examined each of the medication containers in turn. There was no helpful label on any of the packets or bottles, no indication of what they contained or where they had been purchased. The book was a guide to the dolmens of Finistère.

The wall behind the length of the bed was covered in cork placed so that Gosia could look at whatever was pinned to it as she fell asleep. But nothing was pinned. Not a single photograph or postcard.

Mila remembered the drawing pin that had pierced the sole of her shoe earlier. Had Gosia taken down her photographs and mementoes the previous evening?

And where was the journal that Gosia had told Ani was her work?

She shone the torch around the interior of van. That huge book would not be easy to hide in a small space like this. The only places it could be were under the bed shelf or in the shopping trolley. Mila looked. It was not in either.

She picked up a tapestry cushion that had fallen from the bed, replaced it and went outside to check if the book was in the driver's cab. It was not. Neither was there anything beneath the van in which it might have been hidden.

Could the kids have taken it?

No. Mila was certain she'd have noticed if any of them had been carrying anything that large.

She began to feel uneasy. She went to the door and looked around, to check that nobody was watching the van. She held the phone tight in her hand, ready to call for help if she needed it.

She was coming to realise that someone else apart from those boys had been here in the time between she and Ani leaving yesterday evening and her return this morning. Someone had come and they'd taken whatever mementoes had been pinned to Gosia's corkboard and the big old book in which she'd been writing. Of course, they might have taken other things too: money, perhaps. And maybe Gosia had had some valuable items with her – jewellery or antiques.

Mila badly wanted to call Luke, to talk the situation through with him, but the doctor and the police would be here any minute.

She ran through the questions that Luke would ask if he was with her, the observations he would have required her to make. He was meticulous in his approach. He considered every detail.

Three things seemed important to remember. The door had been closed, but not locked on the inside.

The cork board was empty. And Gosia's precious book, her *work*, was missing.

6

Mila took her time going back to the sea house, hoping to shake off the frustration she felt at the attitude of the two gendarmes who had arrived at Gosia's van shortly after the doctor, and who had refused to take her concerns about the missing book and the empty corkboard seriously.

'Photographs and memorabilia?' the less personable of the pair had asked. 'Who'd want to steal photographs and memorabilia from a shithole like this?'

He'd been even less interested in the missing book and he hadn't listened to Mila when she tried to explain how important it must have been to Gosia.

'You're a writer, are you?' he asked, when she said that she was working on her own novel. 'Need a good imagination for that, do you?'

He had an attitude that Luke complained of encountering, sometimes, amongst his colleagues in the UK: a combination of bravado and arrogance; a conviction that the obvious explanation was invariably the correct one, the only one worthy of consideration. The obvious explanation in this case was that the old woman had died in her sleep and no crime had been committed.

Mila was still feeling cross and humiliated when she reached the sea house, and opened the gate into the garden.

Ani had spread one of Sophie's crazy crocheted blankets on the grass and was sunbathing in an acid-yellow bikini, stretched out on her front. Seeing her like this, caught midway between childhood and adulthood, Mila felt a pang of regret, already missing the child Ani who would soon be lost forever.

She pulled herself up sharply. Such regret was the preserve of the child's parents. It was wrong of Mila to appropriate feelings that by rights belonged to Sophie. *Should have* belonged to her.

Berthaud prowled delicately through the buttercups, miaowing a welcome. Mila propped up the bike, gathered the cat into her arms and plied her with kisses.

'She doesn't like that,' said Ani. 'Stop it.'

'Excuse me? *She* came to *me*.'

'Yeah, but she doesn't like you doing that. She only gives affection on her terms. She wants to bite you but she's too polite.'

Mila gave the cat one last kiss between the ears, and then put her down. Berthaud stretched herself out like a draught excluder and crawled into the shade.

'Where've you been?' Ani asked. 'You said you were popping out but you've been gone absolutely ages.'

'Did you put sunscreen on?' Mila asked. She flopped onto the swing-seat. She was hot and flustered. What she needed was a swim, a good, hard sea-swim to disperse the adrenaline in her bloodstream and make her properly tired, but she couldn't go for a swim until she'd had yet another difficult chat with her niece.

Mila had been told several times by well-meaning friends that the responsibility for looking after someone else's child weighed more heavily than the responsibility for looking after one's own.

Given the experience of the past eleven months, she assumed this must be true. Otherwise, why on earth would anyone have children? Or have more than one, at least. Why would anyone willingly burden themselves with the ever-present anxiety about the child's physical and emotional wellbeing, this constant having to put them first; having to think about every single thing you said in case you said something inappropriate or hurtful or ambiguous?

'Have you used sunscreen?' she asked again.

'Yes.'

'Factor 50?'

'I don't *need* it that strong. Maman always said 30 was fine.' Ani flushed at the inadvertent mention of her mother. She rolled over and sat up, cross-legged. She picked up and put on a wide-brimmed straw sunhat that had belonged to Sophie. It was falling apart, bits of straw coming loose in places so that the sunlight made a tartan pattern through the holes onto the skin of Ani's face. The girl reached for her drink. 'Anyway, *where have you been*?'

'To Gosia's van,' said Mila. She pushed the seat back and let it rock for a moment or two, the hinges creaking. She and Sophie had spent hours side by side on this seat, the tips of their fingers touching in the gap between the two cushions covered in a fabric printed with cocktail glasses and colourful cocktail umbrellas; at least, they *used* to be colourful. Now the sun had bleached them to pale pastels.

'Is Gosia okay?' Ani asked. 'Is something wrong?'

'Oh Ani...' Mila leaned forward, put her elbows on her knees and cupped her chin in her hands. 'I'm sorry but no, she's not okay. Sadly, she passed away during the night.'

'Passed away?'

'Died,' Mila said.

Ani's mouth fell open. 'She's *dead*?'

Mila nodded. 'Apparently, she was very ill.'

Ani was silent for a moment, then she said, 'She seemed okay to me.'

Gosia had appeared fit and well to Mila too, but the doctor, when she came to declare Gosia dead, had examined the pills at the side of the bed and told the police that Gosia had incurable heart disease. She said Gosia had been living on borrowed time. That might explain why she had been writing in her book – the book that was now missing – getting everything she needed to say written down while she still had the opportunity to do so. Or it might have had nothing to do with it.

'It's terribly sad,' said Mila, 'but she was quite an elderly woman and... Ani, are you okay? You've gone very pale.'

'It's happening!' Ani said.

'What is?'

'Can I borrow your phone? I need to call Pernille. I need to warn her!'

'Hold on,' Mila said, 'slow down. What are you talking about? Why do you need to warn Pernille?'

'It's the curse of the Kyern Hind!'

'What? But that's a beautiful thing. Why would it be cursed?'

'We've been watching stuff about it on YouTube. When graves are disturbed, there's always a curse.'

'Whoa, Ani, hold on! Curses aren't real! They're something people invented to stop other people from stealing precious objects.'

'If they're not real, why did everyone who went into Tutankhamun's tomb get ill and die?'

'I'm not sure that they actually did.'

'They did! And not just the people who went there, but people close to them too and even their *dogs*! That tomb was *definitely* cursed and Kyern is supposed to be our version of Tutankhamun.'

'Sweetheart, the antelope statuette wasn't taken from a tomb; it was found lying on top of the soil.'

'And now they've started digging trenches in the rest of the field, even though everyone knows it used to be a sacred site!'

Mila had expected this conversation to end in tears and distress over the death of Gosia. She had never, in a million years, thought it would lead to Gosia's death being taken as proof that a prehistoric curse had been triggered. She struggled to untangle Ani's logic so she could begin to tackle it.

'Even if there was a curse,' she began, 'what would it have to do with Gosia?'

'She knew one of the archaeologists! She was reading a book he'd written!'

The dolmen book at the side of Gosia's bed?

'She had a direct connection with someone at the dig so the curse could definitely have affected her!'

'Yes, but...'

'Please,' Ani begged, 'please let me borrow your phone so I can call Pernille.'

Mila gave up. She reached backwards, took the phone out of her pocket and passed it to her niece. As Ani frantically tapped out Pernille's number, Mila took the clip out of her hair and shook it loose. Then she went into the sea house and climbed the stairs to wash the smoke out of her hair.

7

WEDNESDAY, 10 AUGUST

The church was so old it appeared, like the menhirs dotted around the countryside, to be a natural structure, rather than one designed and built by men. The grey stone walls were thick and weathered like the standing stones for which the Finistère region of Brittany was famous; the windows, designed to keep out the Atlantic winds and the summer heat, were so narrow they were barely more than slits.

A little way distant from the church was the cemetery where the blackness of a freshly dug hole gaped against the dazzling green of the grass.

Mila Shepherd was in the cemetery, wearing a dark linen dress, kneeling in the burning sunshine beside a different grave, one that was more established. She'd brought new flowers for Sophie, a bunch of periwinkles cut from her own garden – *Sophie's* garden. The periwinkle flowers were the same colour as Sophie's eyes. They wouldn't last long in this heat, but Mila wouldn't come without bringing something.

Someone had been before her that morning. A beach pebble

and a small posy of yellow and white wildflowers already lay wilting on the grave. Ceci must have been here, although buttercups and oxeye daisies were not blooms Mila would have associated with her stepmother.

Sophie's grave was at the far edge of the cemetery, nearest to the sea that had been her first love, and that, in the end, had claimed her. Her head was close to the boundary wall where the headstone stood, a simple inscription: *Here lies beloved Sophie Cooper.* There was room beneath for Charlie's name but in the absence of a body, it hadn't been included yet.

Mila didn't mind the cemetery. Sitting here, on the cool grass, next to Sophie's grave, made her feel closer to her stepsister. And it was a truly lovely spot; something about the conjunction of sea and sky, grass and the old grey stone of the wall produced a feeling of calm. Gulls flocked overhead, wheeling and calling and the long grasses, gone to seed at the edge of the wall, swayed and shimmied their feathery heads like showgirls.

Unlike her aunt, Ani hated coming here. It was partly because she didn't want to acknowledge the fact of Sophie's death, and partly because she could not help but see the sea. The Atlantic that had claimed her mother was a constant source of torment to Ani. Some days it was so calm and blue it was as if a giant bedsheet had been spread from the horizon to the shore. Other days it was black and green, white horses galloping, boats, even large ships disappearing beneath the enormous waves that swelled beside the vessels. Either way, serene or violent, Ani hated it. It would be a kindness, Mila thought, when she was safely at boarding school in Switzerland, a landlocked country miles from the ocean that held on to her father even now. It would be better for her not to be reminded constantly of her parents' accident. The mountains and forests would heal her. The snow and sunshine would help her to forget.

Summer was in full swing. The grass was beginning to turn yellow after more than a week of dry weather. In the trees around the cemetery the birds were singing, and Mila could also hear the joyful shouts of children playing on the beach. She was grateful for the happy noises: proof that life went on even when death was taking centre stage.

She had come to attend Gosia's internment alone. Pernille's mother was taking the girls out for a picnic and Ceci was meeting with the candidate she'd selected to take over the Sophie/Mila role at the agency. She had asked Mila to join them for lunch at her favourite restaurant after the burial. The prospect of this was hanging over Mila like a cloud.

'I shouldn't be having to do this,' Mila said to Sophie's grave. It was green and still and quiet. Peaceful. In life, Sophie had never been still, quiet and peaceful. 'Why did you have to go out that day, Sophie?' Mila asked. 'Why did you let Charlie take you out in that stupid boat when bad weather was forecast? Were you drunk? Was it a dare? Why did you do it?'

There was no answer. A bee landed on a clover flower amongst the grass. The leaves in the tree rustled softly in the summer breeze.

Mila put the flowers into the jar, which she balanced on the little stone plinth that was roughly at the point where Sophie's folded hands would be if she were lying on top of the earth, rather than beneath it. The blue blooms were sweet against the mottled grey of the headstone. She picked up the pebble and turned it over. The Celtic triskele symbol; the same triple spiral as the tattoo on Sophie's wrist, had been carved into its base. Mila put it back where it had been and sat silently until the sound of an approaching engine cut through the quieter sounds of the summer's day. Then she stood up. Turning, she saw the ancient hearse used by Morannez's only firm of undertakers chuntering at a walking pace down the drive that led through the cemetery.

Mila dusted the creases from the skirt of her dress, picked up her shawl and a second bunch of flowers, and she walked across the graveyard until she reached Jenny from the café, the only other person present.

The two women nodded to one another.

'Are we the only mourners?' Jenny asked in a whisper.

'It looks that way.'

'No family coming?'

'I couldn't find anyone.'

'But you tried?'

'I had nothing to go on. Not so much as a surname for Gosia.'

'But you did try. Nobody can do more than that.'

Mila nodded, but she felt a little ashamed. In truth, she'd made hardly any effort to track down Gosia's family and friends, giving it up as an impossible task.

The two women fell silent as the coffin, having been unloaded from the back of the hearse, began its slow progress on the shoulders of the undertakers' men – a mismatched group, mainly consisting of farm workers, pulled together for occasions such as this – along the narrower path towards the waiting grave.

Jenny and Mila followed, heads down.

'She had a son,' whispered Mila. 'I hate to think of him out there somewhere in the world with no idea that his mother has died.'

Jenny touched the back of Mila's hand. 'At least when he finds out that she's passed on, he'll be able to come to the grave and pay his respects. That'll be some comfort to him.'

'I hope so.'

Cecille had paid for Gosia's coffin and the space in the cemetery and had settled the fees for the priest and the undertaker. She'd had her housekeeper, Madame Abadie, organise it all. When she heard how Gosia had helped Ani, and Mila had explained why she felt the need to do right by the traveller woman, she had insisted.

It was a short service, dignified and unsentimental. There was not much that could be said about an ageing woman who had died in her sleep from a pre-existing condition. That was what the doctor had decided had happened; that was the line that the gendarmes had taken; it was what had been reported in a brief item on the local news; and now the priest used that explanation for Gosia's death too.

When the coffin had been lowered into the grave, and the dust sprinkled on top, Mila decided that Ceci had been right to insist that after the funeral Mila put this whole episode behind her. It was sad, but nothing more could be done for Gosia.

She and Jenny walked together to the cemetery gates and stepped through, rusting wrought iron framing the grand monument beyond with its swags and urns, its carving of a pelican piercing its breast to feed its young.

Jenny took the keys to her 2CV out of her pocket. 'Can I give you a lift anywhere?'

'Thank you, but I'm meeting my stepmother for lunch. I'm being introduced to the man who's taking over my – *Sophie's* job. He's Canadian. Would you like to join us? I'm sure Ceci would be delighted.'

She wasn't at all sure actually but if Jenny was there, at least Mila wouldn't have to make small talk with the man.

'Thanks, but I need to get back to the café before the rush starts. Give your stepmother my regards.'

Mila promised that she would.

Ani's replacement phone had arrived in the post that morning. Mila messaged her.

Everything ok? Xxx

Ani replied with a string of emojis, all of them cheerful. Mila smiled and put the phone back in her bag.

8

Cecille Toussaint's favourite restaurant, Le Liège – known to locals as 'Étienne's', was on the outskirts of Morannez town, at the end of a small track that opened onto the cemetery road, close enough for Mila to walk. The restaurant's location was marked by a small, wooden fingerpost that was so weathered and worn it was impossible to read if you didn't already know what it said.

The restaurant did not shout about itself and two large, smelly and grumpy goats in the field at the start of the track put off all but the most determined diners. That lunchtime, Mila observed something else: a battered and obviously old motorbike. It was propped on its stand behind the fingerpost and looked for all the world like a giant, dusty green wasp. Its owner perhaps wasn't confident the bike would make it over the ruts and potholes all the way to the restaurant.

Le Liège was run by a chef called Étienne Pinet, who on the one hand had been blessed with a brilliant and instinctive talent for cooking but, on the other, was cursed by a crushing shyness, which meant he could never contemplate working in Paris or in one of the glamorous hotels on the coast. Instead, he ran the restaurant from the kitchen of his modest family home, with the help of his mother, Beatrice. There was no menu at Le Liège, as a rule no pandering to the tastes of those who would not eat the flesh of any once-living creature and especially not those who preferred also to avoid the various animal secretions that went to make the cheese, cream and puddings for which the area was famous. Diners at Le Liège ate what they were given. Ceci, who ate anything, who had butter with everything, and who was slender as a reed, loved Étienne and his restaurant with a passion. Étienne, who had a kind heart, made sure there were always plenty of delicious vegetable dishes when he knew Mila was coming along too.

As she drew close to the restaurant, the scent of cooked garlic perfuming the air, Mila felt surly. It was a teenage feeling: a combination of resentment at being dragged along to something the adults had planned, embarrassment at having to be nice to a stranger she had no particular wish to meet, shyness, and there was an element of jealousy too, that this stranger was going to be stepping into her shoes – *Sophie's* shoes.

It was irrational. Mila didn't want to be working with Ceci; she'd *never* wanted to work at the agency. The Canadian was key to Mila's freedom. Because of him, this time next year, hopefully, she'd be a published author. He was welcome to the Toussaint's job and good luck to him.

Mila stopped at the entrance to the restaurant courtyard. She could hear voices, the clink of cutlery on crockery, the tinkle of the water in the fountain. She dusted the soles of her feet and slipped her shoes back on – she'd been carrying them with the straps hooked over her fingers. She wished she'd thought to bring some make-up, a little foundation to hide skin flushed by the heat and the exertion.

You look fine, said Sophie, who knew full well that it always annoyed Mila when she said that, because no matter how fine Mila looked, Sophie always looked finer.

Ceci was sitting alone at a table in the dappled shade towards the back of the courtyard. It was a table that was afforded a little privacy by the flowering shrubs that grew behind it. On the metal table in front of her was a carafe of water, a number of wine and water glasses and a wicker bread basket. Three places were set and it was clear from the breadcrumbs and the crumpled napkin that the one to Ceci's left was already in use, although its occupant wasn't present.

Ceci raised a hand and Mila walked towards her. Her step-mother stood to greet her, reaching up to kiss each of her cheeks in turn.

'Sit down, darling,' she said, indicating a chair that had thoughtfully been placed in the shade of a birch tree that softened the brilliant afternoon light, beside the tumbling geraniums and love-in-the-mist blooms in the borders of the raised garden beds.

'How was the funeral?' Ceci leaned forward to examine Mila's face for signs of stress and tiredness and, finding both, poured a glass of sparkling water for her.

'It was okay,' said Mila. She sat with a small sigh, took a drink of the water, ice cubes clinking against the glass, a slice of lemon pressed against the side. In the branches above her, a blackbird sang. It was a heavenly spot. 'Where's the new boy?'

'Madame Pinet's invited him into the kitchen to meet Étienne. Would you like a glass of wine?' Ceci indicated a bottle of what would undoubtedly be excellent Muscadet chilling in the water of the little fountain in the centre of the courtyard.

'No, thank you.'

'You look like you could use a pick-me-up.'

'I'm fine. It's just...'

'Funerals?'

'Yes.'

'Did you go and say hello to Sophie?'

'Of course. She was good. She sent her love. I guess you were there earlier.'

'Me? No. I haven't been for a few days.'

'Oh. Well, someone had left some flowers.'

Ceci took a sip of water. 'Sophie had many friends.' She put the glass back on the table. 'So, is it over now? Are you going to let that poor travelling woman rest in peace?'

'I am,' said Mila, 'although—'

Ceci interrupted. 'Ah, here he is!'

A man was walking towards them. He was tall, rangy, muscles making half-moons beneath the sleeves of his shirt. Mila recognised him at once; she'd have known him anywhere. Carter Jackson.

Oh my God! cried Sophie. *What is he doing here?*

'Ceci...' Mila began, but Ceci wasn't listening; she was beaming at the man. Beside him, trotting to keep up, was Madame Pinet, mother of the chef, literally half his height and like a sparrow in comparison. She, resplendent in her usual 1940s-esque flowery dress and apron, for once, had a wide smile on her face and was gazing at Carter with the kind of adoration that a Labrador dog reserves for fillet steak. Before he reached the table, he turned to his Number One Fan and took her tiny hand between his large ones.

'Thank you, madame,' he said. 'Meeting your son and watching him work was a privilege.'

'Oh, it was my pleasure! You're welcome in our kitchen any time!'

'That's so kind!'

Carter released Madame Pinet's hand and she disappeared with a spring in her waddle and a slight flush to her cheeks.

'How did you get on, Carter?' Ceci asked. She too was smiling fondly, as one might smile at a favourite nephew.

'It was amazing. The guy, Étienne, he's working in this tiny kitchen, literally smaller than the kitchen in my apartment back home, and... Oh!'

He stopped in his tracks and stared across the table, narrowing his eyes as he peered into the shade.

'Mila?' he asked. 'Mila Shepherd? Is that you?'

'Hello, Carter.'

'You two know one another?' Ceci asked.

'We used to be friends,' said Carter.

'You were Sophie's friend,' said Mila, 'not mine.'

'You knew Sophie?' Ceci asked Carter. 'You knew my daughter?'

'Whoa!' said Carter. 'Sophie Lanson is your daughter? But your name is Toussaint...'

'I've had two husbands since Sophie's father.'

'Good grief!' said Carter. 'Although now I know that you're Sophie's mother, of course I can see there's a strong likeness. Where is she? Where's Sophie now?'

'Sit down, Carter,' said Ceci, patting the empty chair beside hers. 'Before we talk about Sophie, tell me how you and Mila know one another.'

Mila had a memory, a flashback to her teenage self, wearing a blue swimming costume and sitting on the edge of the floating diving board off the main Morannez beach. The water was lapping around her ankles, her feet pale beneath its surface broken up by the sunlight. Carter, sleek as a seal, was in the water, calling to Sophie, who was messing around at the end of the diving board, pretending she was scared to jump when the truth was she'd been throwing herself off that board since she was a child. Carter knew that Sophie wasn't really afraid but he was playing along; they were flirting with one another, teasing. It had been torture for Mila, sitting below, ignored by them both. She'd pretended she didn't care of course. She'd acted as if she was lost in her own thoughts. She had become an expert in feigning indifference that summer.

Carter spoke to Ceci.

'We used to see each other in the holidays when we were kids,' he said. 'I used to come to stay with my grandfather for four weeks every year and Sophie was home from school. And you' – he nodded to Mila – 'you were here sometimes too. We were part of the same gang hanging out together on the beach.'

'La bande sauvage,' Mila said quietly. The wild bunch. She touched her left wrist, in the place where Sophie had had her tattoo. The promise of a summer in Morannez had kept Mila going all year when she was at home with her angry and unhappy mother but she had never really been part of the gang.

'Yes. And then…' He glanced to Mila, who was staring at her plate. 'When Sophie was at the Sorbonne, we, she and I, used to meet up in Paris sometimes.'

Another flashback: Carter and Sophie sitting on the steps outside the Sacré-Cœur Basilica, his arm around her shoulders, her hood pulled up, her head resting against his, a green scarf wrapped around her neck, a full moon rising in the sky behind them and the air bitterly cold. Mila, breath clouding around her, climbing the steps with the paper cone of blisteringly hot chestnuts that Sophie had sent her down to buy, stopping when she saw their closeness, realising in that instant that they were lovers even though Sophie was wearing someone else's parka, and someone else's ring.

She looked down at her hands.

'So where is Sophie?' Carter asked. 'What's she doing with her life? Something brilliant, no doubt!'

'I'm sorry to have to tell you this, but Sophie died last year,' Ceci said.

Carter's eyes widened.

'She's dead? No!'

'Yes,' said Ceci.

'It can't be true!'

'I'm afraid it is.'

'But how? Was she sick?'

'It was a boating accident. She'd gone out sailing with her husband and a storm blew in.'

'Oh God! This is terrible! I can't believe it!'

He's acting, whispered Sophie. *He already knew I was dead.*

'She and Charlie had a daughter,' said Ceci, 'Anaïs. Mila kindly stepped in to care for her.'

Carter looked at Mila.

'Maybe I will have some wine,' she said.

She pushed back her chair and crossed to the fountain. She lifted the wine bottle from the cold water and took it back to the table. She filled each of their glasses.

'I had no idea,' Carter was saying to Ceci. 'I can't believe that Sophie's gone, or that I didn't know. I mean, we lost touch years back, but I assumed she'd always be around. She was a force of nature. People like her don't die.'

He's lying! Sophie hissed. *He was never a good liar. Look at his eyes! See how uncomfortable he is!*

'She was always inclined to be reckless,' said Ceci.

Reckless, Mila echoed in her thoughts. *Idiotic, careless, foolhardy, negligent.*

Mila! For fuck's sake, stop bitching about me and concentrate on him!

'I can't believe it,' Carter said again. 'Jesus, Ceci, I'm so sorry. If I'd had any idea...'

'Of course you had no idea,' said Ceci. 'How could you have? You weren't to know I was Sophie's mother. And I never thought to tell you because I didn't realise you were once friends.' She gave a small sigh. 'I didn't know much about what Sophie got up to when she was home from school as a teenager. She was something of a wild child and I wasn't always as attentive as I should have been.'

Huh, said Sophie, *that's an understatement.*

'Sophie always seemed perfectly happy to me,' said Carter. 'She had no complaints about you as a mother. It's inconceivable that she's gone.'

He does seem really upset about my tragic loss, said Sophie.

Mila returned the bottle to its place in the water beneath the fountain.

What I think, said Sophie, *is that Carter heard that I'd died in what could be described as mysterious circumstances and was so devastated that he came back to find out the truth about what happened.*

Mila went back to her seat; sat down.

Not everything is about you, Sophie.

And it wasn't. But once Sophie had planted the idea that Carter had come back because of her in Mila's head, she found she couldn't shake it off.

9

'Ceci told me you've been living an exciting life in Canada chasing down dirty money,' Mila said to Carter when he had apparently recovered from the shock of hearing about Sophie's death. 'Although, obviously, I never realised she was talking about you.'

'That's right,' said Carter. He fiddled with the stem of his wine glass and would not look Mila straight in the eye. 'I was with the Toronto police narcotics' unit for eight years.'

'So, what made you decide to come back here?'

'My marriage broke up. I thought it was time to come home.'

There you are, said Sophie. *The minute the wife's out of the picture, his thoughts come back to me.*

'Won't you find it a bit dull here after Toronto?'

'Actually, "dull" is quite appealing right now.'

He seemed distracted. Perhaps he genuinely hadn't known Sophie was dead. Maybe, deep down, he'd been holding on to a hope that their paths might cross again, their romance be rekindled.

'It must have been hard giving up your career,' Mila persisted. 'Ceci said you were doing really well.'

'I don't see it as "giving up", rather taking a step to the side.'

'Mila, there's no need to interrogate the poor man,' Ceci said, 'I gave him the third degree in the interview already.'

Carter shrugged. 'I don't mind answering your questions, Mila. The truth is, I was ready for a change. The narcotics work wasn't as exciting as it sounds. Mostly, it involved looking at tax returns and spreadsheets, searching for discrepancies and cash deposits. When I actually got to sit in a car outside a private house for twelve hours waiting for a gate to open so I could follow someone to a bank, that constituted a good day out for me. Coming here, to this beautiful place, and being more or less my own boss, with Ceci's approval of course, well, it was a prospect too good to turn down.'

Ask him when he arrived back in Morannez, Sophie said, *because if it was more than a few days ago, he would have heard about me.*

'When did you arrive back in Morannez?'

'A few days ago. I came by plane. My bike came separately on a ship.'

'Your bike?'

'The Harley. I couldn't leave her behind.'

That explained the machine at the entrance to the track.

Carter always was into motorbikes, Sophie said. And Mila remembered that she was right, he was.

* * *

They were interrupted at this point by Madame Pinet, flushed and with her hair askew, labouring across to their table carrying three plates on a large tray. Mila noticed that she'd applied a strong fuchsia lipstick. It was a little skew-whiff.

'Here we are,' murmured Madame, laying the plates on the table. One held fat white stalks of asparagus, speckled with pepper and garnished with lemon. The second was piled high with crevettes cooked in garlic and wine and the third was tissue-thin slices of raw steak sprinkled with herbs with a spoonful of chopped salsa to the side: Étienne's version of steak tartare. Ceci gave a small sigh of pleasure. Carter said, 'Wow.' Madame Pinet looked immensely pleased.

Ceci unfolded her napkin and spread it on her lap.

'Mila is a vegetarian,' she said to Carter, 'so I normally let her eat the asparagus.'

'No problem,' said Carter. He passed the asparagus to Mila. As he did so, she glimpsed the tattoo on his wrist: the same as Sophie's, the same tattoo all the bande sauvage members had had done the last Morannez summer; the summer Sophie and Mila were eighteen, the summer that Mila missed because she couldn't leave her mother at home alone. Sophie could have told Mila about the tattoos. She could have sent a sketch and Mila could have had one done in England, but Sophie hadn't thought to mention it. Mila had dwelled on this for years afterwards; wondering if it had been a deliberate omission on Sophie's part; if Sophie hadn't told her about the tattoos because she, Mila, had never truly been one of the gang.

'Thanks,' she murmured, taking the dish.

Ceci delicately lifted a slice of the beef and laid it on her plate. The meat had been so thinly cut that the pattern on the dish was visible through it. She raised her glass: 'Here's to you, Carter, and to Toussaint's and to a successful partnership going forward.'

Carter raised his glass too. It was one of the Pinets' finest, a slender, tulip-shaped bowl on the most delicate of stems. It looked fragile in his big hand.

The three of them chinked.

'Cheers,' said Carter. 'Here's to the future.'

He was doing his best to sound cheerful, but his good humour was forced. He was still struggling to process the fact that Sophie was dead: or he was pretending to. Mila couldn't be sure. Carter used to be the kind of person to whom lying was anathema. He would rather hurt someone by telling the truth, as Mila knew from experience, than protect them with a lie. But perhaps he had changed: people did.

Once, during the same winter as the Sacre-Cœur incident, Mila had walked into Sophie's room in Paris to find Sophie and Carter kissing. Her arms had been looped around his neck and he was holding her tightly, pressing her body against his. They had been so engrossed in one another, they hadn't noticed Mila standing there, her arms full of Christmas presents, watching.

'Leave him,' Carter had begged Sophie. 'Tell him it's over. I can't keep doing this; sneaking around; pretending.'

'It's not as easy as that,' Sophie had replied.

Mila thought of Sophie's hand; her wrist; the tattoo. She thought of her, face down in the water. She glanced across the table at Carter at exactly the same moment as he glanced at her. She looked away at once, embarrassed, and he did the same.

I was right, wasn't I? Sophie whispered triumphantly. *He did come back for me! I am the reason he's here!*

* * *

Ceci didn't like talking business over a meal. Partly because of that, and partly thanks to the stream of beautifully prepared dishes that kept appearing at their table, the meal was a quiet one, the clink of cutlery and the soft gurgle of wine being poured only interrupted by delighted exclamations over the sweetness of a clam, or the smokiness of a roasted pepper, or the butter-soft meat flaking from the bone of a tiny lamb chop.

Mila was relieved she didn't have to make conversation with Carter Jackson; the last time they had been together, in Paris, everything had been so complicated and she didn't want to be reminded of that time, nor of her own behaviour.

The quality of the food went some small way to take her mind away from the past.

Before they'd finished one dish, another arrived: mussels cooked in cream and garlic; deep-fried sardines; cured meats; potatoes sautéed with leeks and butter beans; a dressed green salad; olives with herbs; cold roast aubergine in a basil oil; slices of fig and pear sprinkled with walnuts and crumbs of ricotta cheese. Mila hadn't realised she was hungry but each dish set before her was tempting and the bread was salty and soft. Out of nowhere, she remembered how, after Sophie's internment, she'd overhead the priest saying that funerals made him hungry. At the time she'd been appalled: how could he think about food at a time like this, when Sophie, *Sophie!* had just been laid to rest. But later, back at the sea house, alone, she'd opened the pantry door and taken out a stick of bread and, even though it was going stale, she'd torn off fistfuls of dough and stuffed them into her mouth. She wondered now if hunger was a visceral response to death: the body craving the stuff that gave it energy and life to reaffirm its commitment to living.

Following Ceci's lead, Carter Jackson kept conversation to a minimum, mainly speaking to thank Madame Pinet each time she came to the table and to praise the talent of her son. Madame's cheeks became more flushed and her smile wider as the meal progressed.

The only fly in the ointment was the noise from the party at a table on the far side of the courtyard.

A group of men had turned up shortly after Ceci had ordered a bottle of Bordeaux to accompany the meat dishes. Madame Pinet had been wrestling with an antiquated bottle opener, refusing offers of assistance from Carter, when the men came in.

Madame Pinet, hunched over the corkscrew, nodded a welcome. 'I've prepared your usual table,' she said.

The men were sharply dressed and wearing expensive sunglasses and watches. They had taken off their jackets and ties and rolled up their sleeves, scraped their chairs as they pulled them out, and were now talking over one another, competing to tell the funniest stories, some of them vulgar, and to tease one another.

The leader of the group, who had, a few days earlier, cut Mila up in his flashy sports car, ordered several bottles of wine. He was Guillaume Girard; she remembered him from the old days, although he didn't recognise either her or Carter. His elder brother, Arnaud, was there too and had nodded an acknowledgement to Ceci. The men's energy was so intense and artificial that Mila suspected that they'd taken something besides alcohol – all of them except Arnaud who was subdued; out of place. As the afternoon progressed, the others regularly roared with laughter so loud and rambunctious that conversation at the neighbouring tables was impossible. Arnaud tried to quiet his companions several times, then gave up.

At one point, in the middle of a particularly crude story, Carter pushed back his chair ready to intervene but Ceci put a beautifully manicured hand on his arm and shook her head.

'The noisy chap is the younger Girard boy,' she told him.

'I recognise him.'

'Then perhaps you'll remember that his family owns the Morannez holiday park and the grand hotel at Bloemel-sur-Mer. Their custom keeps this place in business.'

'It doesn't justify him behaving like an idiot.'

'No, but let's leave him to it.'

Ceci didn't add that she had a vested interest in not upsetting the Girards. She was friendly with the boys' mother, Monique, and had helped with the legal side of various land purchases and other matters.

Instead, she addressed Mila, subtly changing the direction of the conversation. 'Carter is staying at the holiday park.'

'Couldn't you have stayed with your grandfather?'

'He has dementia. He's gone into a home.'

'I'm sorry.'

Carter shrugged. 'It happens.'

'So have you been and looked at the dig yet?'

'Yesterday evening, I walked over. Met the top archaeologist, a genuine professor. He was a fount of information.'

'Have they found anything yet?'

'Not yet, but they're still hopeful.'

'And it was lucky that Carter met the professor, given what happened today,' said Ceci.

'What happened today?' Mila asked.

'I'll tell you later,' Ceci said.

'Tell me now!'

'Not while we're eating.' Ceci looked across to Carter. 'So what do you think of this place, Carter?'

'I think it's great. And Harry's going to love it here when he visits.'

'Harry?' asked Mila.

'My son. Didn't I say? Emmanuelle, my ex-wife, is from Quimper. She never settled in Canada and now she's come home. She wants Harry to grow up in Brittany. He's the number one reason I'm back.'

10

After the meal, Mila and Ceci parted from Carter Jackson at the entrance to the restaurant and watched him walk back to his motorbike through the clouds of midges that were forming in the late afternoon sunshine. His leather jacket was hooked over his shoulder and he had the bow-legged walk of a cowboy.

'What do you think?' Ceci asked.

'He's massively overqualified for Toussaint's.'

'And?'

'I don't know, Ceci. It feels a bit odd that someone Sophie and I used to know should be taking over her job.'

'Don't you think it's rather nice that someone who used to be a friend is taking Sophie's place? Unless... There wasn't any trouble between Carter and you or Carter and Sophie, was there?'

That last day in Paris. Oh God. Mila couldn't bring herself to think about it. She'd spent years trying not to remember what she'd said to Carter, what she'd done.

'No,' she said. 'Carter didn't do anything wrong.'

'Well then, there's no problem that I can see. His wife moving back to France with the child was my good fortune.'

And it won't make any difference to you, Mila; you'll be back in England. You'll never have to see him again.

That was true of course. It didn't do anything to dispel Mila's unease.

Ceci smiled and breathed in the warm air. 'I had Joe Le Taxi bring me here, but I'll walk back with you for the exercise. The doctor tells me to aim for ten thousand steps a day, frankly an impossible target for anyone who lives their life in heels.'

'You could always buy some trainers.'

'Darling, we both know that's never going to happen.'

Ceci linked her arm through Mila's and they set off, walking at a leisurely pace.

Nobody would ever have mistaken them for mother and daughter. Ceci was small-boned, fair-haired, sharp-featured. Mila was taller and darker and her features were softer. Given the choice, Ceci would surely far rather have been with Sophie, but she never made Mila feel second best. Her kindness was unstinting and Mila became a little less ruffled as they walked and the sunlight and shadows slid over their shoulders. She began to think that maybe it was karma that Carter had returned. Perhaps everything would fall into place and work out for the best. Maybe this was a way for the cosmos to balance things out and make them right.

After a little while, Mila said, 'So, tell me, what happened today to do with the Kyern archaeologist that you wouldn't discuss at the restaurant?'

'Oh, that,' said Ceci.

'"Oh, that," what?'

'The thing is, darling, I don't think you're going to approve.'

'Why aren't I?'

'Well... While Carter and I were in the office this morning, we had a visitor, the wife of the lead archaeologist from the dig, the same archaeologist Carter had, fortuitously, already met; the professor.'

'Okay...'

'She was wearing a white Fendi skirt suit and she wore it very well for an Englishwoman...'

Mila unhooked her arm and leaned down to take off her shoes. 'Ceci, never mind what she was wearing; what did she want?'

'She thinks her husband, Professor Tim Perry, might be romantically involved with one of the students on the dig.'

Mila stood up, enjoying the sensation of liberated feet. 'That's not good.'

'She's not certain but she has an intimation, and spouses are rarely wrong about such things.'

'So, she's looking for proof?'

'"Confirmation" was the word she used.'

'You did tell the archaeologist's wife that we're not *that* sort of agency?'

'Well...'

'Oh, Ceci, you did tell her, didn't you?'

'Listen. She, Mrs Perry, Catherine, wants to know one way or the other if there's any evidence of her husband being on the brink of straying. Which I think is perfectly reasonable, given the circumstances. Professors and students, it's a very difficult area. Far better to nip it in the bud, if there's anything that needs nipping, that is.'

'You said when you set up the agency with Sophie that you would never, ever, resort to that kind of surveillance work! And the agency's doing fine; it's not like we need the money or anything.'

'Darling, with all due respect, it's not really up to you any more. You're leaving in five weeks...'

'Four weeks.'

'There you are. It's up to me and Carter Jackson to take the business forward now.'

'Oh! It was *his* idea to say "yes" to Mrs Perry, was it?'

'No, it was my idea. I thought following the professor for a day or two would be an easy way to ease Carter into the business. He has a huge amount of experience in that field. And Mrs Perry was very persuasive.'

'In her Fendi suit.'

'In her Fendi suit, yes.' Ceci looked at her stepdaughter. 'Darling, I know you don't like the idea, but it's a straightforward job and I can't see how any harm can possibly come of it.'

'The straightforward jobs are always the ones that end up the most complicated.'

They had reached the end of the path. To the right was a small car park that people used to access the coastal footpath and the beach. The road, to the left, led back into Morannez, to Ceci's apartment.

'It's just the one job,' said Ceci. 'To help Mrs Perry.'

'But then word will get out and before you know it, you'll be inundated with people complaining about their neighbours and wanting you to find people who owe them money and you'll be caught in the middle of warring couples and...'

Ceci reached up to put the palms of her small hands on either side of Mila's face. She pulled her stepdaughter down until her face was at a level where she could reach to kiss her. 'Don't worry,' she said softly. 'This is one easy-peasy, teeny-tiny surveillance job, that's all. Everything's going to be fine.'

11

The sea house was empty when Mila returned. When she checked her phone, she saw that Ani had messaged to say she was still at Pernille's.

Please be back by eight.

Can Pernille stay the night? Her mama will drop us off.

Mila replied with a thumbs-up emoji.

Thank U! We're making curse cures.

Curse cures?

Mila smiled. She would miss this kind of craziness when she was back in Bristol.

Not really miss it.

Well, maybe a bit.

She drank a glass of water and then settled herself on the swing-seat in the garden and called Pernille's mother, Melodie Sohar.

'Hey, Mila!'

'Hi, Melodie. Thanks for having Ani today. She says you're bringing her and Pernille back here. Is that okay?'

'It's no problem.' Music was playing in the background, smooth Latino jazz. Mila imagined Melodie wafting about her huge, shiny kitchen, taking vegetables out of the huge, American fridge ready to start cooking some delicious meal for her family. Aubergine and courgette. Big, red tomatoes. The imagining made Mila feel lonely. She pushed herself on the swing-seat so it rocked a little, cradling her phone to her ear. Melodie spoke next.

'Actually, Mila, I was going to call you because I wanted to talk to you about the anniversary.' A pause. 'God, it's hard to even say it, but you know it's the anniversary of Sophie's accident in thirteen days' time?'

'Yes,' said Mila. 'I know.'

'Of course you do! Anyway, I was wondering if you were going to do anything to commemorate it?'

Mila was floored. It had never occurred to her that it might be appropriate to mark the dreadful 24 August anniversary. Not for one minute.

'I'm not sure...' she said.

'Of course, if it's not your thing I completely understand. Only I, *we*, some of Sophie's friends, we thought it might be nice to do something. Nothing mawkish or sentimental, something life-affirming, like a party only not a party. Do you know what I mean? I'm not explaining myself very well.'

'I don't know...'

'For the children's sake as much as the adults'. For Anaïs. Only they say, don't they, that it's good to give children the chance to talk about their parents, when they've lost them, and it must be difficult for Ani to raise the subject normally so I – *we* – thought this would be a perfect opportunity to give her the opportunity to talk about how she feels and...'

'Who says that?' Mila asked. 'Who says that it's good to put children in that kind of situation?'

'Grief counsellors, child psychologists. I've read about it in magazines.'

A silence followed. Mila was biting her tongue to stop herself snapping at Melodie for her tactlessness, for bringing Sophie's death and Ani's grief down to the level of some article written by someone who had almost certainly never been in the situation her family was in.

'You don't have to decide now,' Melodie said, when the silence became unbearable. 'I'm sorry if I—'

'It's fine,' said Mila sharply.

'I'm not trying to take over or anything, I just thought...'

'Really, it's fine.' Mila's emotions were tangled. Anger wrapped up in pain, wrapped in guilt. On the one hand, she felt Melodie had no right to interfere like this. On the other, Melodie had been Sophie's best friend since childhood. She was an original member of the bande sauvage. She wore the same triskele tattoo on the inside of her left wrist as Sophie had.

'Okay,' said Melodie. 'So is that a "yes" or...'

'I can't think about it now. And anyway, I need to talk to Ceci before I agree to anything.'

'Yes, sure. I understand.'

Another long silence.

'I'll bring the girls over in a couple of hours, then,' said Melodie. They finished the call and Mila put her head in her hands.

She knew she'd handled that badly. She knew that Melodie was only trying to help, but she couldn't bear it; she couldn't bear to have the loss of Sophie brought to the fore like that. Plus, they didn't know what had happened to Charlie, so it was a bit premature to be commemorating his death when he might have been picked up by a Chinese container vessel (a theory Luke had propounded) and simply not managed to find his way home yet. And she didn't think Ani would want a party/not-a-party to mark the worst day of her life; why would anyone want to do such a thing? Surely the best way forward, the quickest way to heal, was to put that terrible, terrible time behind them and move on?

Mila wanted to cry. She tried to shake off her distress but she couldn't. So she stood up and she went inside, through the door that looked like it opened into a cupboard but was really the bottom of the staircase, and went upstairs to change out of the linen dress and into a towelling beach robe. She gathered her hair and bundled it into a band as she came back down again, put on the trainers she'd kicked off in the back porch the day before, unpegged her swimsuit from the washing line, picked up Sophie's bike and cycled along the sandy track that led through the woods to the beach, the same track that Sophie and Charlie would have used to reach their little sailing dinghy, *Moonfleet*, on the day of the accident. Charlie loved sailing; it was his passion. He used to leave *Moonfleet* on the beach from spring through to autumn. Then he and Sophie would pull the craft up to the house on its trailer when the winter storms started blowing in and put it inside its tarpaulin coat and leave it tucked into the shed until the weather became more clement again. Of course, *Moonfleet* was gone now, disappeared into the Atlantic. It had probably been sliced to shreds by the propellor of some massive ship and the shreds were being washed up on beaches all over the world and people were looking at the bright yellow pieces of carbon fibre tangled with plastic litter and bits of fishing net and saying how terrible it was the amount of rubbish that found its way into the sea.

Mila had one of her fake flashbacks, literally a nanosecond

glimpse of Sophie's body, face down in the water, but she was ready for it and flashed it straight out of her head.

She had reached the point where the track wound past a small group of menhirs known locally as 'the wedding party' – said to be the remains of a group of merrymakers turned to stone by the Devil. It was Toussaint/Cooper/Shepherd tradition to touch all seven stones, spin round, and say: '*Promenons-nous dans les bois pendant que le loup n'y est pas*,' and because it was bad luck not to do this little routine, Mila did it, just as she always had since she was a child.

It was a load of superstitious nonsense, obviously. But it would be foolish to tempt fate for the sake of a few seconds spent touching the warm granite, and reciting the lines from the ancient children's song – the original curse cure.

* * *

A little way after the standing stones, the track petered out at a small, horseshoe-shaped beach that was so rarely visited by anyone else, the Coopers used to leave their possessions there overnight rather than carry chairs, towels and umbrellas to and from the sea house. They pretended it was their own.

The sand was fine and yellow-pink in colour, but the orientation of the beach meant it was often littered with seaweed brought in by the tide. The seaweed attracted flies, which, although harmless, were annoying to sunbathers, and children didn't like them. Also, the weed smelled fishy. The holidaymakers, if they came once, rarely returned. Why would they when there was the fine, long, unseaweedy, fly-free stretch of beach at Morannez town just a couple of kilometres further up the coast?

The horseshoe beach was enclosed by two rocky spits, one

partially wooded. The other ended at an outcrop that was accessible at low tide, but cut off when the tide was in.

Mila's spirits lifted as she reached the end of the track and emerged from the dappled shade into the warm sunshine.

She dropped the bike at the edge of the sand, changed into her swimsuit and ran into the water, the soft sand warm beneath the soles of her feet. She didn't stop, but plunged headfirst into the breaking waves and swam until she was breathless, then she flipped over and floated on her back in the warmer top ten inches of water, watching the bright silver sunlight sliding over the tops of the waves around her, seeing the swallows darting above, hoping her anxiety would wash away.

But it wouldn't go, this feeling that, when she examined it, was more than a simple annoyance at Melodie's meddling in a tragedy that was nothing to do with her. It was a nagging sense that something was wrong, that something malevolent was approaching and it needed her attention. It was connected to the Kyern dig. There was no obvious link between the death of a vagrant woman and the lead archaeologist's mid-life crisis, if that was what it was. Yet every instinct was telling Mila that she needed to be careful not to leap to conclusions in either case.

Mila swam until she was cold, trying, and failing to pin down her unease. Perhaps she was simply spooked by Ani's talk of curses. Perhaps it was that the return of Carter Jackson had brought back so many uncomfortable memories. By now the moon was high even though ahead of her there was still daylight in the sky. When she turned round, it had grown so dark over the land that she had a momentary panic; she was disorientated, but then she spotted the lights of Morannez town, and the lamps glowing behind the windows of the villas that had been built around the bay, and there was the holiday park; the lights inside the caravans were muted by net curtains and gave a ghostly glow. Presumably Carter was in one of the caravans. Behind the caravans was the Kyern dig site, spotlights mounted on stands shining down on the trenches and the illuminated dolmen behind – like something enormous that was sleeping.

Mila let the tide carry her back towards the shore, being lifted and lowered by the waves, and once she reached the shallows she swam in, shaking off the fragments of weed that fingered her skin. The beach banked sharply where the waves broke and she struggled to gain her footing, but Mila was used to fighting with the breaking waves; she kept her balance and scrambled up the incline. Someone was standing in the gloaming amongst the shallow dunes at the edge of the beach. As Mila drew closer, the figure turned and disappeared in the direction of the town. It was a man, but Mila could see no details although something about him was familiar. When she reached the spot where he'd been, she found a small tower of flat pebbles, one on top of the other. She'd found similar towers on the beach several times in the months since she'd been living in Brittany. They reminded her of her teenage summers. The individual members of the band sauvage used to stack pebbles wherever they went as a signal to one another.

In keeping with tradition, Mila picked up a cockle shell and placed it on the very top.

She put the towelling robe over her swimming costume, and sat on the sand for a while, arms wrapped around her legs, watching the light fade at the horizon. Then she turned and went back to her responsibilities.

12

Mila found Ani and Pernille in the kitchen of the sea house, kneeling at the table and peering into a large bowl. Mila could smell the tang of fresh herbs and green peelings and stalks were curled on the chopping board.

'Are you making a salad?' she asked hopefully.

'It's a curse cure.'

'Of course it is.'

Ani took some sea-salt out of its box and sprinkled it into the concoction. 'Salt has excellent protective properties,' she said. 'It repels ghosts, demons and hell hounds.'

'Hell hounds? Oh, girls, this is getting out of hand!'

'It's only a game,' said Ani.

'I don't think you should be messing around with curses and demons and hell hounds and things.'

'But you've always said they're not real, so what's the problem?'

Mila put a hand to her head. 'Can't you just go back to making face creams and love potions like you were doing last week?'

'Is Luke coming tomorrow?' Ani asked.

'Don't change the subject.'

'I'm not, I'm asking you a question. Is Luke coming?'

'I'll call him,' Mila said, and took the phone upstairs.

She dialled Luke's number straight away but the call went to voicemail. Mila left a brief message, showered and changed into a pair of harem pants and a cotton sweatshirt. She came down and busied herself with the dinner. The teenagers had gone outside and were smearing their curse concoction on the gate posts, giggling.

'Hell hounds!' Mila muttered. 'For goodness' sake!'

We were the same, whispered Sophie. *Don't you remember the Ouija board?*

Mila did remember. She and Sophie upstairs in the sea house with the board they'd found in the attic, a candle casting strange shadows, one of Patrick's antique whisky tumblers, upturned, snatching itself from their fingertips and flying around the board before shattering against the wall. The girls had buried the shards in the woods in the hope that Patrick would never find out what they'd done.

'I don't want Ani and Pernille terrifying themselves like we did,' Mila told Sophie.

It was kind of fun, though.

It wasn't. Not for Mila anyway. For weeks afterwards she'd been convinced there was something in their bedroom, something she couldn't see or touch, but that lurked in the shadows watching – something they had invoked. She couldn't mention her terror to Patrick or Ceci because then she'd have had to admit to the original crime. Even after she returned to her mother, in England, Mila had been worried that whatever-it-was had followed her; certainly, home had felt gloomier and her mother had been more spiteful than ever in the months that followed.

But all that was a long time ago. Mila mixed oil, vinegar, mustard and sugar to dress the salad and drained the pasta. Berthaud jumped onto the table. Mila rubbed the side of the cat's head gently with the knuckle of her index finger and then she called the girls in to eat. She left them to it, poured herself a small glass of wine, picked up her laptop, and curled herself on the settee in the living room. She typed *Kyern archaeology* into the search bar, hoping to reassure herself that, despite her trepidation there was nothing sinister about the dig, and tapped her fingers while the computer did its work. Eventually a list of hits came up.

First there was the dolmen. The prehistoric burial tomb was familiar to Mila. She had always found its great size and age awe-inspiring, and never frightening. Its permanence in the landscape was a kind of reassurance.

Next there was the whalebone statuette. The carving of the antelope was simple, but captured the vitality and spirit of the animal which had been its inspiration. It was a lovely thing. The outline of the statuette had also been used as the logo for the dig at Kyern. Someone had created a rather slapdash website for the archaeology project, and, when she clicked the *Our People* tab, Mila found a picture of Professor Timor Perry wearing a sweatshirt bearing the antelope logo. He was unremarkable in appearance. His hair was receding and he wore glasses. His eyes were small and kindly. He was an ordinary man in middle age, a typical archaeologist – or at least how Mila would imagine a typical archaeologist to look.

There was a video, further down the same page. It showed Professor Perry scoping out the Kyern dig site with a team of students and colleagues. The voiceover told her what she already knew, that the land belonged to the Girard family, who owned and operated the holiday park it bordered. Plans to develop the site had had to be put on hold until the dig was finished. At the end of the video, the face of the narrator appeared on the screen. His name was Alban Hugo and he was the educational co-ordinator for the project and a teacher at the international school. He mentioned that Professor Perry was already an expert in the ancient history of Finistère and had even published a book on the subject. Mila checked online and there it was, the guide to the local dolmens, the same book that had been at the side of Gosia's bed.

Next, out of curiosity, Mila did a search for Professor Perry's wife, Catherine.

It didn't take long to find her. She was active on social media, her accounts full of pictures of herself and the jewellery pendants she made from modelling clay: mainly cutesy ladybirds and bunny rabbits which had garnered plenty of five-star reviews on Etsy. Catherine Perry's profile picture showed a large woman in her mid-forties wearing a voluminous cotton smock and Birkenstocks, unmade-up and heavily browed. She was attractive in a Mother-Earth way but not at all like the woman Mila had imagined given Ceci's description. She certainly did not look the type to spend several thousand pounds on a designer skirt suit.

You shouldn't judge people by appearances, Sophie said.

She was right.

Mila scrolled through Catherine Perry's Facebook feed. Her husband, 'Tim', appeared regularly in photographs taken at family get-togethers – there he was at a wedding, grinning awkwardly in an ill-fitting suit, clutching a paper plate full of cocktail sausages and crisps, clearly a man who preferred to be in the background, an introvert to his wife's extrovert.

The Perrys seemed a well-suited, family-orientated couple. They had two children: a daughter about the same age as Ani, who, Mila discovered, had enrolled temporarily at the international school, and an older boy, a student at Liverpool University. The daughter, Emily, was an apple-cheeked, dimple-chinned girl who took after her mother in appearance.

Mila looked at the pictures, studying the professor's face and body language. He seemed happy. He seemed relaxed. He seemed, to all intents and purposes, to be a committed family man.

If his wife was right, and he was seeing a student – or on the point of getting involved with one – then he was risking everything, not only his marriage, but his career and his reputation. There was never any coming back from a sex scandal for anyone who worked in education. The young woman – or man – concerned would almost certainly be old enough to count as a consenting adult, but there would still be a grossly disproportionate difference in power, not to mention a breach of trust.

Perhaps Mila's first instinct had been right and the professor was having some kind of mid-life crisis.

Mila was interrupted by the ping of an incoming message on her phone. It was from Luke.

Sorry, Mila, I won't make it to Brittany this weekend. Work's a nightmare. I'll call when I can.

She texted back:

No worries xxx

She swallowed her disappointment, went back into the kitchen, took the wine out of the fridge and refilled her glass.

The girls had finished eating their main course and were rummaging in the cupboards, looking for chocolate to grate over the berries and ice cream Mila had put out for dessert.

'Do you guys know a girl at school called Emily Perry?' Mila asked casually. She reached over Ani's shoulder to remove the chocolate from its hiding place behind the rice jar.

'She's in our year,' said Pernille. 'Why?'

'Are you friends with her?'

Ani and Pernille exchanged a glance. Mila couldn't read it.

'Not friends exactly,' said Pernille, 'she only started last term.'

'Don't you like her?'

Ani shrugged. Pernille took the chocolate.

'Come on, Ani,' she said brightly. 'Let's eat this and then we can think of some more ways to ward off evil.'

Ani glanced at Mila, seeking her approval. Mila gave her a small smile.

The girls didn't want to talk about Emily Perry. Why not?

13

THURSDAY, 11 AUGUST

Mila was up at dawn the morning after Gosia's funeral. Sleep had done her good; she felt refreshed and the dread that had plagued her the previous evening seemed to have dissipated. She picked up the book that Ani and Pernille had left on the floor in the living room: *Protective Spells and Counter Curses.*

It was open at a page that suggested using 'poppets', or little dolls to represent those who had been hexed, to draw away the negative energy. Mila posted the book down the back of the bookshelf, a place from where it was unlikely to emerge for some time. Then she put an old jumper of Charlie's over her pyjamas, slipped her feet into flip-flops and went out into the garden. There was dew on the grass, and the yellow Californian poppies were holding their petals closed, like hands over their eyes. High white clouds chased across a periwinkle-blue sky, invigorated by an Atlantic wind. The swallows hunted, chit-chattering above; damsel flies warmed themselves on the stems of the flowers trembling in the breeze.

It was easy to feel close to Sophie in the garden with its charming informality: the rambling roses, the jasmine, the raspberry canes and gooseberries growing amongst the shrubs, the small, dark pond that had been dug for wildlife rather than aesthetics, the windbreak trees that gave glimpses of the low-lying land beyond and the famous ranks of menhirs. The older, more established plants and trees had been put there deliberately, but the more recent planting was accidental.

Sophie was always making plans, brilliant plans, but she never saw them through. She would buy plants that she never planted nor remembered to water, plants that eventually were tipped out of their pots in random places when they appeared to have died. Occasionally, one would survive despite the ill-treatment it had suffered and thrive in an unlikely spot. This was why the garden was so chaotic. It was lovely, but it was crazy too.

With her back to the wind, Mila examined the fruit growing in the shelter of the back wall. The plums were softening and yellowing; the peaches were swollen with a pinkish bloom, almost ready but not quite ripe. Sophie would have picked them anyway. Mila preferred to wait.

She had always loved this time of year even though summer's cresting meant the season would soon be ending. In less than a month, she'd be back in Bristol, sitting in her little house in Totterdown, the house that had, for the past ten months, been rented out to a couple of student doctors. She'd have time to tend to her own tiny garden, to give the house a clean, paint some walls maybe. She'd be able to go and watch grown-up films on her own at the Watershed and take a book and enjoy a glass of Sancerre in the cinema's bar. She'd be able to sign up to lectures or go and see her favourite comedians, and to spend lazy days meandering around the museum and art gallery on her own. She'd be free to make plans to meet up with Luke without having to consider anyone else's arrangements or feelings first.

At the exact moment she was thinking of Luke, her phone rang and her heart gave a little skip to see that it was him.

'Hi,' she said, trying to keep the pleasure out of her voice because she didn't want to sound needy.

'Hi. Listen, I'm sorry about this weekend. We're trying to get to the bottom of this county lines case and it's complicated.'

'You don't have to explain. It's fine. I'm fine. Not long now until I'm back.'

'Is there a lot still to do?'

'I need to sort out stuff for Ani. School uniform, a lacrosse stick, that kind of thing. And I need to talk to Ceci about the anniversary of the accident. One of Sophie's friends thinks we should do something.'

'Like a memorial?'

'More of a celebration is what she has in mind. I don't know. Do you think it would be good for Ani?'

'You're asking me for child-rearing advice?'

'Ha ha. I'm asking for your opinion.'

'Well, don't. How did the funeral go?'

'It was okay. But, Luke, I—'

'Mils, I have to go. Bob's calling.'

'Okay, but I...'

The line went dead.

There you go, said Sophie. *Work always comes first with Luke Hogg.*

Because what he does is important, Sophie.

Yeah, yeah.

Not everyone has wealthy parents like you and Charlie.

Lot of good that did us, didn't it?

Mila couldn't be bothered to argue with the voice in her head. She turned and went back inside the house.

Sophie wasn't finished with her.

What about Carter Jackson? she asked.

What about him?

Aren't you going to see if his story adds up?

Mila glanced at her laptop.

She was tempted, but Carter being an expert in computer technology, he would know how to keep his personal information private, and might also have set up alerts to warn him if anyone was putting his name into search engines.

Oh, go on! Sophie prodded. *Just a quick peek.*

No!

It can't be a coincidence that he's back here, now working with my mother.

Whatever. Carter Jackson and his future career are neither my concern nor my business.

You and I both know that you don't believe that. A pause. *You still like him, don't you, Mila?*

Go away, Sophie. Leave me alone.

You don't want to investigate him in case you find out that he's been lying. You don't want to see him as a bad guy,

Mila walked into the kitchen.

Gosia's shawl, the shawl she'd lent to Ani and that had never been returned, was folded on the back of one of the chairs. To distract herself from Sophie, Mila picked it up and held it against her cheek. She thought of Gosia, lying in her grave. She thought of her son, Tomas, somewhere in the world, not knowing what had happened to his mother. She, an employee of an agency that specialised in tracking down lost people, had spectacularly failed to find out anything about this woman.

She waited half an hour and then she called Luke back.

'Just a quick question,' she said in response to him answering in an *I-don't-really-have-time-to-talk-to-you-right-now* voice. 'How would you set about finding the identity of someone who lived in a van, whose surname you didn't know and who you knew practically nothing about?'

'The traveller woman?'

'Yes.'

'Mobile phone?'

'I don't know where it is.'

'DNA?'

'Not an option.'

'Then the van's numberplate and anything inside it that might give you a clue. Plus speak to anyone who knew her, even had a conversation with her. She might have mentioned something that would help; even the smallest things can point you in the right direction.'

Jenny had spoken to Gosia. And the old horsebox must still be around somewhere.

Mila didn't know where it was, or what had happened to it, but Luke was right; it would be a good starting point.

She'd been lazy. She hadn't tried hard enough. But she would now.

14

Jenny – Mila had only ever known her by this single name – was Somalian, a skilled baker and an excellent maker of coffee. She'd been running the café in Morannez for several years. Jenny had been a good friend to Sophie; even during Sophie's darkest times she'd always been there for her. It was no surprise that she had also helped the traveller woman.

Ani and Pernille had been given the choice of coming into Morannez town with Mila, or staying at the sea house, and they'd chosen to come. The cool morning had turned into a hot day; the thermometer on the wall of the pharmacy was reading 31 degrees. In the early afternoon, the sun was at its zenith. Mila knew the town centre would be quieter then; the heat would keep most of the holidaymakers on the beach or inside, in the shade, beneath their fans.

Morannez was a pretty place, the oldest streets still cobbled, with ancient houses crowded round them, flowers tumbling out of window boxes and from pots placed on steep steps, the grey slate roofs reflecting the sun, lovely views around each corner and the picturesque river running through, the sound of it splashing over its rocky bed providing a musical backdrop to the busier sounds of the town.

In the square, people were sitting at tables in the shade of umbrellas, sipping cold drinks. The doors to the cafés and restaurants were wide open, and from inside came the sounds of laughter as the waiting staff enjoyed their meals now the busy service time was over. A cat stretched luxuriantly on a wall. Doves cooed from the branches of trees and water dripped from the baskets suspended from fancy wrought-iron supports outside the entrance to the marketplace. The girl behind the counter in the Italian gelateria rinsed out the scoops in tubs of water and a young man without a shirt snoozed with his hat over his face in the hammock slung between the two trees where he'd parked his fruit cart.

Mila and the girls went into the café. Mila bought two cans of lemonade for Ani and Pernille, which they took with them to sit on the wall in the shade of the tall trees that surrounded the crazy golf course.

Jenny made coffee for Mila, poured one for herself, and came to sit beside Mila on the stools by the bar. Apart from a man in a fedora reading a book and absent-mindedly stirring a glass of lemon tea, the café was empty.

Jenny was bare-armed, wearing an apron over a polo-necked top and wide-legged cotton trousers. She rested her fingers on the counter, the nails painted the same pale green as her top.

'You'll never be one of the locals, Mila, if you insist on coming into Morannez at this time of day,' she said.

'No, I won't.' Mila paused then added: 'But it doesn't matter because I'm moving back to England at the beginning of September to finish the book I'm writing.'

'Can't you do that here?'

'I tried, but I can't get my head in the right place.'

'And Ani's going with you?'

'No, she's going to boarding school in Switzerland.'

Jenny's eyes widened.

'It's the same place where Sophie used to go,' Mila said quickly. 'Ani's going to love it.'

'I thought Sophie hated school.'

'She did, but it's changed a lot since then. It's a fantastic place now, really *outstanding*. One of the best schools in Europe.'

That was an exaggeration but even so Jenny didn't look impressed.

'Anyway,' Mila said brightly, 'I didn't come to talk to you about that. I came to ask you about Gosia. I'm going to have another go at finding her son.'

'Oh, okay.'

'As far as I know, you were the only person in Morannez who Gosia talked to. She told Ani that she used to come here to charge her phone.'

'That's right. And to use the internet.'

Mila glanced out to the girls. They were still there on the wall, side by side, their heads close together. She and Sophie used to sit exactly like that.

'Do you know what she was doing on the internet? Was she sending emails, maybe?'

'I don't know,' said Jenny. 'I never asked. She used to spend a long time sitting in the corner over there, staring at her phone, lost in concentration.' She sighed. 'If I'd realised she was so sick, I might have paid a bit more attention. I feel awful now that I didn't.'

'You shouldn't feel bad about anything. Gosia didn't give the impression of being ill. I don't suppose she said anything about her condition to you?'

'Nothing. She ate like a horse, always seemed to have lots of energy and I never heard her complain of any pain. She said once that she was looking forward to going home for a rest, but not in a way that made me worry about her. And no, she didn't say where home was.'

Mila remembered the neat shape of the doctor emerging backwards through the door at the back of the horsebox, the same morning that Mila had found the body. In her tan tights and heeled shoes, she had climbed down the ladder with the same fastidiousness with which she'd climbed up. She had stood in a patch of sunlight, peeling blue latex gloves from her fingers and saying, 'Natural causes. There's no need for an inquest.'

Mila turned her attention back to Jenny,

'What about Gosia's book, do you know anything about that?'

'What book?'

'I saw her writing in a large journal. She told Ani it was her work. I think it was stolen from her the night she died.'

'Aren't the gendarmes looking for it?'

'They didn't think it was relevant because it had no monetary value.' Mila sighed. 'Did Gosia ever bring the book in here?'

'I didn't see a book, but she was always asking questions.'

'About what?'

'Everything. Everyone. This town, the international school, the Kyern dig. She used to take my old newspapers to search for stories about it.'

'Ani said she knew one of the archaeologists.'

'Well, there you are. Maybe she came here because of the dig.' Jenny picked up a teaspoon and sipped coffee from it. 'But none of this will help you find her son. Have you looked at her phone? She used to say she had her life backed up on it.'

'I don't know where it is.'

'The gendarmes will have it. They'll have taken it from the horsebox.'

'I don't suppose they'd let me look at it.'

'It's worth asking, though, isn't it? They might at least let you see if there's a number for Gosia's son.'

'You're right,' said Mila. 'They might.'

* * *

Mila paid for Pernille and Ani to play a round of crazy golf and she left them queuing in the shade of the pine trees, while she went to the gendarmerie, a fine building in the middle of the town. She waited for what felt like ages before being seen by the same officer she'd met at Gosia's van the morning she found the body.

He recognised her and was polite but reticent.

'Good morning, madame. How can I help you?'

Mila didn't bother with formalities.

'The traveller woman who died in the horsebox,' she said, 'I'm trying to trace her son, so we can let him know what happened. His details are sure to be on her phone. I don't need to take it away, but could I look at it? It will only take a short while.'

'We didn't find a phone amongst the woman's belongings. If we had, we'd have checked for family contacts ourselves.'

'But Gosia always had the phone with her,' said Mila. 'If it wasn't in the horsebox, it proves that she was robbed the night she died.'

The officer shook his head.

'I don't understand why you're so unconcerned about what is an obvious crime,' Mila said.

'Madame, we're understaffed, underpaid, we're dealing with unprecedented levels of crime and our work levels are through the roof. We have neither the time nor the resources to investigate the death of a vagrant woman in poor health who may or may not have had a few personal items of very little value stolen. It's sad, yes, but it's not important.'

'But her son...'

'If they were close, then he'd have known she was here and he'd have been in touch with us by now asking why he hasn't heard from her. But he hasn't contacted us. Nobody has. Perhaps they were estranged; maybe he was embarrassed by her, I don't know.'

'So that's it?' Mila asked. 'You're not going to do anything about the missing phone?'

'Do you know what make it was? What model? How old it was? Do you know when the woman last had it? Do you know anything about it at all?'

'No.'

'Then even if we apprehended the' – he made speech marks with the first two fingers on each hand – '"thief", and even if he or she still had the phone about his or her person, which is *highly* unlikely, even then we wouldn't recognise it.'

'I suppose not,' Mila agreed.

'Listen, madame,' said the officer, 'I appreciate your concerns but there are bigger, more important things to worry about than one unfortunate, very sick old woman. Leave her be now. Let her rest in peace.'

* * *

Mila spent the rest of Thursday afternoon in the sea house, on the internet, researching the Kyern dig, trying to spot anything that might possibly constitute a link between the dig and Gosia. Nothing jumped out. She went online and scoured digital versions of newspaper stories, hoping to find the article that Gosia had been reading on the evening before her death, but the stories were displayed differently and she couldn't be sure which version Gosia had had nor whose face had been circled in the cutting. The only constant seemed to be Professor Tim Perry, who featured prominently in most of the write-ups and given that Gosia had also been reading a book he had written, it seemed likely that his was the face she had picked out. Likely, but not certain.

Next, Mila swallowed her reluctance to pry, and visited the Toronto police website taking care to keep her searches general rather than searching for Carter Jackson by name. She found no reference to Carter, neither did his name come up on any of the pages concerning the work of the narcotics' squad. But then, if his work involved searching for drug money undercover, it would hardly be advertised on the internet. She pulled up court cases involving drugs but although some of the trials were high profile and featured widely in the media, Carter had never been called as a witness, or if he had, his evidence hadn't been reported.

It was a catch-22 situation. It would be impossible to establish whether Carter Jackson was telling the truth about his career, or whether he wasn't because either way nothing was in the public domain. Mila needed to think of a different route in.

15
_____
FRIDAY, 12 AUGUST

The next morning, Pernille and Ani went back to the Sohars' house to swim in the pool, and Mila took the opportunity to cycle into Morannez.

Friday was the usual crossover day for accommodation at the campsites and holiday parks, which meant the roads were busy with campervans and cars with foreign and French plates coming and going. The small army of local people who worked as cleaners, gardeners and maintenance operatives for rental properties and caravans were out and about too, some carrying their buckets and brooms on the backs of mopeds, a quicker way of getting through the traffic.

In the shady area beside the square, old men and women were already congregating around the tables where they played chess or cards. Others were standing talking around the boules court, unpacking cases of traditional Breton boules.

Mila cycled into one of the tiny back streets, route de Rosnuel, where the Toussaint's Agency offices were located.

The door that led up to the offices was to the left of Morannez town's most bijou patisserie, its windows lined with displays of baked goods: millefeuilles, kouign-amanns, macarons, slices of opera cake, perfect little buttery pastry tarts and tiny paper cups containing marzipan fruit that were exquisite miniatures of the real thing. All these delights were arranged immaculately on laced paper, inclined slightly towards the glass. The smell around the shop was of caramelised sugar with undertones of vanilla and chocolate. Mila was always tempted to go in and buy something ridiculously expensive (although not when you considered the work that had gone into producing each wonderful morsel), but on this occasion she resisted. Instead, she opened the door to the side of the patisserie and trotted up the narrow staircase to a second door at the top. This door was also unlocked which meant Ceci was at work.

'Hello!' Mila called. 'It's me.'

Mila's stepmother didn't answer, and when Mila looked round the door of her office she saw her standing by the window looking out over the street, with her phone pressed to her ear. She was immaculate in a pair of cream linen trousers with a high-necked blouse, blue drop earrings and a matching necklace. She raised a slender hand in greeting. Mila waved back and went into the tiny kitchen area. She took a bottle of Orangina out of the fridge and poured its contents into a glass, which she took into her office.

It wouldn't be hers for much longer. Not that it ever really had been. When Mila first moved in, it had felt like an intrusion. It still did. A framed photograph of Sophie holding a rosy baby Ani in a field full of sunflowers was the only personal item in the office, but still Sophie cast a strong presence. It had taken months of being here for Mila to stop expecting Sophie to open the door and breeze in, saying in mock annoyance: 'Mila! What are you doing sitting at my desk?'

It had been Sophie's office and now it would be Carter Jackson's.

It was hard to imagine the tall Canadian with his big, booted feet in this small room. He'd do away with the potted plants, which were Ceci's passion, but perhaps he'd leave the picture of Sophie hanging where it was. Or maybe he'd replace it with a picture of his own child. Even so, it seemed, to Mila, more than a little weird that he'd be here, in a place that had been Sophie's. It didn't feel appropriate.

Many years have passed since Carter and Sophie were lovers, she reminded herself. And it was unfair to assume that Carter's being here was for some perverse reason. It was feasible that he genuinely hadn't known that Ceci was Sophie's mother. It wasn't as if the bande sauvage ever went into one another's houses as teenagers. All their growing up during the six or seven summers they spent together had taken place at the beach.

And yet, given Carter's background, wouldn't he have done some research into Toussaint's agency when he applied for the job? Wouldn't he at the very least have checked out Ceci's personal history?

Mila looked at the picture of Sophie and Ani amongst the sunflowers and made up her mind that she wouldn't leave it for Carter.

She would take it with her when she left and hang it in the hallway of her house in Bristol.

* * *

Mila opened the blinds to let in the sunlight, switched on the computer and was waiting for it to boot up when Ceci came in.

'Sorry, darling, that was the solicitor, Madame Gide,' said Ceci. 'She has a client, a member of the aristocracy, no less, who wants to leave his considerable wealth to the families of the men his father served with during the war. All he has to go on is an old photograph and some names.'

'That will be interesting work.'

'It's a job that would have been right up your street, darling, but I'm sure, in your absence, Carter will be able to handle it.'

Ceci couldn't have meant to hurt Mila, but that last comment stung.

'Speaking of Carter, where is he?'

'Out watching Professor Perry. Now don't you pull a face, Mila Shepherd, it's perfectly legitimate work. Anyway, I thought it would be useful for him to start familiarising himself with Morannez and the holiday park and the dig site and all the rest of it so he can find his way around.'

He's staying at the holiday park. It's literally ranks of caravans. How could anyone not find their way around that?

'Ceci, can I ask you something?'

'Of course.'

'The van that Gosia used to live in... the old horsebox. What would have happened to it after the gendarmes had finished with it?'

'It would have gone for recycling.'

'They wouldn't have kept it in case they needed it for evidence later?'

'Evidence for what, darling? There was no crime, officially.'

'Okay. So, who would they have called to take the van away?'

'Monsieur Bourran. He runs the breaker's yard behind the furniture store on the outskirts of town.'

* * *

Monsieur Bourran, or at least the man who answered the phone at the yard, was not an easy person with whom to converse if, like

Mila, your French was not fluent and you didn't understand Breton colloquialisms. She also had the distinct impression that whoever she was talking to was enjoying making life difficult for her. Mila had encountered this phenomenon before.

He's messing with you. Be more assertive, Sophie said.

But Mila didn't want to get on the wrong side of Monsieur Difficile at the other end of the line because she needed the information he eventually, after leading her down many garden paths, provided.

The van in which the old woman had died, he told her, was supposed to have been collected and taken to the authorised facility where the various components would be separated and sent off to specialist recycling centres, but that hadn't happened. Why hadn't it? Because Madame Bourran's cousin, Madame Rigaud, who, with her husband, owned a smallholding out on the Bloemel road, had been on the lookout for a similarly sized van for some time. She was expanding her free-range-egg-producing business and needed new accommodation for the former battery-farm chickens she was intending to rehome. The old horsebox was exactly the size she had requested so the van had been set to one side and Monsieur Rigaud had come with his tractor to collect it and tow it away.

Mila would have been interested to know how much money had changed hands, because she was sure there'd have been a fee paid by the municipality for the disposal of the vehicle. To make a further profit from selling it on sounded dodgy – the kind of cash transaction in which Carter Jackson would have been interested in his former role. She didn't ask, though, because she didn't want to alienate the man.

'Was there anything left in the van?' Mila asked.

'Not much. Few bits and pieces.'

'I don't suppose you found anything that might help identify the old woman who used to live in it?'

'Nah, there was only rubbish inside. Old lady stuff. Crap. Nothing of any value.'

'What about the registration plate?' Mila asked. 'Did you check that?'

'Took a photograph in case anyone ever came asking,' said the man. 'If you give me your number, I'll text it to you.'

16

Mila looked up the address for Madame and Monsieur Rigaud and found they didn't live on the main road that linked the towns of Morannez and Bloemel-sur-Mer, as she'd been told, but on a smaller link road. The smallholding was not far from the AquaSplash water park on land that backed onto the grounds of the old chateau that Sophie used to call 'Jonestown' because it was now a commune. Mila couldn't find either a telephone number or an email address for the Rigauds, so decided to make the most of the fine weather and cycle there herself.

'Just popping out!' she called to Ceci.

'Pas de problème, ma chère!'

It was a pleasant cycle ride out towards Bloemel, past the entrance to the water park, which was marked with two large floppy inflatable people, one in a pair of trunks, the other in a bikini, who were permanently participating in a wild, flappy dance. Holidaymakers were still queuing to get in despite the breeziness of the day. An ice-cream vendor was doing a roaring trade along the queue. Inside the park, Mila could see the shadows of kids circling down the tube slides and heard screams of joy as they splashed into the pools at the bottom. Sophie had thrown a party for Ani there once. Ani's birthday was on 29 December, not the best day for a child to have a birthday, and that particular year her actual birthday party had been a disaster. Ani, and almost all her friends, had been suffering from bad colds and the heating wasn't working in the sea house so they couldn't even take off their coats. Sophie felt so bad about the disastrous party that she'd decided to give her daughter a second celebration in the summer to compensate.

Mila, who was over from Bristol for the weekend, had been enlisted to make sure none of the kids drowned but, as it turned out, the park staff were well organised and had the health and safety aspects covered. It had been a scorching hot day and the dozen or so nine and ten-year-olds invited had run riot in their swimsuits, having a blast. Mila had been persuaded by her niece to have a go on the largest, twistiest and fastest slide: the Terminator. It involved climbing up a towering set of stairs, following in the slippery footsteps of a constant stream of noisy little children who were practically climbing over one another to get to the top first. Once there, Mila had to wait until the child in front of her had been dispatched into the mouth of the tube before it was her turn. The teenager who was supervising told her to sit down, lean back, and to keep her hands crossed over her chest. When the bell went, he gave her a shove and she was off.

She had enjoyed the experience for the five or six seconds of open tube before it plunged into complete darkness. Mila was afraid of the speed with which she was being corkscrewed downwards and, despite the warning about her hands, was attempting to slow herself down by grabbing on to the sides, conscious that she might become accidentally wedged in the tube and have other thrill-seekers pile on top of her in the dark.

A few seconds after that, she careered into the splash pool, was completely submerged, and emerged, swimsuit askew, feeling like a sock released from a spin drier.

'What did you think of that, Mila?' Sophie asked, reaching down her hand to help Mila out. Sophie, who had excused herself from any getting-wet activities on the grounds that she was mother of the birthday girl, still had dry hair and intact make-up and was wearing proper clothes.

'Oh, it was great, Sophie, brilliant.' Mila shook back her hair and held on to Sophie for balance. Behind her, little kids bombed into the pool and scrambled out to re-join the queue at the steps to slide again.

'I *knew* you'd love it!' Sophie had said.

How did you do it, Sophie? Mila wondered. *How did you always manage to make everyone do exactly what you wanted them to do?*

On the far side of the water park, about a kilometre further on and down a small turning, Mila found the Rigauds' smallholding. The entrance was cluttered with ornaments, cement animals and ceramic jugs and urns, an ancient petrol pump, a huge, sun-bleached resin model of Marilyn Monroe trying to hold down her skirt, and various rusting pieces of railway memorabilia. A long-haired woman in hippy clothing was walking along the lane lugging a basket of windfalls. She smiled and nodded a greeting to Mila. All the commune people were friendly but Sophie wasn't the only person who privately called them 'freaks'.

Mila parked her bike by the gate and walked down a drive towards an old farmhouse with land on either side. Vegetables and flowers were growing in organised beds, and beyond those were paddocks with sheep, goats and alpacas. Beyond, the turrets of the chateau were illuminated by the sun.

The door to the farmhouse was ajar. Mila knocked and shouted, 'Hello!' A cacophony of dog-barking ensued and a number of animals of varying shapes, sizes and shagginess bounded around the corner to greet her. They accompanied her along the path to the back of the building. Outbuildings and garages housed various pieces of farm machinery, some old caravans and other bits and pieces of agricultural and leisure kit. Most of it looked as if it had been left to rot. The fact that dozens of chickens were roaming around the yard seemed promising.

Amongst the chickens, a swarthy man in overalls was attaching a spraying mechanism to a dusty tractor. The dogs ran over to him and set to sniffing around the tractor.

'Bonjour, monsieur!' Mila called.

'Salut!' He raised a hand in greeting but did not straighten his back. Smoke was caught in tiny gusts from the cigarette clenched between his lips. 'What can I do you for?' He was small and squat and appeared very strong, his skin tanned a deep brown, and he was wearing a peasant shirt and canvas trousers held up with braces. 'Have you come about the eggs?'

'Eggs? No!'

'If you want to buy eggs, there's a kiosk at the front with an honesty box.'

'I haven't come for eggs, monsieur.'

'Ours are the best eggs. Free range. Happy chickens. We sell at all the local markets, and we even supply Monsieur Girard's Grand Hotel at Bloemel.'

'That's fantastic,' said Mila. She decided it would be easiest to get straight to the point. 'Monsieur, I understand you took possession of an old horsebox recently that your wife intends to use as a chicken house.'

'Who told you that? We didn't do anything wrong. It was all perfectly above aboard.'

'I'm sure it was and please don't worry, I'm not from the authorities. It's just, I knew the lady who used to live in the van; her name was Gosia. Before you put the chickens in, I was wondering if I could have a quick look inside.'

The old man stood up. He took the cigarette out of his mouth and pinched it between two huge fingers. 'The hens are already in it,' he said. He nodded towards a paddock where dozens of chickens were pecking around in the dirt, or sitting on the branches of the low, overhanging trees, squawking at their sisters. The van was there; Mila just hadn't recognised it. The wheels and cab had been removed and hens were all over and around it.

'Oh,' said Mila. 'Well, I'm sure Gosia would be glad that it's being put to good use.' She hesitated. '*Was* there was anything left in it when you brought it here?'

The man shrugged. 'A few bits of rubbish. Some wood. I burned everything we couldn't use. The cab went to the breaker's yard.'

'You burned everything?'

'Apart from a few pots and pans that my wife wanted to keep. I assure you there was nothing valuable.'

'I don't suppose you found anything with a name on it? A shop receipt or a library card for example? Anything? I'm trying to identify the woman so that we can let her family know what's happened.'

Monsieur Rigaud threw the end of the cigarette on the ground. 'There was a photograph.'

'A photograph?'

'Yes. It had slipped down the back of the bed shelf.'

'May I see the photograph, monsieur, or...' Mila paused, realising suddenly what might have become of the picture. '... did you burn that too?'

'No, of course I didn't burn it. I wouldn't burn anyone's precious memento. That'd be asking for trouble – bad luck and all that. Hold on, I'll fetch it for you.'

He set off at a painfully slow pace towards the farmhouse. Mila propped herself against a pile of wood while she waited. A particularly old, smelly dog came and leaned against her knees and she patted the top of its greasy head. The dog sighed with pleasure. After a few minutes, Monsieur Rigaud appeared again clutching a small image between his filthy finger and thumb. He passed it to Mila. It was an old-fashioned print framed by a narrow white border and it showed a boy of Ani's age or perhaps a little older. He was standing in a garden, a flower border behind him, holding the collar of a large dog similar to the one currently scratching its ear beside Mila. The boy had dark hair, and was wearing pale blue jeans and a long-sleeved shirt beneath a leather bomber jacket. Mila turned the picture over. On the back was a single word: *Tomas*, and a date, *1992*.

'That's Gosia's son,' Mila said. 'He wanted to be a vet. It's all I know about him.'

She looked into the boy's face. It was such a sweet, hopeful face, the chin flushed with acne.

'They buried her in the cemetery, didn't they?' asked Monsieur Rigaud, crossing himself.

'Yes. And I'd really like to find this boy and let him know.'

'He won't be a boy any more. If he was, say, sixteen in that picture, 1992, that would make him in his mid-forties now.'

Which would make Gosia mid-sixties to seventies. Not really old at all.

'Also,' said Monsieur Rigaud, 'there's this.'

He passed Mila a CD in a rigid plastic case. The sleeve inside was faded so that the writing was almost impossible to read, but Mila could just make out a word written in black marker in the top left-hand corner of the CD.

'"Speakeasy",' she said. 'What does that mean?'

'Don't look at me,' said Monsieur Rigaud. 'I haven't a bloody clue.'

Mila and Ani sat at the kitchen table together, Ani drawing the cat, Mila sipping coffee and watching her niece, thinking how beautiful she was with the light from the window shining through her hair, admiring her small, sharp features. Berthaud jumped onto the window ledge and stretched in the sunlight, pawing half-heartedly at a butterfly on the other side of the glass.

The photograph of Tomas lay on the table between them.

'Is that the same picture that Gosia showed you?' Mila asked.

'One of them.'

Mila held the photograph up. She studied it as hard as she could but she couldn't see anything new in it: no clue as to where it had been taken, or the second name of Tomas or Gosia. It was so frustrating, to have such a strong connection and for it to be no help at all.

'What time's Luke coming?' Ani asked suddenly, out of the blue.

'He's not. He texted me last night. Sorry, I forgot to tell you.'

'He shouldn't leave it to the last minute to tell you his plans.'

'He can't help it when things outside his control go wrong, Ani.

That's what happens when you work for the police. He has to work overtime to support his colleagues.'

'He doesn't actually *have* to work overtime, though, does he? I mean, they wouldn't sack him if he said "no".'

'Probably not but when there's a big case, everyone pulls together. That's what teams do.'

'And that's really shit telling you by text.'

'He called me as soon as he could.'

'If he really cared for you, he'd be more considerate.'

'Oh yes? Since when did you become a relationship expert?'

'Maman always said family was more important than work.'

'That's true,' Mila said. She thought, but didn't say, that Sophie thought almost everything was more important than work. Besides, Luke and she weren't exactly family – not yet. Although after ten years, perhaps couples became related by osmosis.

She was quietly pleased that Ani had said 'Maman', and didn't seem to have realised she'd done so.

'Even Mamie says Luke messes you around,' said Ani. 'She says he doesn't give any thought to your feelings.'

'Mamie Ceci said that?'

Ani nodded. Mila had no inclination to pursue the conversation. She didn't like the thought of Ceci and Ani discussing her love life; it was none of their business. And Ceci had no right to criticise Luke when he, like the rest of them, was a victim of circumstance. It wasn't his fault that he and Mila were living on different sides of the Channel. Out of everyone, he'd had the least control over the situation.

Anyway, if she looked at it objectively, it was a good thing Luke wasn't coming this weekend. Mila and Ani rubbed along without too much friction most of the time, but on the few occasions Luke had come to stay at the sea house, Ani had been awkward and things had been less simple, more like they had been in the aftermath of Sophie's death.

Luke didn't belong in the sea house. It was not his fault but he didn't fit into it; he was always trying to impose order and fix things that Sophie had broken or Charlie had bodged and Ani didn't like that at all.

Luke didn't like it either. He didn't like the haphazardness of the place, the fact that none of the plates or mugs matched, the disorganised heaps of books on the shelves, the second-hand saris that Sophie had bought at the market in Bloemel and hooked over the windows to form makeshift curtains. He didn't look right sitting at the kitchen table, which was wonky, having been crafted by Charlie out of driftwood; he walked in frustration around the garden pulling up plants that he considered weeds but which Sophie had loved. His ankles were bitten by what he said were cat fleas, although neither Mila nor Ani were ever affected. When he was in Mila's bed, the mattress dipped inwards and neither of them were comfortable. Sex was out of the question given the bed's squeaky springs and Ani in her bedroom just down the landing and so was conversation because what could they talk about that wasn't relevant to Ani? How could they discuss a future when any future would impact on her?

* * *

When she'd finished drawing her portrait of Berthaud, Ani went into the garden. She curled up on the swing-seat with her phone in her hands and her hair shielding her face.

Mila made more coffee. She tapped her fingers on the tabletop and stared at Tomas looking out at her from the photograph that had been taken three decades earlier. Who had been behind the camera? she wondered. Gosia? Tomas's father? Somebody different altogether? Berthaud came and padded at her fingertips with her soft little paws, barely bigger than pennies. Mila crooked a finger and rubbed the cat's cheek. Berthaud closed her eyes and rubbed back, pressing her hard little head against Mila's hand.

'Speakeasy,' Mila said. 'What does that mean?'

She did a search on her laptop.

Mila had of course heard the word 'speakeasy' before, but hadn't realised until Wikipedia helpfully explained that it had come into common parlance in America during Prohibition to represent an illicit establishment that sold alcoholic drinks. The patrons of the saloons would have had to whisper or 'speak easy' in order to be admitted.

One of the songs in the musical *Bugsy Malone* was called 'Speakeasy', or maybe it was the name of the scene in which the song was set. A click on the link showed little girls performing a complex tap routine and wearing sparkly costumes that wouldn't be considered appropriate today.

Nowadays, the word 'speakeasy' was used to denote a bar that replicated the old-fashioned, stylish décor and slightly louche ambience with which the original establishments were associated. In Covid times, people had also used the term to refer to places where people met to drink, when meeting wasn't allowed.

Mila couldn't see how any of this could possibly help her identify Gosia or her son.

She turned the CD over in her hands. It was one of those that used to be bought as part of a large pack of blanks in the last part of the twentieth century before the full-on onset of the digital age. She hadn't listened to a CD for ages and she couldn't be sure that this even was a music CD – she had an idea that some discs were specially formatted to store information, even videos.

She texted Ceci.

Do you know anyone who still has a CD player?

The reply came almost at once.

Yes. Me.

18

SATURDAY, 13 AUGUST

Mila received a message from the man she'd spoken to at the recycling yard; he'd been good to his word and attached a photograph of Gosia's horsebox's registration plate.

On the plate, the letters SK were printed beneath the golden stars of the European Union logo. It took Mila less than thirty seconds to establish SK represented the country of Slovakia. Apart from that, the plate was white with black digits, two letters followed by a small Slovakian flag, four numbers and a letter at the end. Mila googled the registration, hoping against hope that a dealership number or some other information might turn up, but all she discovered was that the plate had originated in the Ilava district in the west of the country.

This might mean that Gosia was Slovakian, but it could equally be a red herring. Perhaps she'd simply picked up the van while travelling or had acquired it from a Slovakian. Mila could ask Luke if he had access to an international register of EU number plates, but since Brexit, accessing that kind of information would almost certainly have become more difficult. And even if it was possible, Mila didn't think Luke would appreciate being asked to investigate something that was massively out of his remit. Even ten years ago it might have been possible but nobody could do anything on the quiet any more. Any kind of activity left a digital footprint. Mila would never ask Luke to lie on her behalf, and she didn't want to ask him to do anything that would put him in a compromising position; he wouldn't do it anyway. He would refuse.

The numberplate was a dead end. That left the CD.

Mila couldn't take the CD to Ceci's apartment yet because Ceci was meeting a friend for lunch and even if she hadn't left yet she liked taking her time getting ready for such appointments.

Mila felt as if she had to do something, though.

Ani said she was happy spending the morning alone at the sea house; there was a film she wanted to watch and she'd probably meet up with Pernille in the afternoon. Mila studied her niece's face for signs of anxiety, but couldn't see any. Twenty-six days until she went off to boarding school in Switzerland, only eleven until the anniversary of the accident and they still hadn't spoken about either event.

Mila had tried to talk to Ani about her going away to school, but each time Ani had either walked away, or shut the conversation down at the earliest opportunity. Mila didn't want to upset Ani, but if they didn't talk about it soon, they'd run out of time and the longer she waited, the harder it would be.

Mila really needed Ceci's support. Ceci was always good at making things sound like they were going to be fun. Sophie used to say it was her superpower.

For now, though, Mila had some time to herself and she decided to cycle to the Kyern dig site because she wanted to see Professor Timor Perry in the flesh and talk to him if she could. His potential philandering was none of her business but either he, or one of his colleagues, was connected in some way to Gosia and the professor was the most likely candidate given that Gosia had been reading his book. He might know some snippet of information about the woman, some little clue that would set Mila on the right path towards finding Tomas.

The lane to Kyern was banked on either side, the grassy slopes dotted with wildflowers, trees casting dark shadows that fractured the glare of the sun reflected on the surface of the road. It narrowed into a series of bends before climbing up one side of a hill and ending in a gravelled car park at the top. There was a circular drive, and tourists coming to visit the famous dolmen could reverse into spaces marked out around the drive, in the shade of the trees at the edge of the forest that covered most of the hill.

The car park was almost full. Mila spotted a couple of minibuses from Rennes' university's archaeology department, and a number of small, dusty cars that she thought were likely to belong to people working on the dig. A family was picnicking beneath the awning of a large campervan and there was a handful of vehicles with foreign plates.

A small group was standing in front of the large, weather-worn information board which told the 'story' of the Kyern dolmen. Someone would have to update it now, given the discovery of the statuette. Presumably marketing people were right now planning new boards with pictures of the antelope taking centre stage. Or perhaps they were waiting to see if the dig turned up any further treasures.

Mila left her bike behind the trees at the edge of an area designated for picnics and followed the narrow path down through the woods towards the dolmen. The sun was at full height now and crickets were chirping in the undergrowth. When she stepped out of the shade of the trees, the air was warm on the skin of her bare arms and her head.

She felt a frisson of excitement as she walked down the hill. She did not know why Gosia had been so interested in the dig, or what connected her to one of the people working here, but she hoped she might soon find out.

If she was lucky, she could even find the key that would unlock the mystery of Gosia's identity, and help Mila track down the traveller woman's son.

19

The dig was at the bottom of the hill on land that ran behind the holiday park, land that was still being used for agricultural purposes. As Mila approached the end of the path, she could see how one corner of a huge field had been cleared. The rest still contained line upon line of corn plants, each taller than a man, standing like a ranked army on their sturdy stalks, whiskery heads of maize opening up amongst great, papery leaves. When the breeze ran through the field, the corn whispered and performed a Mexican wave in its wake.

The dig area was bigger than Mila had been expecting, a large, rectangular patch of land divided into a series of trenches. Around these were tents and kiosks, portable lavatories and a marquee, with a hand-painted wooden sign saying: *Refectory*. People were milling around, some crouched in the troughs of soil, others moving between the tents. Black plastic sheeting weighed down with old tyres covered some of the site, to protect what lay beneath from the weather, and keep it out of sight of prying eyes.

Mila wandered into the site – there was no physical barrier and nothing telling people to keep away. She approached a woman who was rinsing small items in a plastic bowl on a trestle table in the shade of a small pagoda with its legs pegged into the dry ground. The cleaned items were drying on a rack.

'Can I help you?' the woman asked, without looking up. Her hair was very short and dyed bright pink. Her earlobe shone with piercings and her bare arms were covered in tattoos.

'I just wondered how the dig was going,' Mila said.

'It's not going badly,' the woman answered. She gently worked at some dried-on mud on something that looked like a pebble with the bristles of a small brush. 'We found a couple of prehistoric blades today. A nice burin.'

'Burin?'

'Like a chisel. For carving. It's the kind of tool they'd have used to make the whalebone sculpture.'

'Wow. So, it might possibly have been the same tool that was used to carve the antelope?'

The woman smiled sideways at Mila. 'Nothing's impossible.'

'It must be exciting, waiting for finds,' said Mila.

'I wouldn't use the word "exciting". You're right about the waiting, though. If you want to work in archaeology, the most important attribute you need is patience, and a willingness to be disappointed. I've been on some digs where we haven't found a single thing. Not. One. Thing. Which is frustrating. Especially when you know there's probably some good stuff down there.'

'I can imagine. How long will you be here for?'

'We've got ten more weeks.'

'That's not very long.'

The woman shrugged. 'Sometimes we don't even get as long as that.'

'So, anything you don't find in the next ten weeks is going to be buried for the next however-many thousands of years beneath tonnes of brick and concrete?'

'Yep. Unless we hit the jackpot, archaeologically speaking, and then we might get an extension.'

'I would have thought the carving that's already been found would be enough to halt any development on this land.'

'You'd think. But the tourist trade suffered so badly during the pandemic that the authorities are keen to boost it however they can. This' – she gestured around her, indicating the dig site with the cornfield beyond – 'is prime money-making land. We were lucky we were given permission to dig at all.'

The woman carefully laid the piece she had been cleaning on a cushion of folded paper towels on the drying rack. She fished in the washing-up bowl and took out another piece.

'Is it okay if I look around?' Mila asked.

'Feel free. Just don't go too near the trenches. The team gets very protective of them.'

Mila wandered over to the fringes of the main trench and watched as a variety of people of different ages meticulously worked at the soil, scraping it in tiny increments into buckets, which were passed back to waiting colleagues who tipped it into a pile, to be replaced later. The people doing the digging were working in direct sunlight, but all were wearing hats and their complexions were veiled by a thick layer of sunscreen. As Mila watched, a young man came out with a jug of iced water, which he used to replenish the various water bottles. Everyone officially present at the dig was wearing a particular type of lanyard and most had T-shirts with the antelope logo.

Mila hoped she might witness a cry of astonished delight as something rare and precious was found, but there was no such luck, only the quiet of concentration as the archaeologists worked. After a while, she turned away and wandered amongst the tents and kiosks, looking for Professor Perry. She heard voices inside the refectory marquee, and approached quietly. As her eyes grew accustomed to the gloom inside, she could see that tables had been arranged around a wooden podium. An electricity supply had been brought in via a number of electrical leads and sockets connected to a generator outside. Young teenage children, all dressed in identical cream-coloured polo shirts and khaki shorts, were sitting around the tables, cheeks resting on their hands, their focus on a man who was talking in front of a whiteboard. Mila crept closer. She caught the odd word and phrase coming from the lips of the speaker and soon was close enough to recognise him as the man who had narrated the video she'd watched online: the education co-ordinator, Alban Hugo. He was an animated and entertaining teacher: the students were hanging on his every word as he described the evidence that pointed towards a significant Mesolithic community inhabiting this very site. Mila stood close to one of the wooden poles supporting the marquee, interested to hear what the teacher had to say, but not wanting to draw attention to herself. He was describing how the region, with its fertile soil, ample freshwater sources and plentiful supply of granite would have provided everything the ancient people needed to thrive. Mila lifted a hand to brush a fly from her face and Monsieur Hugo glimpsed the movement and looked towards her. He smiled and then broke eye contact and continued with his explanation of how fragments of bone could reveal all kinds of information about how the ancestors lived and died and even the meals they ate.

Mila listened for a little longer and then she turned and came out of the marquee, almost bumping into a man walking the other way. His body was bony, but he had a pot belly. He was wearing a pair of creased shorts and a baggy shirt. Two hairy, knobble-kneed and bandy legs emerged from the bottom of the shorts and ended in rather large, flat feet encased in brown ankle socks and worn Jesus sandals. The man had neither presence nor charisma but he looked terribly worried. Mila recognised him at once: Professor Timor Perry.

The professor oozed anxiety. His head was held low and furtive. He had a gait that could best be described as scurrying. It was evidently not a good moment to stop him and interrogate him about Gosia.

'Sorry,' Mila said, moving to one side at the exact moment the professor stepped the same way. She gave an embarrassed laugh and went the other way. So did the professor.

'After you,' he said, holding out a hand that held the rim of a sweat-stained canvas hat and a mobile phone. Mila passed him and then turned to see the professor put the hat back on his head, and continue walking across the site in a peculiar, forward-leaning gait, glancing over his shoulder every now and then, as if to check that he wasn't being followed. He was a parody of a man with something to hide.

Mila waited a moment or two, and then headed after the professor. She lost sight of him as he disappeared behind a long tent, in which a number of students were poring over their laptops, and spotted him again on the other side. He was walking quickly, almost tripping over his own feet. He went through a gate into the fenced-off area where the Kyern dolmen stood, the enormous cap-stone balancing on the points of three vertical supporting stones. Mila slowed her pace and followed. The brightness of the day and the position of the sun meant the shadows around the old tomb were dark. Mila could see the professor's silhouette, and she could see that someone else was there with him, someone who must, in fact, have been waiting for him. Her heartbeat quickened.

The noise from the crickets was deafening and behind that was the thrum of the generators powering the dig site. The professor and his companion were speaking but Mila couldn't hear anything they said. At last, they moved out of the shadows and into the sunlight and she saw that the professor was with a young woman. She was short but heavily built, and her multi-coloured hair was cut raggedly. She was wearing sunglasses, a T-shirt, shorts and trainers. She was obviously distressed and appeared to be pleading with the professor. She kept reaching her hands towards him, and whenever she did this, he stepped backwards, away.

Mila still couldn't hear their conversation and she doubted she could get any closer without being spotted. Professor Perry and the girl stayed close to the dolmen, mostly hidden in the shadows, only occasionally coming into the sunshine. Mila crept a little way forward, treading carefully, like a hunter. Dead foliage crackled beneath the soles of her shoes and at one point the girl looked back. Mila thought she must have been spotted and froze but soon the girl turned again and her attention was back with the professor. She was becoming more agitated, gesticulating with her arms and then clasping her hands together, apparently begging for something. The professor put the fingers of one hand to his forehead in a gesture of despair.

There was no breeze down there in the hollow of the valley. The sea, blazing blue beyond the ranked caravans of the holiday park, was as still as a pond and the few wispy white clouds above it were motionless in the sky. In the last hour or so, the wind had given up altogether. The heat was intense, heavy with the peppery perfume of the ripening corn. There was a fluttering of sparrows come to feed on fallen maize heads. Mila had a good clear view, not of the girl, who was angled with her back to Mila, but of Professor Timor Perry. His doughy, unremarkable face was contorted in panic. The girl was upset but he seemed desperate.

What mess have you got yourself into, Professor? Mila wondered, and at almost the exact same moment she spotted a light glinting behind the professor some thirty metres away on the other side of the dolmen, a light that came from amongst the ranks of the corn.

She narrowed her eyes and realised that what she was seeing was the sun reflecting from the lens of a camera, and the camera had to be being held by someone who, like her, was observing the couple.

Carter Jackson.

* * *

Mila had been disturbed by what she had witnessed. She couldn't make sense of it. Yes, the professor was definitely involved in some way with a much younger woman, but their assignation, furtive as it had been, had not appeared the least bit romantic.

Puzzling over the professor's behaviour, Mila walked back up the hill to collect Sophie's bike, cruised downhill, enjoying the breeze and then made her way back to Morannez, to Jenny's café.

The German girl Jenny employed part-time as a waitress, Betty, was busy bobbing amongst the tables taking orders, serving drinks and ice creams and collecting money. Mila ordered an espresso and a glass of sparkling water and took a seat in the sunshine. She checked her phone while she drank her coffee; there was a message from Luke:

Another bust in Bristol last night. Six arrests.

Mila smiled. Most people's partners, if they were distant, would be sending them messages saying: *Missing you, Love you,* kissy-face and heart emojis. She got updates about gang-related crime.

Jenny came to sit beside Mila. 'Any luck with Gosia's son?'

Mila showed Jenny the picture of Tomas copied onto her phone. 'That's all I've got so far. I'm no nearer to identifying him or his mother.'

'What if you posted the picture and an appeal on Facebook?'

'I'm not sure it would be the right thing to do. They're not my family and I can't ask permission of anyone.' She gave a small smile. 'Ceci and I always tread very carefully with social media. You can never be sure that when you ask for information, you're not going to open a Pandora's box.'

'There's always the Morannez community forum. You could ask if anyone knows anything about Gosia. I mean, she must have had a reason for being here, in the town.'

It was a good idea.

They talked a little longer until they were interrupted by the roar of a motorbike engine, a sound so loud that Mila actively feared for the safety of some of the older and more rickety buildings in the town square. A few seconds later, the sound reached a crescendo. Carter Jackson in his *Mad Max* motorbike helmet and leathers was slowly driving along the road at the far side of the square, heading back towards the route de Rosnuel.

'There goes the cavalry,' said Jenny.

Mila didn't smile. Carter was heading back to the office, no doubt to upload the pictures he'd taken of Professor Perry and the girl. What he'd just done, at Ceci's bidding, felt wrong on every level to Mila. It was cheap and voyeuristic and heavy-handed. A picture was no more or less than a moment frozen in time. It never told the whole story. It did not allow for nuance.

She hoped that the Perry family wasn't about to be riven apart, their lives ruined. She wished Ceci hadn't accepted this job. She wished Carter had refused to cooperate.

She thought of the professor, the haunted expression on his face.

He was clearly a man already in trouble, and what he didn't know was that a whole lot more trouble was heading his way.

* * *

Back at the sea house, Mila did as Jenny had suggested and posted the picture of Tomas and a notice on the Morannez community forum. As the network was limited to permanent residents of the town, she couldn't see how it could possibly cause any problems.

The notice read:

I'm looking for help identifying the traveller woman in the van who sadly passed away on 29 July. This is believed to be a picture of her son. Very grateful for any information.

Beneath the words, she added her phone number and her address.

20

SUNDAY, 14 AUGUST

'But *why* are we going to Mamie's?' Ani asked.

'Because Madame Abadie is going to cook us a delicious meal and I want to listen to the CD that was found in Gosia's van,' said Mila.

'What's she cooking?' asked Ani, some way to being seduced. Madame Abadie, Ceci's housekeeper, was probably the second-best cook in Finistère, next to Étienne Pinet.

'I don't know exactly, but you and I both know that it'll be something you like. Everyone knows you're her favourite.'

'Obviously,' said Ani.

Mila took a deep breath. 'And, also, we were wondering, well, Pernille's maman was wondering if we shouldn't talk about doing something the Thursday after next. Something to remember Sophie and Charlie, your maman and papa, and mark the anniversary of the accident.'

'Why?'

'Melodie thinks it would be a nice thing to do. So that we can all think about Sophie and talk about her and...'

'No,' said Ani. She was silent for a moment as all the colour slowly drained from her face. Then she picked up her phone and threw it across the room. '*NO!*' she screamed as the phone bounced off the wall.

Oh mon Dieu, thought Mila, *please don't let that one be broken too!*

Ani ran from the room and slammed the door. The cat, alarmed, jumped onto the bookshelf and hid behind a plant pot.

Mila checked that the phone was still in one piece, then sat down and put her head in her hands.

'Shit,' she whispered. 'Shit, shit, shit, shit, shit.'

Well, what did you expect? asked Sophie. *You've spent eleven months doing everything you can not to mention me and Charlie to Ani and then you land her with that!*

What do I do now, Sophie? How do I deal with this? How do I help her?

Talk to her.

Talk to her?

Just you and her. Not a whole party-full of people.

The sly and Sophie-esque thought crept into Mila's mind that if she could avoid doing anything for another four weeks, Ani would be in Switzerland and she'd be in Bristol and Ani's grief would no longer be her problem.

Don't even think about it! said Sophie. *Besides... have you ever thought that it might be good for you to face up to what's happened too?*

* * *

Mila only managed to persuade Ani to come with her to Ceci's apartment by the prodigious use of emotional blackmail.

'Ceci's your grandmother, sweetheart; she hasn't spent any quality time with you for ages and all we're going to do is listen to the CD and eat something delicious as prepared by Madame Abadie and maybe play a few games of cards. And you know that

Mamie can be really funny when she wants to be. It's going to be fun.'

'We're not going to *talk*, are we?'

'Well...'

'If we're going to talk about what Melodie said, then I'm not coming.'

'If you don't want to talk about it now, we won't. I promise.'

'Really promise?'

'Ani, when have I ever broken a promise to you?'

Silence. Then: 'I don't want to talk about school either.'

'Boarding school?'

'Any school.'

'Okay,' said Mila. 'No school talk either.'

Ffs, how much longer can you leave it?

I don't know, Sophie. I honestly don't know.

* * *

Ceci's apartment was part of a block that had been built in the 1930s and epitomised all the style and glamour of that era. It resembled a cruise liner, with a huge, curved prow. One whole wall, on the side that faced the sea, was made of glass and was horseshoe-shaped to give spectacular 180-degree views of the coastline. A spacious balcony ran along the window. The inhabitants of the apartment above, and the one below, had filled their balconies with plants but Ceci's was empty; she said it had been designed to make the most of the vista and she didn't want anything, not even a potted camellia, to interfere with that. And Ceci adored pot plants. The rest of the apartment was full of them.

There was a lift to one end of the block, an old-fashioned cage lift with a fierce door that clicked shut, which ascended and descended painfully slowly on rickety chains and which Mila thought was a health and safety risk, given that it was almost impossible not to catch one's fingers, hair and clothes in the mechanism. Mila, inclined to claustrophobia at the best of times, in any case always took the stairs, which were wide and sweeping, made of white marble. Ani, dressed in pink cotton that made her look young and vulnerable, slapped up the stairs in her flip-flops, grumbling behind her aunt. Mila had spent the afternoon making an apricot tart from fruit from the garden. It was rather messy, but the caramel sauce was truly delicious and the pastry was suitably French and buttery. Madame Abadie had nothing to worry about and she hoped the woman wouldn't be offended but she had felt she ought to make some kind of effort.

Ceci had left the door to her second-floor apartment on the latch and Mila and Ani went in to find Madame Abadie putting the finishing touches to a meal.

'Chicken with a truffle and champagne sauce and steamed vegetables for you mon ange,' she told Ani. 'And there's some vegetarian paella for you, Mila.'

'Thank you,' Mila said. 'That's so kind.'

She put the tart on the counter in the kitchen – 'Don't look at it, Madame Abadie; it's not close to being in the same league as yours!' – and then laid the CD on top of the sideboard in the living room. Ceci eyed it with suspicion.

'We'll eat first and listen to that later,' she said. 'It looks so old it'll be a miracle if it still plays.'

'Fingers crossed,' said Mila.

'Why are you interested in what's on the CD?' Ceci asked.

'It belonged to the traveller woman?'

'Oh, Mila,' said Ceci, 'you promised me that you'd forget about her.'

Mila thought back and although Ceci had asked her to put the tragedy of Gosia behind her several times, she didn't remember promising anything of the kind.

* * *

After they'd eaten, and the adults had enjoyed a glass of pastis, Mila, Ceci and Ani went into the living room, where Ceci kept the Bose music system that Patrick had once given her as a birthday gift.

'It's ancient,' Ceci said, 'but quality always prevails.'

Mila wondered, as she often did, how it was her father had always managed to buy such thoughtful presents for Ceci – he still sent mementoes now, years after their divorce – when he couldn't even remember the date of his daughter's birthday, *hers*. And for as long as Mila could remember, her mother, Ava, had complained about Patrick's selfishness; the fact that he never considered her feelings, ever. Never mind. She passed the CD to her stepmother. Ceci popped open the case and slotted the disc into the player. After a few moments' almost silence during which there was much crackling and scratching, there was the sound of a guitar being strummed, and then a male voice started singing.

It was the Green Day track 'Good Riddance'. Mila knew it well.

'Do you think that's Tomas singing?' Ani asked.

'It could be.'

Ani leaned against the side of Mila's chair to listen. They were silent until the end of the song. After that, there were some more background noises and then the CD finished.

'That used to be one of Maman's favourites,' said Ani.

'I haven't heard it since she...' Ceci trailed off, holding her fingers to her lips.

Grief settled on their shoulders, gentle as falling snow, a

memory at a time. They all knew how Sophie used to love that song.

On the wall was a photograph of Sophie, aged eighteen, standing on the rocks beside the sea beneath the rugged cliffs of Pointe du Raz, close to where her body would later come to shore, her arms spread wide like a bird's wings and her head tipped back in laughter. Her strong pose, her vibrancy, echoed the position of the lifeless body washed ashore in Mila's false flashbacks. In the picture, the white sails of boats interrupted the green-blue of the sea behind Sophie. Ani couldn't bear to look at that image but it captured the essence of Sophie so well that it was as if she was in the room with them.

Mila stood up and crossed the room to stand on the balcony. The wind was whipping up the tops of the waves on the ocean, making them dance an informal ballet. She wished she'd spoken more to Gosia while she had the opportunity. But more than that, much more than that, she wished she could speak to Sophie again, even one more time, just to tell her not to go sailing that day almost a year earlier, not to take any unnecessary risks no matter how much fun it might be – for once in her life, only once, to be sensible, to do the right thing.

* * *

Later, while Ani and Ceci played cards, Mila sat on a foldaway chair outside the window with her legs pulled up to her body, half watching the seagulls following a fishing boat into the harbour, and half searching the internet for more clues about the song. She typed 'speakeasy' and 'Green Day' and 'Good Riddance' into the YouTube search bar and got plenty of *Bugsy Malone* hits and mentions of a group called the Speakeasy Girls but nothing that helped explain the link between the word and the song on the CD.

The usual search engines were no help either.

It was frustrating, and she spent more than an hour looking, until the sun was kissing the strip of haze that hovered above the horizon. The day was almost over, she and Ani needed to get home, she was not one iota closer to finding out who Gosia really was and it seemed that both the word 'speakeasy' and the song recorded on the CD were red herrings. Like the photograph of Tomas, they were no help at all.

21

Mila and Ani caught a taxi back to the sea house from Ceci's apartment. Mila would have been happy to walk but Ani was tired. They'd left the bikes at home. Even though Ani's bike was fixed now, she'd not been so keen to ride it since the accident and Mila saw no need to nag her into using it. She wouldn't need her bike at boarding school. It would all be skiing and hiking and pony-trekking there.

'I've never been this way before,' the taxi driver said as he bumped slowly down the narrow lane that led to the sea house. He'd already told them he was from Bloemel. He'd made it sound as if driving the ten kilometres to Morannez was a huge inconvenience. A barn owl was flying parallel with the taxi, making its way along the line of the hedgerow. Mila was worried it might make a sudden turn and fly into the side of the car; she'd heard of it happening, the lovely birds, large-spanned but light as sparrows, suddenly turning and thudding head-first into vehicles as if they were intending to kill themselves. Of course they weren't. They only wanted to cross to the other side of the road and their brains didn't understand cars; they hadn't evolved quickly enough.

Be careful, she willed the owl and the driver. He was an older man, wizened. She didn't know how he might react to her pointing out the vulnerability of the bird. She wished he would slow down, let it go ahead so that it would be safe but she feared that if she asked him, he might, out of bloody-mindedness, take the opposite approach.

'Is it just the two of you?' he asked. 'Living all the way out here on your own?'

'No,' Mila said brightly, 'it's not just us.'

'No?'

'No,' she said with a glance to Ani, who was looking anxious.

'I wouldn't like to live out here,' said the man, 'so far from everywhere. It would give me the willies.'

'Each to their own,' said Mila briskly.

* * *

Back home, the taxi driver paid and gone, feeling conscious of their isolation, Mila picked up the cat and cradled her until the animal would tolerate the fussing no longer and wriggled free. Mila went upstairs and changed into a hoodie and a pair of sweatpants, even though it was still warm, said goodnight to Ani, promised her they'd spend the next day together – thinking that tomorrow she really would broach the subject of school – and came down again.

She braced herself against the loneliness of the surroundings – she wasn't going to allow herself to start being jumpy now – and went outside to call Luke; he answered and for a while they were united by the small screens of their phones as night settled in across the north-west corner of France and the south-west of England – another day over. Moonlight was illuminating the garden and Mila kept an eye on the boundary: there was no movement on the track, there never was.

Berthaud was hunting in the long grass at the fringes of the garden and moths were batting the outside lamp. An owl, not the same one they'd seen earlier but a tawny owl, was calling from the trees; they heard it almost every night. Mila lit a citronella candle and went to sit on the swing-seat, still holding the phone, talking to Luke. She had a glass of wine in her hand and he told her he had one in his. They'd been apart for so long, and that night she missed him terribly, him and his body and his big hands and his dry, quiet humour. That night she craved the touch of another human being; she longed for adult company, a companion, sex.

'I wish you were here,' Mila said to Luke. She didn't usually say that sort of thing.

There was a silence. Any kind of intimate talk always floored Luke. He could talk for hours about his work, about the law, about Manchester United or Bristol City football clubs, about politics, about music. He could not talk about matters of the heart, not even obliquely.

That, of course, was one of the things that had attracted Mila to him in the first place.

'I'm dog tired,' said Luke eventually. Mila hadn't expected him to say anything reassuring or emotional. Even so, she was disappointed by the mundanity of this comment.

'I guess the case you're working on takes it out of you,' she said.

'Yeah,' he said. 'You know, I always try to see the best in people, but some of these people... Some of them, I look as hard as I can, Mila. I find reasons for them being the way they are because most of the time there are reasons. But some of them, it's hard finding anything good.'

Mila had balanced the wine bottle on the grass beside the swing-seat. She leaned down to pick it up by the neck, to top up her glass, and that was when she saw a movement on the lane.

'Hold on,' she said to Luke, 'someone's there.'

Clutching the phone tightly, she stood up, went to the gate and looked over. She couldn't see anything. The lane petered out beyond the boundaries of the sea house and after that there was only the sandy track winding through the woods to the beach. Whoever had been there was gone.

'Who is it?' asked Luke.

'I don't know. A man walked past but I can't see him now.'

'Perhaps it was an animal you saw. A deer.'

'No. It was a man. Why would anyone come this way, at this time of night, without a torch? And where did he go?'

'Has he definitely gone?'

'I can't see him.'

'Go inside, Mila, just in case.'

'Yes. I will.'

She picked up the half-drunk bottle of wine and the glass from the grass and, clutching the phone, she went inside. She pushed the door shut with her hip, then put down the wine, locked the door behind her and bolted it. The windows were all still open. She kept talking to Luke as she went around the ground floor pulling them shut, telling him about the Green Day song that had nothing at all to do with the word 'speakeasy' and the frustration she felt at having reached another dead end, all the time peering into the darkness, but seeing nothing untoward outside.

She didn't mention that 'Good Riddance' had been one of Sophie's favourite songs. Luke might remember, though. He had an encyclopaedic knowledge about music.

'The young man singing the song might be Gosia's son,' said Mila. 'He's singing in English but he has an accent and it's the same as Gosia's as far as I can remember. She might just have kept the CD so that she could listen to his voice again from time to time.'

Saying it out loud like that made her feel sad. For weeks after Sophie's death, she had dialled Sophie's number so she could connect to Sophie's voicemail, and hear Sophie thanking her for calling and telling her to leave a message. It was heart-breaking to think that the CD might be the only way Gosia could listen to her beloved Tomas.

'Was there anything else written on the CD sleeve?' Luke asked.

'It's pretty badly faded.'

'It'd be worth looking.'

'Okay, hold on, I'll do it now.'

Mila went into the kitchen, found her bag, and brought it back to the sofa. She tipped out its contents, picked up the CD case. She popped the disc out of the plastic casing, and examined the paper insert through the transparent shell.

'Take the paper out,' said Luke. 'It's usually folded on the inside.'

She did as he said and he was right about the fold. Tucked between the two sides of the folded paper was a small, white card, about as long as Mila's index finger.

'There is something there,' she said. 'It looks like a business card.'

She turned the card over. 'Oh my God!'

'What?' Luke asked. 'What is it?'

'It *is* a business card,' Mila said. 'And it belongs to someone I kind of met yesterday.'

'Who's that?'

'The lead archaeologist at the Kyern dig. Professor Tim Perry.'

22

MONDAY, 15 AUGUST

Mila was woken early by the sunlight coming through her window. She hadn't slept well; she'd drunk too much wine the night before and she'd kept thinking about the man who'd walked past. She was almost certain it was the same man she'd seen watching her from the beach when she'd gone for her swim; someone who had seemed familiar, but not familiar enough for her to recognise in the darkness. She'd tried to tell herself it was no big deal. There was no law against anyone using the track, or going to the beach; neither was private. Whoever it was had been furtive, or at least had seemed so to Mila, but maybe it was because *they* were afraid. Maybe they feared they were trespassing and that someone might come after them with a shotgun. Maybe there was absolutely nothing sinister in them being there at all.

Yet hardly anyone, ever, came down that track after nightfall and it was equally rare to see anyone else at the beach; especially a lone man.

Perhaps the man was a vagrant, living in the woods. Oh God, Mila hoped not. She didn't want to share this place with a stranger. She didn't want to keep spotting him lurking in the shadows. But she was almost certain he wasn't a stranger. She knew him, or she had known him. She felt if she tried hard enough she might realise who he was, but no matter how hard she racked her brains, she couldn't place him.

It wasn't only the thought of the man that had kept Mila awake that night. The 'Good Riddance' song had kept playing in her mind, like an obsession. As she slept she'd heard Sophie singing it, her voice tremulous and thin as oxygen and she'd dreamed again of the fake vision of Sophie's body being washed ashore. The dream had been worse than usual because this time, Mila had been standing on the shore, right next to the place where the sea had brought the body in, and she'd been about to bend down and turn Sophie's head over, to lift her face out of the water, so that Sophie could breathe. As she'd bent to touch the body, someone behind her had screamed '*Don't do that!*' and she'd woken with a ferociously pounding heart.

Then there was the card hidden inside the CD case, confirmation that Gosia's connection with the Kyern dig was Professor Tim Perry. How had the traveller woman come by the card? He must have given it to her, or sent it to her, or she must have attended some event where he was also present.

But why would a woman like Gosia keep a card belonging to a man like the professor? Why would she need to be in touch with him?

There must be some reason yet Mila, tired and anxious, couldn't see it.

She looked for her phone and found it down the side of the easy chair in the living room where she'd left it when she'd finished talking with Luke the previous evening. The battery was flat.

You idiot! It was a good job the stalker didn't come back and you didn't need to call for help.

Shut up, Sophie.

Mila plugged the phone in to charge and then she made coffee.

It was too early to call Ceci, too early to wake Ani, yet Mila didn't want to be on her own. She paced, drinking a glass of water and swallowing back a couple of paracetamol pills, looking through all the upstairs windows and seeing nothing out of place. She kept looking at Professor Perry's business card. It had an email address, a UK work phone number that was an extension at Cambridge University, and a mobile.

She could simply call and ask him.

That's what she'd do. Or perhaps she'd go to the dig and confront him in person – no, not *confront*, talk to him, over a cup of tea maybe.

She checked the community forum website to see if there'd been any response to her notice, but there was nothing apart from a smattering of sad-face emojis and three useless responses.

MadameB: The woman in the horsebox was a gypsy. She's been pestering people to buy lucky heather.

Violala: my brother's a cop. He said the old lady died in her sleep.

DB: These travellers are a blight on our beautiful country. They should be sent back to where they came from.

Mila thought it wasn't a good idea to have her address on display like that; she edited the post to remove it, then, on second thoughts, deleted the whole post. Perhaps that was what had brought the visitor to the track last night. Perhaps someone was curious to look at this isolated house close to the sea. Or perhaps someone knew something and had come to tell her but changed their mind at the last minute.

Even though it was so early, the opportunist Berthaud was

miaowing for her breakfast. Mila fed her, and ate two supermarket pains au chocolat straight from the packet.

The phone, revived, pinged. It was a message from Luke.

Speakeasy was an album by the 1980s new wave band Zagreb. They were from Yugoslavia/Croatia.

Bingo, thought Mila.

She could see what had happened. Someone – Tomas, perhaps – had recorded the Speakeasy album onto a blank disc and put it in the case. Over time, a different disc, the one with the 'Good Riddance' song, had found its way into the case. None of that mattered. What mattered was that Gosia had hidden the card there, and Mila now knew that Gosia almost certainly came from somewhere within the former Yugoslavia and that she was connected, somehow, to Professor Perry.

* * *

Later, when the day had properly begun and the sun was up, Mila checked the mailbox and found a large brown envelope with Swiss stamps and postmarks. It contained a welcome package from the boarding school. There was a brochure listing all the clubs Ani could join and all the fun activities she could do in her leisure time. There were different questionnaires for her to fill in about her likes and dislikes so the matron and other pastoral care staff could 'know a little' about her. There was also a booklet with cheerful cartoon illustrations telling Ani what to expect when she arrived at the school and a list of what she could and could not bring.

It was all very friendly and chatty and proved that boarding schools today were nothing like boarding schools used to be – evidence that Ani was going to have the best time ever there.

Despite this, Mila shoved the whole lot in one of the kitchen drawers, beneath folded tea towels and tablecloths, a place where she could absolutely guarantee Ani wouldn't look.

Mila sat at the table and checked the time. It was half past eight, not too early to call the professor. She dialled the mobile number on the business card but the call went directly to voicemail. Mila didn't leave a message. She'd try again in fifteen minutes.

She went outside and picked a couple of fat, yellow peaches directly from the tree. She sat in the kitchen, eating slices of sweet fruit, drinking coffee, and reading a tatty old copy of a Jackie Collins novel she'd found on Sophie's bookshelf. She and Sophie had first read the book as teenagers and the pages were heavily annotated with scribbles and lists of names. Looking back, Mila couldn't remember if they were the names of boys she and Sophie had fancied, or those of the horses from the stables over at Bloemel-sur-Mer, where they used to have riding lessons in the school holidays. It was strange that something that had seemed so important at that time could be so irrelevant now.

When she'd finished the peach, Mila tried the professor's number again with the same result, then she went upstairs to shower and dress. She was brushing her teeth when she heard her phone ringing but it had stopped before she could reach it. She pulled a T-shirt over her head and stepped into a long cotton skirt. The phone rang again. This time she picked it up.

'Morning, Ceci!'

'Mila, I need you to come into the office now.'

'I can't; I need to be here with Ani.'

'Darling, I'm sorry but I need you.'

'Is something wrong?'

'Something's terribly wrong. Can you come right away?'

'Ani's still asleep. I don't want to leave her alone.'

'She'll be okay for a few hours. Just come. Please, darling. Come now.'

'What on earth has happened?'

Ceci sighed. Then she said slowly, 'The photograph that Carter took of Professor Perry, with a girl... Someone's copied it, and stuck the prints up all over town.'

23

Mila's head was ringing with questions. How could anybody outside the agency have got hold of a photograph that Carter Jackson had taken? Was he so careless that he'd dropped a memory stick or had his camera stolen? And why would anyone copy the picture, presumably a compromising image, and post it for everyone to see? Students maybe, for a joke? Only this wasn't funny – not for the professor, for his wife, for the girl, for those involved with the dig. Nothing about it was funny at all.

She called Melodie Sohar to see if she could come and pick up Ani, but Melodie didn't answer – perhaps she was annoyed with Mila for being so curt with her the other day. Then she went upstairs, picked up Ani's phone from the side of her bed and checked that the battery was charged. She shook Ani gently by the shoulders and, when she stirred, said: 'Ani, I've got to go to the agency. Mamie needs me. I don't know how long I'll be. I'm going to lock the door behind me and I'll try to get Pernille's maman to pick you up and if she can't Ceci will come and fetch you in her car.'

'Mmm,' Ani mumbled.

'Don't go anywhere. Stay here and wait until Melodie or Mamie comes.'

''Kay.'

'Ani, promise me!'

'I promise.'

The girl shrugged off Mila's hands and wriggled over in the bedding so that her back was towards her aunt.

'Thank you,' Mila said.

She almost leaned over and kissed Ani's forehead, but remembered in time that she and Ani didn't have that kind of relationship.

She grabbed a jumper and her bag, went downstairs again, picked up the bike and set off towards town. As she stood up to pedal harder and gain some momentum, she muttered to herself that this would never have happened if Ceci had listened to her in the first place. She *knew* the agency shouldn't have got involved with Mrs Perry's request to follow her husband. They should have stuck to what they were good at: investigations that didn't involve the messy business of human emotion. And again, she wondered how the photographs could have found their way into the public domain. Carter Jackson was supposed to be a surveillance expert, wasn't he? If he was such an expert, how on earth had this happened?

Unless they weren't Carter's pictures. What if someone else had photographed the professor and the girl? They'd been together at the dolmen for anyone to see. Any of the students or even a passer-by with a half-decent camera or smartphone who'd happened to be in the cornfield and spotted the professor with the girl could have taken a photograph.

Mila put on the brakes and the bike screeched to a standstill. She took her phone out of her pocket and called Ceci, who answered at once.

'How do we know they're Carter's pictures?' Mila asked.

'He stuck our logo on the bottom of the images he sent to Catherine Perry.'

'Our logo? The Toussaint's logo?'

'Yes.'

'Why would he do that?'

'Because I told him to.'

'And the logo's reproduced on the prints too?'

'*Yes!*'

'And the prints are all over town?'

'Carter's out now collecting as many as he can, but they're everywhere.'

'*Mon Dieu!*'

'Where are you, Mila?'

'I'm on my way.'

Mila disconnected the call and set off again. Her heart was pounding. This was terrible! Not only had the agency, somehow, breached Professor Perry's privacy in the most awful way, but the fact that it was their mistake was being advertised on the prints too! This could be the end of the business.

She cycled as quickly as she could, feeling self-conscious, as if the occupants of every car that passed her might be looking at her, saying: 'That's the woman who works for the agency that's responsible for ruining someone's life.'

Perhaps it's not as bad as Ceci thinks, she told herself, but in the next breath she rounded a corner close to the junction with the road that led to the international school and there, right in front of her, was a poster fixed to the wall that ran alongside the road. The image was a blown-up close-up of two people standing beside the Kyern dolmen. It showed the back of the young woman's head, and Professor Timor Perry's face tilted forward towards hers; his expression was impossible to read but it was clear the encounter was emotional. The girl was leaning towards the professor and her hand was on his shoulder. The image was black and white with striking red text beneath.

'Oh no,' Mila breathed as she read the caption.

Professor Pervert.

At least the girl wasn't recognisable; that was something. But *Professor Pervert!* That was libellous, wasn't it? Or slanderous? Oh dear God!

She tore the poster from the wall, screwed it up, and shoved it in her rucksack. She cycled on and soon enough she found more posters, three of them, stuck over the advertisements at the bus stop. She ripped them into pieces, put the pieces in the waste bin just as a bus pulled up and people piled out. They were students, wearing the Kyern dig lanyards and T-shirts with the antelope logo: young people who knew Professor Perry personally.

Mila looked down the road. A small gang of teenage boys was coming towards her, one on an electric scooter, another carrying a skateboard. The third was holding a poster, laughing at the image, giddy with the craziness of seeing an adult, someone in a position of authority, being ridiculed in this way.

Beyond, Mila could see more posters. They had been stuck to street furniture, lamp posts, bare patches of wall. They were everywhere. It was as if the town had been afflicted by a plague of flyposting.

There were too many for one person to take down. Mila decided to abandon them instead, she climbed back onto the bike and cycled into the town centre as fast as she could.

When she reached the route de Rosnuel, she saw that Carter Jackson's vintage motorbike was parked in the only place in the narrow street big enough to accommodate it. Mila freewheeled past it, bringing the bike to a stop outside the patisserie beneath the agency offices. A poster had even been stuck to the wall beside the patisserie where a queue had formed, waiting for it to open. She said, 'Excuse me,' grabbed the poster, opened the door at the side of the patisserie with her shoulder and heaved the bike into the tiny space beyond. She propped it on the stairs and pulled the door shut behind her.

'It's me,' she called.

She could hear voices above. She trotted up the stairs. Ceci and Carter were in Ceci's office. A pile of posters was on her desk. They both turned to face Mila as she came in.

'What's going on?' Mila asked. 'What's happening?'

'I wish I knew,' said Carter.

'It has to be Mrs Perry who's done this,' Ceci said. 'It can't have been anyone else.'

'Have you spoken to her?' Mila asked Carter.

'I've been trying to call her for the last hour. Her phone's unavailable.'

And so was the professor's. Mila dreaded to imagine the conversation taking place in the Perry household right now. And she knew Tim Perry would never agree to speak to her once he realised she was connected to this mess.

'How could you have let this happen?' Mila asked Carter. 'How could you be so incompetent? Are you really what you say you are? Did you really work for the Canadian drugs squad or was that all a pack of lies?'

'Mila!' said Ceci sharply.

'He's supposed to be a surveillance expert, Ceci, and on his first job, his *very first* job with Toussaint's, he messes up – not just a teeny tiny mess-up but a catastrophic mess-up, the biggest mess-up in history!'

'I did everything by the book,' said Carter.

'Evidently you didn't!'

'I only sent the pictures to Mrs Perry. I didn't even copy them to Toussaint's. I encrypted them. I don't see how they could possibly have been hijacked.'

'Carter and I have been through this a dozen times, Mila. Catherine Perry must be behind it; there's no other explanation.' Ceci put a hand to her forehead. 'Although I can't believe she'd do this. I can't believe she'd be so vindictive.'

'She in her Fendi suit,' Mila muttered.

Ceci held her finger to her lips. 'Shh, Mila. I'll try Catherine's number from my phone. Perhaps she'll speak to me.'

She lifted her phone, found the number, and called it. They all heard the electronic voice that stated the number was not available.

'She's probably turned her phone off, knowing the shit was about to hit the fan,' said Carter.

Mila rounded on him again.

'This has to be something to do with you, turning up out of the blue, making out you don't know anything about anything, acting like Ceci being Sophie's mother is all a big surprise to you!'

'What?'

'I know you're lying, Carter! I can tell! Did you come here to ruin the agency? Is it some kind of twisted revenge because you couldn't have Sophie?'

'Mila!' Ceci was angry now. 'That's enough! I mean it! Let's deal with the problem in hand.'

'I told you taking on this job was a bad idea! I *told you!*'

'And you were right about that but taking it out on Carter isn't helping.'

Ceci reached for Mila's hand. Mila's instinct was to snatch it away but Ceci held tight.

'It's okay, Mila,' Ceci said. 'We've been through worse than this and we have survived. Let's calm down and try to work out what's going on here.'

Carter, who had backed as far away from Mila as he could in the small room, nodded. He was wearing a loose shirt. Mila could see the triskele tattoo on the inside of his wrist, beneath the watch strap. The very sight of it revived all manner of old hurts and slights; reminded Mila that wounds she'd thought had scarred over, were still raw after all.

Ceci's voice brought her back to the matter in hand.

'We're agreed the image used on the poster could only have come from Mrs Perry via Carter,' said Ceci, 'so the next question is why would she do this?'

Mila slowed her breathing. She tried to concentrate.

'If the professor *has* been unfaithful, she might be trying to get her own back on him.'

'Except she didn't seem that sort of woman,' said Ceci, 'did she, Carter?'

'No, ma'am,' said Carter. 'She seemed very much as if she wanted to avoid a scandal, not cause one.'

'There must be some explanation that we're not seeing,' said Ceci.

'We need to talk to Mrs Perry,' said Carter.

'She obviously doesn't want to talk to anyone.'

'We'll pay her a visit then.'

'Agreed,' Ceci said. 'We'll go together, Mila, you and I. Carter, you concentrate on taking down as many of the posters as possible.'

'Hold on,' Mila said, 'I don't want to be involved in this. It's not my case. It's nothing to do with me.'

'The fact that you're not directly involved will make it easier for you to talk to Mrs Perry.'

'No! I won't do it. Ani's alone, Ceci. I need to get back to her. I promised her we'd spend the day together.'

'We'll pick her up on the way back.'

'Ceci! This isn't fair!'

'You'll be leaving soon. You'll do this one last little thing for me, darling, won't you?'

Distraught as she felt, Mila found it impossible to refuse.

The Perry family were renting a new-ish house on a small estate halfway between the towns of Morannez and Vannes. The house had white walls climbing up to a steeply sloping grey-slate roof with dormer windows, and a front garden comprised solely of lawn that had been cut too short and had browned in the sun. A basketball hoop was fixed to the side of the garage and a pair of roller skates was tumbled together outside the front door.

A dusty old maroon Volvo estate with British plates was parked on the drive. Someone was standing outside the front door, having apparently rung the bell.

'Who's that?' Mila asked as she and Ceci drove slowly past.

'Rana Bhan. She's a journalist with the local TV.'

'What's she doing here?'

'She lives in Morannez. She must have seen the posters. I saw her on television interviewing Professor Perry at the dig the other day; she probably thinks he'll talk to her.'

'It doesn't look as if anyone's going to open the door.'

Mila, in the passenger seat, looked up and clearly saw a movement at an upstairs window of the Perrys' house: a woman on her telephone, pacing, one hand in the air making a gesture of disbelief. Mrs Perry was at home and it seemed as if she was distressed. If she had put the posters up herself, perhaps she hadn't anticipated such a quick reaction from the media.

Ceci pulled up her car at a bend in the road.

'This is dreadful,' she said. 'A dreadful situation.'

Angry as she was, Mila was worried for her. Ceci shouldn't be having to deal with this kind of problem on top of everything else. She should never have let Carter Jackson – because it *had* to be his fault – talk her into taking on this job in the first place.

'I don't know how we can fix this,' said Mila, 'but the agency hasn't actually done anything illegal. If Carter emailed the images to Mrs Perry, like he said, and if he used the secure connection, then you're right, the only person who could have made those posters and put them up is Mrs Perry herself. Unless her computer has been compromised, or her email address hacked, which of course is possible. But if that's the case, Toussaint's can't be blamed.' She tailed off miserably, knowing full well that while they might be legally in the clear, morally the waters were extremely murky.

'I would have bet my bottom dollar that she wasn't the kind of woman to do such a thing!' said Ceci.

'You want to believe she's not, but why has she switched her mobile off? If she didn't put the posters up, don't you think she'd have called you by now? Don't you think she'd be demanding to know what's going on?'

'There'll be a witch-hunt against her husband. Professor Pervert! Oh, Mila, how could she do that to him?'

'Perhaps she thinks he deserves it,' said Mila.

'I wish she'd stuck to throwing paint over his car or... or chopping up his clothes or one of the other more conventional forms of revenge.'

Ceci seemed diminished. Despite her bravado, she was flailing and Mila, who had been absolutely determined that she wasn't going to get involved, found herself relenting.

'I'll go and talk to Mrs Perry,' said Mila. 'I'll convince her that this strategy for punishing her husband is a really bad idea. She and her husband need to sit down and talk.'

'He might be there, in the house.'

'He might be. Could you try the phone again, Ceci? I saw Mrs Perry upstairs talking to someone just now.'

Ceci pressed the redial button. A moment later the same electronic voice repeated that the call could not be connected because the number was unavailable.

'She must have more than one phone, then. Hold on...' Mila took out her own phone and found Catherine Perry's Etsy page. 'Is this the same number you have?'

'No.'

'Well, let's try this one.'

She dialled the alternative number and saw movement inside the house: the shape of the same woman at the same upstairs window. After a moment a tentative voice said: 'Hello?'

Mila switched the phone to speaker and nodded to Ceci, who was still sitting in the driver's seat, strapped in, with her fingers resting on the wheel and her back to the Perrys' house.

'Catherine, hello, it's me, Ceci, from the agency...'

'What agency?'

'Toussaint's.'

'You? You're the one who took the pictures of my husband?'

'It was my colleague, Carter Jackson. I introduced you to him when you came to our offices.'

'What are you talking about?'

'The husband must be there with her,' Mila whispered. 'She doesn't want him to know she's involved.'

'Catherine, is your husband there with you?' Ceci asked.

'No. He's not here. And don't call me Catherine! Why did you follow my husband and take those horrible photographs? Why did you set him up like that, to humiliate him, *us* in front of everyone, the whole town?' The woman's voice was thick with anger and tears. 'My daughter is here. My fourteen-year-old daughter. Can you imagine how she's feeling now? Can you imagine what it's going to be like for her going back to school after this? What did we ever do to you for you to treat us so badly?'

Ceci and Mila exchanged glances.

Ceci spoke quietly. 'You came to our office, Mrs Perry. You said you had concerns about your husband. You thought he might be involved with one of the students working on the dig. You asked me to arrange for him to be followed. I introduced you to my colleague, Carter Jackson, an expert in surveillance. You said you wanted to know the truth, not because you wanted to humiliate your husband, but because you were trying to avert a scandal.'

'What? I've never been near your office! I don't know what you're talking about!'

'We have your visit recorded on CCTV. We can prove you were there. There's no point trying to deny it.'

'Are you crazy? I've *never been to your office!*'

'Mrs Perry...'

'No! That's enough. Don't you "Mrs Perry" me. I don't want to talk to you any more. Don't contact me again. I'm going to tele-phone our solicitor. Right now. This minute.'

The line went dead.

Ceci stared at the phone, confusion written all over her face.

'Why would she deny it?' she asked. 'Why would she say she hadn't come to our office? Does she have amnesia or something?'

An awful realisation was beginning to dawn on Mila.

'Turn round, Ceci,' she said quietly. 'Look behind you. Look at the Perrys' house. Now look at the large upstairs window.'

Ceci turned slowly. 'That window up there?'

'Yes.'

The woman, the same woman whose photographs Mila had seen on Facebook and other social media was standing at the window, both palms pressed flat against the glass.

'Who's that?' Ceci asked.

'That's Catherine Perry.'

Ceci gave a brief laugh, more like a bark. 'No, it's not. That woman doesn't look anything like Catherine Perry. She's the wrong shape. She has the wrong hair. Everything about her is wrong.'

'It is her,' Mila said. She showed Ceci her phone. 'Look, there's a picture of Catherine with her husband and children on holiday in Norfolk.'

Ceci stared at the screen. The colour drained from her face. 'That's not her,' she said quietly. 'That's not the same woman who came to see me at the office.'

'Then the woman who came to see you wasn't Catherine Perry.'

Ceci exhaled shakily. She was silent for a good minute as the implications of this sank in.

'So, the woman who commissioned us to follow Professor Perry, the woman to whom Carter sent the photographs, was not Professor Perry's wife?'

'No,' said Mila.

'She was an imposter?'

'She must have been.'

'Mon Dieu,' said Ceci. 'What have we done?'

25

There was nothing for it but to take the new information back to the office, to regroup. Ceci was in shock and Mila couldn't think straight. *Why* anyone would go to so much trouble to do this; the Perrys seemed such a nice, ordinary family?

If Professor Perry was in a relationship with the girl he'd met at the dolmen, then perhaps it was someone connected to her who wanted to ruin him. But Mila didn't believe the professor was having an affair. She'd seen him with the young woman. The body language had been all wrong. The photograph made the situation appear more intimate than it had been in real life; something about a pixelated image, obviously taken without the consent of the subjects, inevitably hinted at sleaze and sexual impropriety.

Everything about the situation stank.

Carter was out when they reached the office. Ceci headed for her computer, to access the app that controlled the CCTV, while Mila filled the coffee pot and put it on the stove to percolate. She poured two glasses of water from the cooler, took one to Ceci and placed it on her desk. Her stepmother was dreadfully pale.

'Ceci, why don't you go and fetch Ani and go home, leave this to me and Carter. We'll figure out what's going on and...'

'I need to check the CCTV,' Ceci said. 'I need to show you the woman who said she was Mrs Perry. You need to see with your own eyes how convincing she was. You'll understand why I fell for her story.'

'I believe you, Ceci.'

'That woman knew how to manipulate me,' Ceci said. 'She knew how to impress me. It was almost as if she knew me. What will people think of me, Mila? What will they say? How could I have let this happen?'

Mila put a hand tentatively on her stepmother's shoulder.

'People know you, Ceci. They know you're an honest business-woman and an ethical one. They'll know this wasn't your doing.'

Ceci covered Mila's hand with one of her own.

'But the professor, Professor Pervert... That name is going to plague him for the rest of his career.'

'Not if there's no truth in the accusation...'

'The truth won't make any difference. People will say there's no smoke without fire. What's it going to do to his family... his wife? His daughter? School starts in what...?'

'Three weeks.'

'Three weeks! Imagine what that poor child is going to go through!'

Mila pulled out a chair and sat down. She sipped her water. Her mouth was dry as dust.

They heard the door open downstairs, and then Carter Jackson's footsteps thumping on the stairs. Moments later he came into the office smelling of fresh air, engine oil and leather. He dropped a pile of posters on the floor. 'They're fucking everywhere,' he said.

'Ceci doesn't like swearing,' said Mila.

'Sorry, ma'am.'

Ceci waved the apology away.

The coffee was bubbling urgently. Mila went into the little kitchen, took the coffee maker off the hob and shared the black liquid it contained between three cups, which she took back into Ceci's office.

'Thanks,' said Carter. The cup looked very small in his big hand. 'Has something else happened?' he asked. 'What is it? Is it Mrs Perry?'

It must be very different for him, thought Mila, coming from the high-pressure, high-adrenaline world of the narcotics squad. There, presumably, he had been part of a large, macho team who wore guns and kicked doors open in dawn raids and told evil drugs barons to get in the back of the van. Now he was hunched in a small office with two women stressing over the fact they might be obliquely responsible for destroying a man's good name. If the story he'd told Ceci was true, that was.

She remembered an argument she'd had with Sophie years earlier, Mila telling her stepsister to stop manipulating Carter. '*He trusts you!*' she had cried, furious with Sophie and also with Carter because he couldn't or *wouldn't* see how he was being used. But just because he used to be trusting and naïve and honest, didn't mean he was now.

Carter was leaning forward, his arms resting on his knees.

'Are you feeling okay?' he asked Ceci. 'No offence, ma'am, but you don't look too good.'

'There's nothing wrong with me, Carter,' Ceci said, 'and I do take offence to you commenting on my appearance. Please don't do it again.'

Carter held up a hand in apology.

'More importantly, there has been a significant development,' Ceci continued. 'Mila and I went to visit Mrs Perry this morning and the woman who came to the office, the one you and I spoke to, was not her. The woman in Fendi was a fake.'

'Surely,' said Carter, 'you asked for some ID before you spoke to her?'

Ceci flushed. Mila had never seen her colour like that before. Of course she wouldn't have asked an apparently respectable woman in a Fendi suit for identification! In the normal course of the agency's work, there was never any need but this wasn't normal work. Ceci should have been super cautious and she knew it and now she realised the extent of her carelessness she was mortified.

Carter, seeing Ceci's discomfort, said quickly, 'It wouldn't have made any difference. She'd have had something fake, anyway.' A pause. 'I don't suppose she gave you any bank details?'

Ceci put a hand to her eyes. 'She offered,' she said. 'I said we'd email an invoice later.'

'Okay,' said Carter calmly. 'So, if the woman was fake, that means the phone number and the email address she gave us were fake too. I sent the photos directly to the scammer.'

Ceci nodded.

'You've got to give it to whoever's behind this,' said Carter, 'it was well planned.'

'It's all on CCTV,' said Ceci.

'Does the camera record twenty-four-seven?'

'It's motion sensitive but only triggered by people, not foxes or birds. It was last Thursday, wasn't it, when fake Mrs Perry came?'

'Wednesday. I left for the funeral at 9.30,' said Mila. 'It must have been after that.'

'Let's start at 9.30, then.'

Mila came to stand behind her stepmother. She looked over Ceci's shoulder and watched a video of herself coming out of the door next to the patisserie and walking along the cobbled street on her way to Gosia's funeral. After a few paces, she stopped and slipped her shoes off, hooked the straps over her fingers and walked on barefoot.

'I wish you wouldn't do that, darling,' Ceci murmured. 'The road are filthy.'

After that, there were various comings and goings of people visiting the patisserie; most of them, even the passers-by, spent a long time gazing through the window glass at the displays inside. Some went into the shop and came out holding a white cardboard box tied with a satin ribbon. Some simply stared at the cakes, and then shook their heads and walked away.

Ceci sped up the video and the people moved in jerky, fast motion, then she slowed it down.

'Here she is,' she said.

'That's her,' Carter Jackson agreed.

Mila leaned closer to get a better look.

Fake Mrs Perry did not resemble the real Mrs Perry at all. Her hair was short and blonde and expensively styled. As well as the beautiful clothes, she wore pearls around her neck and on her earlobes. Her legs and arms were slim, she was tastefully and comprehensively made up and although she could not see the detail, Mila *knew* she would have been well manicured.

Before she approached the door to the Toussaint's office, the woman paused outside the patisserie and looked in the window, not to admire the cakes but to check her own reflection. She turned to the left and then to the right, smoothed her hair, wiped away a smudge of lipstick with the tip of her finger, then stepped across to the Toussaint's door and disappeared through it.

'Do you have CCTV inside too?' Carter asked.

'Only in the reception. Here.'

This file opened with Ceci coming out of her office to greet the visitor – there was a bell attached to the door at the top of the stairs, which the visitor had pressed. Fake Mrs Perry looked around and noticed the camera because she immediately turned so that it was pointing down at the back of her head.

'I'm pretty sure that's a wig she's wearing,' said Mila. 'And the outfit – she didn't buy that in Morannez. If you isolate a still, Ceci, I could ask Melodie Sohar. She might be able to tell us where it came from.'

'She's wise to the cameras,' said Carter. 'You don't have a single good image of her face. We're not dealing with an amateur here.'

'She treated us like amateurs,' said Ceci. 'Why didn't I notice that she was keeping her back to the camera?'

'But it's not *us* who were the targets of this scam,' Mila pointed out, hoping to make Ceci feel a bit better. 'We, *Toussaint's*, was just the weapon used to get at the Perrys. What we should be asking is why someone would want to hurt the professor.'

'You're right,' said Carter.

'We should revert to Plan A,' said Ceci. 'You must go and talk to the real Mrs Perry, Mila.'

'She'll never agree to talk to me now.'

'If we're going to sort this mess out, darling, at the very least you have to try.'

26

The queue for the patisserie had dwindled to two people so Mila joined it and when it was her turn, she went into the shop and bought a selection box of delicacies from Mademoiselle la Caze, the patissier, a woman who, with her immaculate hair, pristine clothes and perfectly manicured fingers always made Mila feel like a pony, heavy-footed and shaggy by comparison. She balanced the box carefully in the basket over the front wheel of the bike while she typed a text on her phone.

Mrs Perry, my name is Mila Shepherd & I'm cycling over to your house because I want to help you. I'm not a journalist, nor am I connected to the dig. I have brown hair tied in a headband & I'm wearing a green skirt. It's fine if you don't want to let me in but if you'll give me a chance I might be able to help you sort this out.

Then she climbed onto the bike, and headed back towards the estate where the Perrys lived.

Most of the posters en route had been taken down now; Mila only spotted one or two and these she removed herself. She didn't know how much damage had been caused already, but she hoped with all her heart that the worst of the crisis, the initial shock and the subsequent reaction, was over.

The morning was rolling on. Most people were going about their daily lives oblivious to what had occurred. Cars were queuing for space in the supermarket car park; campervans were pulled over in the laybys so their occupants could have a snack, or take their dogs for a quick walk; delivery vans pootled by, their drivers resting their elbows on the frames of the open windows, different music singing out.

Mila knew the lanes around Morannez so well now that she hardly needed to think about where she was going. She knew where the worst of the potholes lurked; she knew which were the difficult junctions; she knew the straight road where the bikers liked to open their throttles, where she had once nearly come to grief.

On an impulse, she stopped at the little Turkish supermarket and bought fresh milk, sliced bread, cheese, chocolate, a packet of Yorkshire tea bags and six fat, white peaches, all of which she placed in her bicycle basket with the little cakes before setting off again.

The air was still beautifully warm but there was a faint promise of autumn, the first time Mila had noticed it that year. Wasps were buzzing amongst the fallen fruit at the feet of the trees at the side of the road. The blackberries on the wiry arms of the brambles that wove through the hedgerows were sticky and flyblown; the breeze coming off the Atlantic had the subtlest hint of a chill.

Mila could imagine this mess dragging on for weeks. Thank God there were only a finite number of days for her to be involved. Only three more Mondays after this one and she'd be back in Bristol where she could concentrate on her writing, and return to the emotional stability she'd worked so hard to achieve, and which she now craved. She'd had enough of drama, of teenage angst, of grief. And never mind commemorating next week's anniversary; if Ceci couldn't be bothered to think about it, then Mila wouldn't either.

She cycled on and soon reached the approach to the estate.

She slowed the bike as she turned in to the Perrys' road and coasted towards their house. Nobody was standing by the front door, but a dusty Peugeot was parked by the kerb that ran around the front lawn and a man was in the car. Mila was as certain as she could be that he was watching the house; she'd put money on him being a press photographer.

Merde.

A face looked out of an upstairs window. A girl. Mila waved and the girl moved away from the window.

A gull flew down and landed on the pavement beside Mila. A juvenile. It squawked hopefully, put its head down, extended its throat and flapped its wings in that nagging 'feed-me' way that young birds did.

'I'm not your mother,' Mila told it. She took out her phone, typed a quick message to Ani, checked it had sent, put the phone in her pocket, propped the bike against the garage wall and, holding the cake box and the bag of groceries, walked to the Perrys' front door.

27

There was a gate at the side of the Perrys' house, which led into the back garden; Mila considered using it, so she'd be out of sight of whoever was sitting in the Peugeot, but then she saw a corner of the blind in the front window twitch and a moment later the door opened a crack.

'Who's that?' a voice called urgently.

'It's Mila, I sent the text.'

'Come in, quick.'

The door opened just wide enough for Mila to squeeze in, and then it slammed shut behind her.

She found herself with Catherine Perry in a smallish hallway, the only natural light coming through a window halfway up the stairs. The space was cluttered: jumpers piled on top of one another on pegs, shoes by the door, a dog bed, a school bag, empty reusable shopping bags and a large plastic exercise ball. The air smelled of female sweat and stale talcum powder.

An old, overweight spaniel heaved itself up and wagged half-heartedly around Mila's legs. The girl who had been at the window was now sitting at the top of the stairs with her elbows on her knees and her chin cupped in the palms of her hand.

'Hello,' Mila said. The girl raised a hand in greeting. The spaniel lay down again. Mila turned to the woman. 'Mrs Perry,' she asked gently, 'are you all right?'

'No, I'm not all right,' Mrs Perry said. 'The whole town is either laughing at us or appalled by us. I don't know where my husband is and he's not answering his phone. I'm going out of my mind with worry and I can't see how anything is ever going to be all right again! What is happening to us?'

'I don't know,' said Mila, 'but whatever it is, we'll get to the bottom of it.'

'Even if we do, it won't change anything. This is going to kill Tim. He's never going to get over it.'

'Don't say that about Daddy!' said the girl. 'Don't say he's going to die!' She slid down the stairs, put her arms around her mother and pressed her face into her chest.

'I'm sorry,' said Mrs Perry. 'Sorry, my angel. I just... I'm in such a state.'

'It's absolutely understandable that you're distressed,' said Mila.

'I don't believe Tim would be unfaithful,' said Mrs Perry. 'I don't believe he'd do that to me' – she glanced at her daughter – 'to *us*. I know this is some kind of attempt to discredit him. But still, he let this happen. He let us be humiliated like this!'

'Your husband had nothing to do with the posters, Mrs Perry,' said Mila. 'I don't know why this has happened or who's behind it, but I'm here to help.'

She held up the bag. 'I brought you a few bits and pieces for lunch. I thought it'd be one less thing to worry about. I'll put them in the kitchen, shall I?'

'Thank you.'

Mila located the door to the kitchen, switched on the light, put the groceries into the fridge, filled the kettle and put it on the hob to heat.

Mrs Perry's craft-making paraphernalia was laid out on the kitchen table: lots of little pots of paint and glue and tiny hooks, ring settings and studs for earrings as well as numerous Tupperware tubs of differently coloured clay. She began to clear them away absentmindedly into plastic crates.

Mila asked, 'When did you realise something was wrong this morning?'

'Early. Tim's deputy called, from the dig. He kept blathering on about posters and reputations and we didn't understand what he was talking about. And then five minutes later our neighbour, Paulette, she's an older lady but she goes to the same church as us, came round. She'd gone out for her walk this morning, like she always does, and she brought one of the posters back with her. She said: "I'm ever so sorry to have to show you this, but I think you ought to see it." Tim looked at the poster, he held it in his hands and his face kind of *collapsed*; the only other time I've ever seen him look like that was when he got the phone call to say his mother had died. When I saw the poster I asked him what the hell was going on and he said: "I have to go and sort this out," and I said: "You're not going anywhere until you've told me what's going on," and he said: "Catherine, I'm truly sorry to put you through this, I had no idea they would go this far," and he said "See you later, alligator" to Emily and he left. That was about seven o'clock. *Hours* ago.' She paused for breath. 'I don't know where he's gone, and I don't know why he hasn't called or why he hasn't come back!'

Mrs Perry was veering between anger at her husband and concern for his well-being. Mila knew the feeling; she'd been through it many times with Sophie.

'I bet the battery in his phone's flat,' said Emily.

Mila looked at the teenager approvingly. 'I'm sure that's right,' she said. 'Mrs Perry, you said your husband said something about how he didn't think "they'd go this far"?'

'That's right.'

'Do you know what he meant? Do you know who "they" might be?'

'I hadn't thought about it. Do you think he's in some kind of trouble?'

'I don't know.'

The water in the kettle was beginning to bubble. Mrs Perry looked at it in surprise, as if she'd forgotten it had been put to the boil.

'I know it's difficult, but we need to understand what's been going on in your husband's life,' said Mila. 'There must be a reason why someone would go to so much trouble to ruin his good name. Has he mentioned anything to you about any problems? Anything to do with the dig?'

Catherine Perry was quiet for a moment.

'He hasn't *said* as much, but I know he was worried about getting everything done within such a tight timescale. And no decent finds have come up so far, nothing even remotely of the quality of the whalebone carving.'

'Has anyone been putting pressure on him to speed things along?'

'Not exactly. But with any dig, the sponsors always expect results. It gets a bit tense if they're nearing the end and they have nothing to show for their investment.'

'And he's worried about Jake,' said Emily.

'Jake?'

'I don't think we need to bring Jake into this.'

'I'd be interested to know about Jake,' said Mila.

Mrs Perry sighed. When she next spoke the tone of her voice had become bitter.

'Jake was our son, Emily's older brother. He was at Liverpool University but he was failing the course. About a month ago he sent his father a text to say he was dropping out. A text! Can you imagine?'

'You said he "was" your son. Has something happened to him?'

'I washed my hands of him,' said Mrs Perry. 'He's dead to me now. If people ask, I say I only have one child.'

She had stiffened. Her jaw was clenched. 'It sounds harsh, but you don't know what that boy has put us through over the years. He's been trouble since the day he was born. If there was a wrong crowd to be in with, he'd make a beeline for them. He's been convicted of theft, minor drugs offences, all sorts. One Christmas, he turned up at the church, drunk! Can you imagine our shame? It was a miracle when he got the place at uni, but he was never going to make a success of it. I wasn't surprised when Tim received the text. If Jake can find a way to mess something up, he will.'

Emily nodded sagely. Mila had the impression she quite enjoyed hearing her brother being criticised.

'So, to be clear, you don't talk to Jake, but he's still in touch with his father?'

'Tim calls him. I don't approve. I believe that sometimes it's a parent's duty to put their foot down. Children, even grown children, need boundaries. They need to know when certain lines have been crossed. And if they cross those lines too often, there need to be consequences and those consequences should be adhered to. I'm a traditionalist like that. Don't you think that's right?'

'I don't have any children of my own,' Mila said, 'so I'm not really in a position to comment.'

'You don't have children?' Mrs Perry asked. 'Aren't you married?'

'No,' said Mila. 'It never really appealed to me.'

'Oh,' said Mrs Perry. She looked around her miserably as if being married was beginning not to appeal to her either.

28

Mila made the tea.

'I bought some cakes from the patisserie in town,' she said, indicating the white box, the cardboard only slightly dented from being carried in the bicycle basket.

'We don't really like French cakes,' said Mrs Perry. 'We find them rather rich.'

She took a tin from a cupboard and prised open its lid. It contained the remnants of a Mr Kipling Battenberg cake folded into its wrapper. She offered the tin to Mila, who took a piece even though she would have preferred one of the tiny coffee éclairs she'd brought from the patisserie.

'Have you spoken to the police, Mrs Perry?' Mila asked.

'Why does Mum need to talk to the police?' Emily asked.

'It's not as if Tim is missing,' said Mrs Perry. 'We don't know where he is but he hasn't been kidnapped. And he's only been gone hours. Aren't you supposed to wait for a day?'

'I was thinking more about reporting the malicious posters,' said Mila. 'It's up to you, of course.'

'If we involve the authorities, won't it make things worse? More official?'

'It might do, yes.'

'The absolute worst thing would be if news of this was to find its way into the British press. I think it's best we make as little fuss as possible.'

Mrs Perry lifted a small piece of cake to her mouth then changed her mind and put it back on her plate. Bright pink crumbs spilled onto her bosom.

'I can't eat,' she said. 'I can't eat a thing.'

Emily was picking at her cake, delicately removing the marzipan and making a small pile at the side of her plate. Mila smiled at the girl.

'I think you know my niece. She goes to the international school too. Her name's Anaïs Cooper – Ani.'

'Yes, I know her. Pernille's friend.'

'That's right.'

'She's kind of quiet.'

'She is.'

'Isn't she the girl who was being bullied?' asked Catherine Perry.

That was news to Mila.

'Has Ani been bullied?' she asked Emily.

Emily looked uncomfortable and Mila regretted firing the question at her. Emily turned to her mother. 'Is it all right if I go and get my stuff ready for the sleepout?'

'Yes, you carry on.'

'Come on, Buffy,' said the girl. The ancient spaniel shuffled to its feet and followed her out of the room. Mila got up and closed the door quietly behind them.

'Sleepout?' she asked Mrs Perry.

'The whole of the middle school. Wednesday night on the town beach. It's all Emily's been talking about for days. Surely Anaïs has mentioned it?'

She hadn't.

'I'm not that keen on Emily going,' Mrs Perry continued. 'I don't want her turning out like her brother so we generally keep her on a pretty tight leash, but Tim thinks she'll be all right as long as she has her phone with her. A couple of the teachers will be there to supervise and he says he'll pop down every now and then to make sure things aren't getting out of hand.' She looked at Mila. 'He will be back by then, won't he?'

'I really hope so.'

Why hadn't Ani said anything about the sleepout? Because she didn't want to go, probably. It would be a particularly cruel form of torture for her, to be exposed so close to the breaking waves in the dark – especially if she had school bullies to contend with too. Mila felt a pang of pity for her niece, quickly followed by relief that she wasn't going to be down on the beach all night with God-knows-how-many drunken and vulnerable teenagers.

'Don't you like the cake?' said Mrs Perry. 'I guess your tastes are more attuned to French cuisine. Don't get me wrong, I'm not against it as such, it's just all that butter and cream messes up my system.' She sighed. 'Battenberg is Tim's favourite. He always likes a slice with a cup of Earl Grey when he comes back from the dig.' She tailed off and when she looked up her eyes were full of tears. Mila stared hard at her cake, hoping Mrs Perry wouldn't realise that she'd noticed. Strange how a woman who had found it easy to sever ties with her son was clearly so fond of her husband.

The professor's wife reached across the table, pulled a man-size tissue out of a box, blew her nose and wiped her eyes.

'You do believe me that Tim's not the sort to have an affair?' she asked.

'Of course.'

'You really think it's a smear campaign?'

'Yes.'

'Whoever it is, they know exactly how to get to Tim. His reputation is everything to him. He can't bear to have people thinking badly of him. He'd do almost anything to avoid unpleasantness and this... Oh God, I don't know how we're going to get through it, I really don't.'

Mrs Perry sniffed and looked up to Heaven. 'You asked if he'd mentioned any problems at the dig, and he hasn't, but I've had a feeling something was wrong for a while now. Tim's been staying out late and when he comes home, he disappears upstairs to work on his laptop instead of watching television with me or building Lego models with Emily like he used to. He's been short-tempered and that's not like him. I even asked him, a few days ago, if anything was going on that I ought to know about.'

'What did he say?'

'That everything was fine. I could see that he was lying. I should have pushed him but he looked so tired.'

'Do you think he might have fallen out with someone? One of his colleagues?'

'Tim doesn't fall out with people. He's not like me; I speak my mind and I don't care who I upset. Tim's not like that. He's mild-mannered, that's what he is. Kind.'

Mrs Perry thought for a few moments, then said, 'Actually, now you mention it, he did fall out with someone: me!'

'Oh?'

'We had a disagreement over the traveller woman. The one who lived in the horsebox.'

Mila's heartbeat quickened. 'Do you mind if I ask why?'

'I found out he'd given her some money without discussing it with me. A *lot* of money. Three hundred euros.'

'Why would he do that?'

'So she could get her horsebox fixed. There was something wrong with the gear box. It was ridiculous; the van was falling apart and she would have been much better off in a home; she was clearly not quite all there. But would Tim discuss getting the authorities involved? Oh no, he insisted on going to see her, getting the problem diagnosed and then giving her the money to have it fixed.'

'Has he ever behaved like this before?'

Mrs Perry nodded. 'He picks up waifs and strays everywhere.'

'But this thing with the traveller woman, it started about the same time as your husband began behaving differently?'

'That's right. And next thing we heard, she had died and after that he got really… I don't know… *twitchy*.'

'As if he was afraid of something?'

'Maybe.'

The faint sound of music came from one of the upstairs rooms. Mila recognised it as the latest K-pop band; Ani liked them too.

She asked. 'Have you checked your husband's laptop, Mrs Perry?'

'Tim took it with him.'

'So, he went out this morning with a purpose. Maybe to go into the university to work?'

'Not to the university. He didn't take the car.'

It was a statement of the obvious, but something Mila had overlooked. The Volvo was still outside the house. If the professor was on foot, he couldn't have gone very far.

29

Mila didn't leave the Perrys' house until Catherine Perry had convinced her that she would be all right. She had her daughter with her, and her mother had already been summoned and was on her way over from England.

'Will you call me as soon as you hear from your husband?' Mila asked. Mrs Perry promised that she would. 'And if you need anything in the meantime, you have my number.'

Mila was relieved to be out of the clammy claustrophobia of the Perrys' house.

She gave a dirty look to the paparazzo as she pushed her bike past the Peugeot – he had his arms folded over his chest and looked to be snoozing. He raised his middle finger to her, which didn't help her mood.

She turned the bike away from him and freewheeled down the incline, cycled out of the housing estate and waited until she was out in the countryside, out of earshot of anyone, before she stopped the bike and called the agency. Carter picked up at once.

'Professor Perry left home at about 7 a.m. on foot,' Mila told him. 'He took his laptop and phone with him. He's been concerned about something for some time and...'

'Somebody was threatening him?'

'Sounds like it. He hadn't taken a warning seriously enough, is how I interpreted it.'

'Okay,' said Carter. 'So, our next step is to find out if the professor was involved in something dodgy.'

He sounded as if he was in charge of this investigation, if that was what it was. Mila tried not to bristle. If Carter Jackson wanted to take the lead, that was fine by her; *she* certainly didn't want to be at the helm – in fact, she didn't want to be involved at all.

'And there's some kind of connection to Gosia, the traveller woman. I don't know what exactly but the professor knew her and was concerned about her.'

'How is Mrs Perry?' Carter asked.

'Confused and worried that people are going to think badly of them both. She's going to call me if her husband gets in touch.'

'Is she worried that he might harm himself?'

Mila groaned. 'Oh God, Carter, please don't put that thought into my head!'

'You didn't ask her?'

'No, of course I didn't. I didn't want to put the possibility into *her* head. But she told me that the professor cares massively about his reputation. If someone wanted to make him so ashamed that he might be driven to do something stupid, this was the way to do it.' She paused, then added, 'She did say this would be the death of him, or something like that.'

'Okay,' said Carter, 'let's not read too much into that. As long as the professor is thinking straight, his priority is going to be to clear his name. He can't do that unless he's alive and well and has access to means of communication.'

'That's true.'

'So, let's assume he's holed up somewhere working on a come-back strategy. Ceci's scouring academic talkboards and archaeology groups to see if she can find him online.'

'Did she manage to speak to Ani?'

'Hang on... Ceci, Mila says did you speak to Ani? No? But they texted. Ani's fine. Are you coming back to the office?'

'I need to go back to the sea house. I need to make sure Ani's okay.'

Carter started to say something else, but Mila's finger had already pressed the button to disconnect the call.

She slipped the phone into her rucksack. She didn't want to talk to anyone for a while. She wanted to be quiet.

She stood, breathing the soft summer air, gazing out to the milky sea in the distance, feeling the sun on the skin of her face. She would be back in England soon; Bristol in autumn would be very different to this and she wouldn't have to think about difficult situations concerning slandered professors and women who lived in horseboxes and teenage girls who were struggling at school.

After a few moments, she put her leg over the bike, and set off again, cycling at a steady speed.

Swallows were lined up on the wires outside the big old hay barn close to the Bloemel turning. Others were darting above a large dung heap steaming amongst ancient farm machinery, picking off the flies. Swallows, the prettier *hirondelles* in French, had been Sophie's favourite birds. Mila preferred starlings. She liked the petrol sheen of their plumage close up. She loved the way they murmurated in their tens of thousands in Somerset during the winter months – hiking across the Levels was one of her and Luke's favourite pastimes.

Sophie preferred swallows because they were small, fast, and delightful. Also, because they travelled so far and because they always knew where they were going. Which was ironic, when Mila thought about it, because her whole life Sophie had never seemed to know in which direction she was headed. It was tragic but absolutely fitting that Sophie's death should have come about because she and Charlie were lost at sea.

Mila's mind segued between memories of Sophie and wondering where Professor Perry might have gone with his laptop when the peace of the day was interrupted by what started as a distant buzzing and soon escalated into a roar that sent the swallows flying up into the air. A few seconds later, Carter Jackson's motorbike pulled up alongside Mila's pushbike. He was so close she could feel the road vibrating through the sole of the foot she put down to steady herself, and the heat from the Harley's engine blew warm against the side of her leg.

'What are you *doing?*' she yelled.

Although the bike was stationary, the engine was pounding like a jack-hammer.

'You cut me off and then you weren't answering the phone. We need to talk.'

'I told you, I have to get back home for Ani.'

'We can talk at your place then.'

Mila didn't want Carter coming to the sea house. She didn't want to have to deal with all the memories and feelings that his presence would prompt. She didn't want to be on her own with him. But they couldn't stand here yelling at one another and she couldn't think of a way to refuse that wouldn't seem desperately surly.

A tractor that had been slowly making its way towards them, on the other side of the hedge, slowed and turned. The air was sweet with the honeyed smell of hay-making.

'Okay,' said Mila. 'Do you know where to go? Turn right at the next junction, and the one after that, then take the little lane just beyond the spot where the kids have built a bike track. I'll see you there in a few minutes.'

Carter raised two gloved fingers to the visor of his helmet, nodded, and roared off. Mila turned her head and closed her eyes against the sting of the fumes ejected from the bike's exhaust.

'It's only carbon emissions,' she muttered, 'bringing about the end of the world. Who cares about climate change? Not him, with his stupid, show-off, dumbass bike.'

She wafted her hand in front of her face to disperse the toxins in the air, then remounted the pushbike and continued on her way.

30

Carter was waiting on the grassy area beyond the sea house, in the same spot where the man who had gone past in the night had disappeared from view. Mila, who'd been pedalling as fast as she could on the pushbike, was glad to see that although he had parked his motorbike up on its stand, dismounted, and removed his helmet, he hadn't come through the gate.

Mila went through into the garden, holding on to the handlebars, the pushbike bumping along obligingly beside her. Berthaud was lying on the path in a patch of sunlight. She flicked the end of her tail in the laziest possible greeting to Mila, but didn't attempt to get up. As she passed the washing line, Mila grabbed her swimming costume and pulled it off. She crumpled it and shoved it behind the folding chairs in the porch. Then she opened the door with her key and called: 'Ani! I'm home!'

There was no response, no sound at all from inside the house, and it had the empty feeling it only had when nobody was there. Ani's trainers were missing from their usual spot by the front door. Her rucksack was gone too.

Merde. So, on top of everything else, Ani had gone out without letting Mila know where she was going, which meant that she was punishing Mila for deserting her that morning. Fair enough, Mila supposed, but this, on top of everything else, was another burden Mila didn't want to have to carry. She was annoyed with Ceci, who had promised to make sure Ani was okay. She was annoyed with herself for having been talked into going to see Mrs Perry when she should have been looking after her niece. She felt a mixture of guilt and frustration; it was an uncomfortable cocktail.

Mila put her rucksack down on the seat of the rocking chair in the corner of the kitchen. Carter had followed her to the door.

'Is it okay to come in?'

'I'll be with you in two minutes.'

He withdrew back to the garden.

Mila called Ani's number but she didn't pick up. Mila sent a message.

Sorry about this morning. Please call me.

She called Ceci.

'Did you actually speak to Ani earlier?' she asked, without attempting to disguise the irritation in her voice.

'We texted. She said she was going out to meet a friend.'

'Which friend?'

'Darling, I didn't ask. Ani's a sensible girl. I trust her to make the right decisions.'

'If she gets in touch, will you ask her to call me?'

'Of course. Is something wrong, Mila?'

'Ani's gone out,' Mila said, 'and I don't know where she is.'

'She'll be fine.'

'She's fourteen! She's lost both her parents; she's being bullied by little shits at school; I've been out all morning and you, Ceci, you promised to make sure she was all right, and all you did was send a couple of texts.

'Mila, calm down! You worry too much! You and Sophie used to be at the beach on your own all day when you were Ani's age.'

And you didn't know who we were with or what we were doing. You never even laid eyes on Carter Jackson, for example, even though he was there with us all summer, every year, watching Sophie while I was watching him.

At least 'Sophie and I had each other,' Mila said.

'And Ani has her friends.'

'Didn't you hear what I just told you, Ceci, she's being bullied at school.'

'But she's not going back to that school, is she? And she'll be out now with young people she likes, not the ones who cause her grief.'

Mila didn't answer.

Ceci sighed. 'Listen, darling, I need to get back to work. Is Carter with you?'

'Yes.'

'Good! You have a talk with him and I'll see if I can get hold of Ani. But you mustn't be so stressed about her. We'll talk soon, okay?'

She cut off the call. Mila looked out through the window. Carter, looking dreadfully out of place, was standing staring into the middle distance with his thumbs hooked into his pockets. He was preoccupied with his own thoughts which was good because Mila needed a moment to calm herself down. She was frustrated that after all these months, she still couldn't seem to balance her responsibilities towards Ani with the rest of her life. She was no good at being in loco parentis. She was a crap carer.

How many times, she wondered, had she tried to make things better for Ani over the past year? Dozens! She had been constantly trying to compensate for the loss Ani had suffered and she had been destined to fail. She could never replace Sophie and Charlie. She couldn't come close. It would be better for Ani when she was at boarding school in the care of professionals who had experience of dealing with bereaved children. And Ceci was right, she'd be away from the bullies at the international school; she'd be able to start again with people who knew what they were doing. Ani would be better off without Mila. Really, Ceci should have taken the boarding school route sooner. If she had, Ani would be settled by now and this would all be over.

Mila poured herself a glass of water from the tap and drank most of it. Then she filled another glass and went outside. Carter was sitting on the swing-seat, pushing it backwards and forwards with his enormous feet in their enormous boots with buckles at the side. Mila passed the glass to him.

'I don't have anything else,' she said, even though Carter had not asked for anything at all.

'Water's good.'

He was wearing a T-shirt that was a khaki-grey colour with a large black peace symbol in the middle. Something about the logo pricked Mila. What was it?

Of course! Sophie used to have it printed on a poster stuck to her bedroom wall. How could Mila have forgotten? In her mind's eye Mila could see Sophie sitting cross-legged on the bed beneath the poster, plaiting her hair into micro-braids. She was wearing denim cut-offs and a cheesecloth shirt, long, beaded strings wrapped around her neck. And her skin was tanned, her hair sun-bleached, everything about her so... so *Sophie*.

She wondered if Carter had ever been into Sophie's bedroom; if he had seen her poster and if, subconsciously perhaps, that was why he had chosen that T-shirt. Or perhaps he and Sophie were so similar in personality that they were inevitably drawn to the same things.

Or maybe it meant nothing. Peace symbols were hardly uncommon.

'Do you want to sit here?' Carter asked. He indicated that he would stand up to let her have the swing-seat.

'No. I'm okay.'

Mila fetched a wooden chair from the old bench table and dropped onto that instead.

'You said you wanted to talk,' she said.

'Is that okay with you?'

'Well, you're here now.'

'I wanted to fill you in on what happened while you were with Mrs Perry.'

'Go on then.'

Carter narrowed his eyes. Mila held his stare.

'I went to Kyern.' Carter said. 'Everyone at the site is seriously stressed. Nobody would talk to me. I guess they've been told not to say anything to anyone. But the professor's not there and I got the impression nobody had seen him. I had a good look round the town too but there's no sign. I checked out the train station; there's a guy painting the fence outside and he's been there since seven and said he hadn't seen Tim Perry today. It doesn't mean he's still here, of course. He could've caught a bus out.'

'But why do that when he had access to a perfectly good car?'

'Exactly.'

Mila pulled her legs up onto the chair. 'What about the girl in the poster? Did anyone at the dig site recognise her?'

'Like I said, they wouldn't talk to me. But I met a couple of students in the town. They said the girl's not connected to Rennes university but they had seen her before. She'd turned up a few times at Kyern asking for Professor Perry and making a nuisance of herself if he didn't come to see her straight away. People were getting annoyed about her hanging around. The professor had been asked to make her stay away.'

'They blamed him for her being there?'

'They thought she was his responsibility.' Carter rubbed his fingers across the stubble above his upper lip. 'But nobody I spoke to thought their relationship was romantic. One of the girls said they seemed more like people who were related; the students had speculated that she might be a black sheep daughter.'

'She's not. The Perrys only have one daughter and she's the same age as Ani.' Mila took a drink of water. 'Is the girl French?'

'I'm guessing English if people thought she was related,' said Carter.

'I don't suppose anyone's seen her lately?'

'Not since Saturday, no. Meanwhile, the powers that be are shutting the dig for the rest of this week and the sponsors are putting together a statement that will be issued to the press with regard to the professor's position going forward.'

'Are they standing by him?'

'I suspect they'll distance themselves from him until an internal inquiry has been carried out.'

'That's unkind. There's no proof he's done anything wrong.'

'No organisation wants to be associated with an alleged pervert, especially an organisation involved in educational out-reach.' He considered for a moment then said, 'If the point of all this was to get Professor Perry off the dig, then whoever was behind it has succeeded.'

Mila wrapped her arms around her legs and pressed her face into her knees. 'The only people I can think of who would benefit from the dig being wound up early are the Girard family. An early conclusion would mean they could get going on their restaurant and leisure park without losing any more money.'

'But?'

'But why pick on Professor Perry? Ceci's told me all kinds of stories about the Girards and when they want something, they always take the most direct route towards achieving that goal. This feels too personal and convoluted for them to be behind it.'

'And the dig is over half way through. If they'd wanted to stop it, it would've made more sense to do something earlier.'

At that moment, Mila's eye was caught by a movement along the lane – a slight figure walking through the sunlight: Ani. She was alone, dawdling, lost in a world of her own thoughts, earbuds in her ears, trailing one small hand along the side of the hedgerow, disturbing a few small, yellow leaves and a family of goldfinch.

Carter had spotted her too.

'Is that your niece?'

'Yes.'

'I'll get going then,' he said, 'give you guys some space.'

'Thanks,' said Mila.

Carter stood and picked up his jacket.

'By the way, Mila, did you ask Mrs Perry if her husband had made any unusual financial transactions lately?'

'Should I have?'

He shrugged. 'Asking about money is a habit you get into when you've been on the money-laundering team for a while.'

'She told me her husband had given a few hundred euros to Gosia, the traveller woman, so she could get her van fixed. Mrs Perry wasn't happy about it, but she said he's always helping people randomly. And I can't see how that could be connected to this.'

'Was there anything else?'

'Not that she mentioned.'

'It might be worth double-checking,' Carter said.

'Okay.'

Ani had spotted them now. She was hovering by the gate, unsure if she should come in. Carter saluted her. She looked away.

Mila prayed he wouldn't try to talk to her, wouldn't say anything about how he used to know her mother. She walked with him back to the bike, catching Ani's eye, giving her a reassuring smile.

'It feels like there's something we're missing,' Mila said as Carter pulled on his helmet.

'It always feels like that,' Carter said. 'At a certain point in any case, when you start to get invested in the people you're dealing with, you always get this "if only" feeling. "If only I could work out why she said this...", "If only I could figure out why he said that."'

'When does it stop feeling like that?' asked Mila.

'When you've figured out the answers,' said Carter. 'That's when.'

31

When the sound of Carter Jackson's motorbike engine had finally dwindled to nothing, Mila looked at her niece and said, 'I'm sorry, Ani. I'm sorry I went out so early and I'm sorry you've been on your own all morning.'

'I don't care.'

Okay.

'Where've you been?' Mila asked, keeping her voice as warm as she could. 'Ceci said you'd gone to meet a friend. Was it Pernille?'

'She was out.'

'Right.' Mila paused. 'I met Emily Perry this morning.' She studied Ani's face for any reaction to the mention of Emily's name, but Ani looked disinterested.

'She mentioned that there were some not-very-nice students at your school.'

Ani shrugged.

'You won't have to deal with those particular people again, not when you start your new school but you know, Ani, if you're ever having any trouble you can always...'

'Do you have to do this now?'

'Do what?'

'Have a go at me!'

'I'm not having a go at you, I'm trying to help!'

'By pointing out that nobody likes me?'

'No! That's not what I'm doing at all! I'm trying to tell you that I'm always there for you!'

Ani glared at her aunt. Mila realised how patronising and also dishonest that statement must have sounded.

'Okay, obviously I haven't always been there for you but if you'd said something...' *No! Now you're blaming Ani for the situation.* 'I'm sorry, Ani. Let me start again. This is not your fault. There's nothing you should have said or done. This is down to me. *I* should have paid closer attention.'

'It doesn't matter, does it? Like you said, I'll be at my new school soon. I won't be your problem any more.'

'Ani, you're not a problem, don't say that!'

'I don't know why we're even having this conversation. What's the point?'

Mila opened her mouth and then closed it, trying to find the right words.

I'd back off, if I were you, said Sophie.

'All I'm saying is that I don't want you to feel alone.'

Ani frowned. Mila again sensed her own hypocrisy. Ani had been on her own all morning and would soon be packed off to Switzerland.

Mila tried again. 'Perhaps we could do something together this afternoon. Is there anything you'd like to do?'

Even as she was speaking, a voice in her head was telling her she should be concentrating on finding Professor Perry.

'Not really,' said Ani, cagily.

Mila hoped the professor was, as Carter had suggested, in some quiet room somewhere writing the emails and pulling the strings to put the things in place that would clear his name and exonerate his reputation. But what if he wasn't? What if he was lost and desperate?

'Okay, well, if there isn't anything you want to do, perhaps you could watch some videos while I get on with some work?'

'If that's what you want me to do.'

'I didn't say that. It's just that a man has gone missing...'

'Emily's dad?'

'How did you know?'

'I saw something on our class WhatsApp.'

'What did it say?'

'That Emily's dad was a pervert.'

'It's not true,' Mila said. 'Someone is trying to make people think badly of him.'

'Why is everyone saying it if it's not true?'

'I don't know. Is Emily in this WhatsApp group?'

'Yes.'

Mila needed to contact Mrs Perry to make sure she was aware of this. Thank goodness it was the holidays. At least Emily wouldn't have to run the gauntlet of the school corridors.

She tried to take a step back to consider the situation.

Ceci was looking for the professor. Carter was looking for him. No doubt countless numbers of his colleagues were looking for him. His wife was poised by the phone. Mila spending the afternoon online was hardly likely to make much difference to the outcome, whatever that might eventually be.

What was driving Mila, if she was 100 per cent honest with herself, was the fact that she preferred doing internet research to spending time with her teenage niece.

It was easier and less hassle.

And she could perfectly well do it this evening when Ani was asleep.

'Ani,' she said, 'shall we have some lunch and then get changed, and go into Morannez and be tourists?'

Ani brightened. 'Seriously?'

'Well, yes. Why not? If you'd like to.'

'What about Emily's dad?'

'Lots of people are looking for him. And we can look out for him while we're being tourists.'

Being tourists was a game that Mila and Sophie used to play when they were teenagers. It meant enjoying all the overpriced delights that Morannez laid on to tempt incomers to part with their money. It was a guilty pleasure. When Sophie and Mila were young, they observed how Patrick and Cecille, not short of money by anyone's standards and normally the most generous couple, used to complain over the inflated cost of ice cream or sunscreen or bottled water purchased from the town's small shops, how they wouldn't let the girls play on the games machines in the little arcade because it was a 'waste of money', how they would make detours of several kilometres to buy something more cheaply from a supermarket rather than line the pockets of the merchants who were ripping off the tourists. The game had been Sophie and Mila's response to this particular form of tight-fistedness.

Mila watched and saw how quickly Ani's eyes brightened at this prospect. Part of the fun was knowing how badly Ceci – and Patrick, were they to get wind of what was going on, would disapprove.

'Just you and me?' Ani asked.

'Just us,' replied Mila.

'Okay,' said Ani.

While Ani was changing, Mila called Catherine Perry.

'Is there any news?' Mrs Perry asked before Mila even had the chance to frame a question.

'Not from this end. You haven't heard anything from your husband?'

'Nothing.'

'I don't know what I can say to reassure you, Mrs Perry,' Mila said, 'but please try not to worry. Is your mother still on her way?'

'She'll be here in the morning.'

'Well, that's good. You won't be on your own for much longer.'

Mila told Mrs Perry about the WhatsApp group and suggested she keep Emily away from social media if she could. Then she asked if she and her husband had joint bank accounts.

'One for the bills, and we have individual ones too.'

'And can you access them online?'

'Of course.'

'Then would you have a look to see if there's been any unusual activity on either your joint, or your husband's account lately – money coming in, or going out, anything that's out of the ordinary.'

'Why? Do you think Tim's being blackmailed?'

'I don't think anything. My colleague, who has more experience in this kind of field, said it would be a good idea to check, that's all.'

'All right. I'll let you know if I find anything.'

'Thank you. If I haven't heard from you, I'll call you in the morning. Let me know if your husband comes back in the meantime.'

Mrs Perry promised that she would.

Mila finished the call as Ani came downstairs in her hippy flares and a fringed tank top.

'Ready!' she cried, doing a twirl.

She looked so like her mother that Mila took a sharp intake of breath.

That's my girl! said Sophie.

'What?' Ani asked. 'You look like you just saw a ghost.'

She smelled of mango and coconut and she looked so young and vulnerable that Mila had a strong urge to open her arms and wrap her up and protect her from all the nastiness in the world.

The feeling was so compelling it was almost painful.

You won't be able to help her once she's in Switzerland, Sophie whispered.

But she'll be in the best place, with the best people to look after her.

Keep telling yourself that, Mila, and maybe one day you'll believe it.

No! It wasn't Mila's job to look after Ani; this was – and always had been – a part-time role she'd taken on to help in a crisis. She'd been here for near enough a year, which was way over and above what anyone could reasonably have expected her to do. She'd dropped her whole life to help out: left Luke behind, her book, her friends. She'd done her absolute best, beyond the call of duty. Nobody could accuse her of shirking her responsibilities.

It's true, said Sophie. *So why is it, Mila, that you're feeling so bad about everything?*

Mila didn't know the answer to that question.

It wasn't like she was the one who'd gone sailing a year ago.

It wasn't as if she was the one who had never come back.

32

When they were ready, Mila and Ani wandered into Morannez town. It would have been quicker to go to the horseshoe beach and then follow the coastal path along to the main resort, but Mila didn't want to do anything that might upset her niece, which meant staying away from the sea as much as they could.

Because their route took them close to Kyern, Mila asked Ani if she would like to take a quick look at the archaeological dig. Ani said 'If you like,' which wasn't a 'no', so they made a small detour along the road that encircled the bottom of the hill. A group of tourists who had obviously come by coach were grouped around the dolmen listening to a presentation by a guide; the odd word in German being broadcast via a loudspeaker occasionally made its way to Mila and Ani on the breeze. Only one or two people were at the actual dig site and nothing much appeared to be going on. There was no sign of the professor.

'That's my teacher,' said Ani.

She was pointing to Monsieur Hugo, who was standing close to one of the trenches, with his sleeves rolled up and his hands on his hips, talking to a woman in heels and a navy-blue peplum dress with a black folder tucked under one arm. From her days in the NHS comms department, Mila recognised the uniform; the woman was almost certainly worked in public relations.

Ani had hooked her arms over the railing at the viewpoint where they were standing, lifted up her feet and was absentmindedly swinging herself to and fro, humming.

'Do you like Monsieur Hugo?' Mila asked.

'He's okay,' said Ani.

'Damned by faint praise,' said Mila.

'He's not one of my favourite teachers,' said Ani, and then she went quiet and Mila knew it was because she was remembering that she was never going back to her old school. Or perhaps she was thinking about the bullying.

'Ani...' Mila began but there must have been something in the tone of her voice that alerted the girl to the fact that she was about to raise an uncomfortable topic, because Ani jumped down and wandered away from her aunt.

Mila jogged to catch up with her and they headed back into town. They couldn't avoid walking partway along the seafront. The lights that were strung along the promenade had been turned on and reflected beautifully in the water. The tide was in, the smallest of waves washing the sand, smoothing over the footprints, the holes that had been dug, the castles that had been built during the day and the sand kicked over by older children playing beach ball. The town was entering the quiet phase, immediately before it became busy again. Waiters with their hair slicked back and aprons tied tight around their waists were laying the tables outside the restaurants ready for the early evening rush. Shopkeepers were sweeping up and rearranging their outside wares. Residents were watering their window boxes and hanging baskets: trails of small leaves and tiny blue flowers, the blood-red of the pelargoniums growing in repurposed olive oil cans and splashes of water darkening the pavements where the baskets were dripping.

Somewhere, in one of the back streets, Mila heard a motorcycle roar and a dog barked after it. It was almost certainly Carter Jackson, once again disturbing the peace of the little town.

Ani was cheerful. Her eyes were bright. She looked healthy and relaxed, for once, so Mila relaxed too. She tried to put Professor Perry and Gosia from her mind.

'Can we get something to eat?' Ani asked.

'We're tourists, remember?' Mila said. 'We can do whatever you like in whatever order you like!'

'Anything?'

'Anything.'

'Can we eat something sweet before something savoury?'

'Absolutely.'

'All right, then. I'd like an ice-cream sundae, please. Not from Jenny's – from the Milk Bar.'

This was a place that specialised in dairy treats – milkshakes, sundaes, ice-cream sodas and knickerbocker glories. It was done up in 1950s Americana, complete with the front half of a Buick apparently crashing through one of the walls. Its prices were extortionate; Ceci couldn't walk past the place without tutting. This, of course, put the Milk Bar on a similar status to Valhalla as far as Ani was concerned.

Ani and Mila went inside and Ani spent a long time staring at the laminated menu before settling on a peach melba deluxe. It came served on a dish shaped like a boat and, as well as fruit and ice cream, featured huge blooms of squirty cream, hot chocolate sauce, chopped nuts and hundreds and thousands in pretty pastel colours.

'Oh. My. God!' said Ani, staring at it wide-eyed. She took a picture with her phone. The waiter lit a sparkler that was stuck into a slot at the front of the dish and it obligingly burst into life, crackling and shooting off zigzags of light. Families walking along the promenade stopped to watch through the window. When the sparkler fizzled out, they applauded. Although Ani said she was embarrassed, Mila could see that she was secretly thrilled.

Mila sipped a ginger beer while Ani ate her sundae and when she'd scraped every last drop of sauce from the dish – 'There was a pattern on that before,' the waiter said approvingly – she looked up at Mila and said, 'I'm *so* full!'

'You'd better not be. We're tourists, remember? We have *way* more to eat yet.'

Ani giggled. 'Maman would have loved this!' she said.

She said it spontaneously, unselfconsciously, and she didn't realise what she'd said because there was none of the usual silence that followed a statement like this one, none of the subsequent sadness. Ani simply wiped her fingers on the paper napkin provided, took a drink from her glass of water and asked, 'Where now then?'

Mila could not have been more proud.

They went outside, walked on past the harbour where a group of young teenagers were gathered, sitting on the longest wooden pier in that part of France, dangling their legs over the edge, laughing in a self-consciously noisy way as if trying to draw attention to themselves and, at the same time, trying to avoid doing so. The pier, stretching out into the sea, with no railings or bars, not even a rope for people to hold on to, always made Mila feel wobbly. It had been damaged by storms the previous winter and a barrier erected just beyond where the boys were sitting warned people to keep off. *DANGER!* it said, and there was a cartoon drawing of a man falling into the sea, arms flailing, to ram the message home. Ani slunk to the other side of Mila so she would be less visible to the boys.

The sharp, burned-sugar smell of crêpes being cooked on the hotplate of the woman who operated the stall set up at the edge of the harbour mingled with the normal fishy smells. The gentle sound of the clanking of ropes against the masts of the sailing boats was background music. A gull stood on the roof of the cabin of a fishing boat and cawed. Ani slipped away from Mila to look at the discounted clothes hung on the rail outside one of the Sohars' chain of shops and, freed from her responsibility for a few moments, Mila let the nostalgia that trailed her come up alongside.

It felt like only a few days ago that she had been here, in this exact same spot with Sophie. Last summer it was, before the accident. Mila had come over to stay at the sea house for a week at the end of July, so she could share the news about her novel being published with Sophie. On Mila's last evening, they'd left Ani behind at the sea house with Charlie, and come into Morannez together. Sophie had been drinking beer from the mouth of a bottle. It wasn't strong beer, but she'd been tipsy. 'High on life,' she'd said, malt on her breath. She'd tripped over one of the raised cobblestones and Mila had caught her by the arm.

'Careful, Sophie!' she'd said, irritated. The bottle was still in Sophie's hand, the glass hadn't broken, Sophie hadn't fallen among the shards and severed an artery... but she might have done.

'Oh, it's these stupid shoes! I should've worn my trainers!' Sophie said. Before they left, Mila had suggested that Sophie might be more comfortable in trainers and Sophie had said, 'But I want to show off my Chloé sandals! What's the point in new shoes if you can't wear them?'

The days had been longer then than they were now. Evening arrived later but Mila recalled that, on the evening she was remembering, although it hadn't yet been dark, the moon had been up and Venus had been shining brightly in the sky.

Mila hadn't been cross about the shoes for long. It had been impossible not to be buoyed by Sophie's mood. Sophie had been thrilled about Mila's success, genuinely thrilled – almost giddy with happiness for her stepsister. She knew how long Mila had wanted this, how hard she had worked for it.

'I'm so proud of you,' she had said. 'So proud and happy!'

She'd been in a wild mood. Some time later, she'd taken off her shoes and run down the beach into the sea, splashing in the shallows, soaking the hem of her dress, which had been a gift from Ceci: expensive, panels of pastel-coloured silk in ice-cream pink, mint green, eggshell blue. Mila, watching, had wondered if Sophie was all right, if she was perhaps teetering on the brink of one of her manic phases.

But then Sophie had come back up the beach, laughing, the wet dress clinging to her legs. She took Mila's arm and leaned close.

'I've got something to tell you,' she'd said.

'What?'

'A secret! I'll tell you later!'

'Sophie! You can't tease me like that! Tell me now!'

'I'll give you a clue,' Sophie had giggled. She'd whispered in Mila's ear: 'It's about someone we used to know!'

'Who?'

'Later!'

She'd dragged Mila across the road to the Sohars' shop, to where Ani stood now, and she'd been holding up different clothes against herself and adopting fake fashion poses. 'What do you think? Does it suit me? Does it make me look like a sex goddess?'

'Mila? *Mila!*'

'What? Sorry, Ani, I was miles away. What did you say?'

'This. Do you think it suits me?'

Ani was holding a denim jacket against herself. The jacket was still on a hanger. It was embroidered with a peace sign. Mila was disorientated. For a moment she wasn't sure if she was looking at

Sophie or Ani. Time seemed to kaleidoscope; it contracted and expanded like the bellows on an accordion. Mila felt as if she was spinning. Sophie was there, whispering about her secret, and then she was not. Someone asked, 'Mila? Are you okay?'

She turned and Carter Jackson was standing behind her, the same peace sign on his T-shirt clear between the two halves of his jacket. The world swung from side to side once or twice more and then gravity returned to normal.

Mila looked at Carter's big hand on her arm.

Someone we used to know.

'Sorry,' he said, removing it. 'I thought you were going to fall.'

'I wasn't,' she said. She rubbed the spot where he'd touched her. He backed away.

'Mila?' Ani asked, pointing her chin towards the jacket.

'Yes,' she said, 'it's perfect, sweetheart. Give it to me. I'll buy it for you. My treat.'

33

'Promise me,' Mila said to Ani as they approached the sea house, 'that you won't tell Mamie what we did this evening until we're all together.'

'Why not?'

'Because she won't approve but she won't go mad at me if you're there.'

Ani hugged the huge, squashy rabbit that she'd won at the tombola in the little fairground that was erected each summer at the far end of the town. The toy was made of some soft, probably highly combustible, definitely environmentally disastrous, plasticky fake-fur fabric. It had almost certainly been constructed in a sweatshop. It was the epitome of tackiness with its great big stuck-on eyes and its very existence made Mila feel guilty, but Ani was thrilled with it and Mila could not begrudge her niece a moment of her pleasure.

'I won't tell Mamie if she doesn't ask,' said Ani.

Mila smiled. She was carrying the clothes she'd bought for Ani – a skirt and a couple of T-shirts as well as the jacket – some glo-stick jewellery and pink-and-white chunks of coconut ice sweets in a plastic bag. Evening had fallen now and she was using the torch on her phone to light the way back down the track to the sea house. To one side, the white owl dipped into the long grass and something small and invisible screamed. The owl glided back up into the bough of a tree holding its prey in its talons. Mila shivered. The air was cooler now. High summer was over; they were on the gentle downward slope through the remaining warm days into autumn.

'Was that man following you?' Ani asked.

'What man?'

'The motorbike man. He was at our house earlier and then he was at the clothes shop.'

'He wasn't following us. It's just that Morannez isn't a very big place. You can't help bumping into people sometimes.'

'Why don't you like him?'

'Who said I didn't like him?'

'When he offered to buy you a glass of wine, you said no.'

Mila laughed. 'I didn't want a glass of wine, that's all.'

'Maman said you should never say no when someone offers you a glass of wine. She said it was rude.'

'I don't think Carter was offended by my refusal, Ani. You don't need to worry about his feelings.'

By this time, Mila and Ani had reached the wooden gate in the hedge at the entrance to the sea house garden.

The gate was open. Mila was certain she'd closed it behind her when they left. She remembered checking to make sure the latch had caught. She shone the torch from her phone on the grass beyond. A dew was settling. The grass was trampled between the gate and the house, but of course she and Ani and Carter had walked over it several times already; it didn't mean that anyone else had been there.

Then she saw something that made her catch her breath. She put out a hand to stop Ani in her tracks.

The door to the sea house was ajar.

The door to the sea house was ajar.

34
―――――――

Mila was certain she hadn't forgotten to close and lock the door on
the way out. She put her hand in her pocket. The house key was
there; she could feel the metal fob in the shape of a letter S.

She stood, the light of the phone pointing at the grass at her feet,
holding Ani slightly behind her, out of sight. The choices she had ran
through her mind: turn round and retrace their footsteps back into
town and find someone to come back with them. But who? And
anyway, Ani would be exhausted if Mila dragged her all the way back
to Morannez. Call the gendarmes – and say what? *The door to my house
is open but I don't know if anyone is inside.* That would be ridiculous. Call
Ceci. What could Ceci do? Call Luke. Luke would tell her to call the
local gendarmerie. Call Carter Jackson? No, she couldn't. She couldn't
impose on him like that simply because he was a man. It would be
unfair on him and it would make her appear pathetic and weak and
also he might think she had staged the scenario on purpose to get him
over to the sea house. He might think she still had designs on him.

The last option, the only option that was viable, was to be brave
and walk up to the door and yell and if anyone was inside, hope-

fully they'd be more afraid than she was and come barrelling out and go away.

She had to act. She couldn't have Ani out here with the night falling, and the air growing damp, clutching the hideous purple rabbit and she being too scared to go forward.

'Ani,' she said, 'I'm going to go to the door and bang it loudly and shout: "Is anyone in there?" and if somebody answers, I want you to wait here, this side of the hedge until they and I come out again. If nobody answers, I'll have a quick look round inside and then call you to let you know it's okay to come in.'

'Okay,' said Ani. 'But you probably just left the door open. Maman used to do it all the time.'

'I'm not like your *maman*,' Mila said and regretted the comment at once in case Ani interpreted it as a criticism of Sophie, which, of course, it was. 'Not like your *maman* in that way, I mean. I don't forget things.'

'Do you really think there's a burglar in the house?'

'I don't think there is but I want to be sure.'

'But what if you go in and there is one and they grab you and you don't come out? What shall I do then?'

'If I'm not out in five minutes, run back down the track to the junction and then call Mamie. Okay?'

Ani nodded.

Mila crept towards the house. When she reached the door, she pushed it open so that it banged against the wall behind it and then, heart thumping, she reached her hand forward until she found the light switch. She pressed with her fingertips and the light came on. The interior looked exactly as it had when Mila and Ani had left some hours before.

A movement from the kitchen made her jump, but it was only Berthaud, creeping around the door edge, miaowing a welcome.

'Is anybody there?' Mila called. Her voice sounded small and pathetic. She tried again.

'*Is anybody there?*'

There was no answer. No sound at all. She picked up Berthaud, held the cat close to her heart, sharing her warmth, and went inside. She turned on the light in each room as she reached the relevant door: kitchen, living room, dining room, snug. She opened the door to the staircase and switched on the light that lit the stairwell. She ran up the stairs, still holding the cat, and checked the bedrooms and the bathrooms. They were all empty.

She went back down and called Ani. 'It's okay, you can come in now.'

Ani ran across the grass, threw herself and the rabbit into the hallway, and Mila closed the door behind her and jammed the bolt into place. They were both half-laughing, half-crying. A moth batted itself against the paper lampshade that covered the hall light and Ani squeaked in alarm and grabbed hold of Mila, and they laugh-cried some more.

While Ani boiled the kettle in the kitchen for peppermint tea – even she was too full for hot chocolate that night – Mila went around double-checking the windows and making certain, just to be extra sure, that nobody was hiding behind the furniture or in the cupboards. They weren't. She checked a second time, caught the moth and set it free from an upstairs window, watched Berthaud, tired of being held hostage, escape into the night via the tiny window in the cloakroom, and finally relaxed enough to pour herself a small glass of blackberry gin.

35

When Ani went up to bed, Mila stayed downstairs, with the gin. She had changed into her sweatpants, a loose T-shirt and an oversized cardigan. She looked in the dining-room cupboard and found Sophie's old slipper socks. She played Lana Del Rey through the speakers, so that the music became a kind of company, and sank into Sophie's soft chair, sipping her drink. She tried not to think about anyone being outside – a predator, in the darkness, circling the sea house, looking at the thin lines of light around the edges of the windows. She tried not to think about being watched, but she couldn't put the thought from her mind altogether. She couldn't decide if something had happened that justified her fear, or if nothing had happened at all; if the man-on-the-track incident had been completely innocent; if her memory of closing and locking the door earlier, and her distinct recollection of checking the gate was latched were false memories or those of a different evening. When one repeated the same action day after day, it was almost impossible to pin down specific memories, because each was identical to the one that preceded or succeeded it.

Think about it. Why would anyone have gone to the trouble of breaking in, simply to leave the door open? she asked herself.

It made no sense.

Unless the objective had been to scare her.

Or unless they'd taken something she hadn't noticed was missing.

She went into the kitchen. There were no blinds or curtains in that room, which meant anyone watching from the woods would be able to see Mila moving about inside. She picked up her bag and took it back into the living room, switching off the kitchen light as she left. She resumed her position on the chair. If she did some work, then she would relax.

Firstly, she checked her phone. There were no messages from Catherine Perry.

That didn't definitively mean the professor wasn't home yet; he might have returned and, overwhelmed by the relief of having him back, Mrs Perry could well have forgotten, or simply not have got round to texting Mila. Or they might be having an argument or they might be reassuring one another, or sharing a bottle of wine, deciding on their strategy going forward.

This was a comforting thought.

But although she told herself different versions of the event that might be taking place in the Perry household, Mila was worried by the lack of news. Deep down, she was pretty sure Mrs Perry would have let her know if her husband had come home.

It was night now, real night. Professor Perry had left home some fifteen hours earlier, and there'd not been a word from him since. With every minute that passed, his absence, to Mila, felt more sinister.

'It's not like him,' Mrs Perry had said. 'He's the most thoughtful man. He always lets me know where he is.'

But he didn't tell his wife everything, did he? He hadn't told her about the young woman, whoever she was, turning up and making a nuisance of herself at the dig site; he hadn't told her what it was, lately, that had been worrying him, playing on his mind.

On an impulse, Mila found the professor's number on her phone. She pressed the redial button, but again, the call went straight to voicemail.

Mila topped up her drink and looked for her laptop. She always left it charging in the living room, out of sight of the windows, when she went out. It was one of the first things she'd checked was still in place when she'd come into the house. It was where it was supposed to be, but the connector plug had come out of the port. Perhaps Berthaud had moved the wire.

But the laptop was on the floor, close to the electric socket. There was no need for Berthaud to have touched the wire.

Mila's heart began to pound again.

Was this proof that someone *had* been inside the sea house?

Had they been looking at her laptop?

Mila looked around the room, trying to see if anything was out of place, but she'd had several measures of gin now and her mind wasn't as sharp as it should be. She noticed a smear on the table, close to the vase, as if the vase had been tipped and some water spilled out. But that *could* have been Berthaud, or even Ani.

Stop it! You're being paranoid!

If anybody had been inside the sea house, they wouldn't have unplugged the laptop and left it; they'd have taken it.

She opened the lid of the laptop, tapped in her password: *Mila&Sophie123*. Not the cleverest password in the world but difficult enough for anyone who didn't know her well to guess. The computer opened and for a second, for the briefest instance, Mila saw a picture of Gosia's face on the screen. Not her live face, but her face as it had been lying on the pillow in her makeshift bed in the horsebox the day Mila found her there, dead.

She jumped back, spilling some of her drink on her wrist.

'Jesus!' she cried.

She hadn't taken a picture of Gosia's dead face. It must have been the gendarmes, recording the scene for posterity. How had a gendarmerie photograph found its way onto her laptop?

What if it wasn't a gendarme's photograph?

Nobody else was there apart from the doctor and I don't think she...

What if someone killed Gosia and then took the photograph and they've put it on your computer as a warning?

No! Mila thought, backing further away from the laptop. *No, no, no, no, no. That was a stupid, overtired, paranoid thought.*

She told herself she was being foolish; she couldn't have seen what she thought she'd seen. How could she have? She picked the device up and looked again. On the screen was the last document she'd been looking at before she went out – the document that contained what little information she knew about Gosia.

Mon Dieu, she must be stressed. She must have seen Gosia's name and her mind automatically inserted the image of the old woman lying dead in her van.

It wasn't that at all. You saw the image. You saw it.

If it was on the computer, where is it now?

Mila took another drink of gin. Then she turned the laptop off and rebooted it, her eyes fixed on the screen. It opened to the usual screensaver, a picture of Sophie and Charlie on their wedding day with the toddler Ani, looking cute as a button, standing between them holding a wicker basket of flowers.

There was no dead woman.

It must have been a flashback.

Mila was more stressed than she'd realised. She ought to go to bed. She ought to try to sleep. She ought to try to forget all about this stuff. The sooner she was away from here, back in Bristol, doing her writing, the better.

But Sophie's voice was insistent in her head. *Why are you doubting yourself, Mila? Someone's trying to scare you. First it was the man in the night, and now someone's putting pictures of dead people on your laptop.*

It was a flashback.

You know that it wasn't.

Mila got up and checked the doors and windows again. They were all firmly closed. She tried to calm her nerves; wishing that she hadn't had alcohol, and craving more. She told herself that this night was no different to any other night since Sophie's death. She had never been afraid to be the only adult in the sea house before. If someone was trying to make her uneasy, they were succeeding. But why would anyone do that?

Because they don't want you looking into Gosia's history. They want you to leave it alone. They know who you are and where you live – you put all the information on the community forum. They won't stop. You don't know how far they will go.

Was that true? Mila wondered. Was Sophie right?

She ought to go to bed. She ought to try to sleep.

But the facts that she knew kept playing on her mind even if she didn't understand how they were connected. Gosia and Professor Perry had known one another. Tim Perry had paid to get Gosia's van fixed. And Gosia had kept his card safe; hidden away. She had been reading his book. She had been interested in the dig. And she was dead and he was missing.

Curiosity was a more powerful incentive than fear.

First, Mila disconnected her laptop from the internet and ran an anti-malware program.

Then, when she knew her computer was clean, she launched the software she used at the agency when making a file on a new subject; the software automatically connected to a number of international databases to which Toussaint's Agency subscribed. She named the file 'Professor Timor Perry'. She logged into the British register of births, marriages and deaths. And she started work.

36

Mila was in bed; not the double bed with the super-soft mattress, the huge feather pillows and the antique quilt that she slept in in the sea house but the king-sized bed with the hard, orthopaedic mattress that she and Luke shared whenever she stayed over at his loft in the Paintworks complex in Bristol. It was a hot night and they'd left the windows open to benefit from the cooling breeze. The voile curtains were inflating like lungs and she could hear sirens on the Bath Road heading towards the cemetery at Arnos Vale. She tried to rouse Luke to tell him but he was sleeping naked, his legs tangled in the single top sheet, one arm thrown above his head; his chest was broader and more muscular than usual and his hair was dreadlocked and black, and there was a triskele tattoo on his wrist. It wasn't Luke but Carter Jackson lying in Luke's bed.

It was confusing but she had to go. She went out into the darkness and soon she met two children holding hands: Jake and Emily Perry.

'Is your father okay?' she asked and Emily, who was wearing a pink dress and white ankle socks, said, 'No.'

The night was clammy, the moon milky. She tried to call Sophie but her fingers wouldn't press the right buttons on her phone; she misdialled a hundred times and when she went into her contacts list, Sophie wasn't even there and the realisation that she'd never speak to Sophie again because she'd lost her number was the worst frustration she could imagine.

She went into the top entrance of the cemetery, and began to walk down the hill, along the twisting, turning pathway, knuckled roots tripping her and the brambles reaching out for her; fingers of ivy and birch brushing her face and the gravestones crooked. The path narrowed and it was difficult to breathe but she saw a movement ahead of her; the shadow of a giant pendulum and heard the creaking sound of a rope stretching under a heavy weight. Someone was hanging from the bough of a tree.

Mila awoke, heart crashing inside her chest, struggling to catch her breath. She was in her room in the sea house. She was all right.

It was a dream! she told herself. *A stupid dream, that's all.*

But she felt cold and afraid and the memory of the sound of the creaking rope and the shape of the body hanging from the limb of the tree in the old cemetery lingered in her mind.

She sat up, switched on the lamp and tried to shake off the image, but she couldn't; it had felt too real. Everything about the night felt sinister now; the shadows cast by the old furniture; the darkness outside, pressed against the windows; the fear that somebody was outside, watching.

She could not bear to be alone. She slipped out of the bed and picked up her duvet and pillow. She'd go and sleep on the floor in Ani's room; she'd done it before. In the morning, if Ani woke before she did, she'd make up some jokey excuse about a mosquito plaguing her.

She was at the door, with the soft pile of bedding in her arms, when the phone on her bedside table buzzed.

She wanted to ignore it; the only kind of news that ever came through in the early hours was bad news. And whatever it was, she couldn't do anything about it now. Ani was safe and Ani was the only person on earth, besides herself, for whom she was directly responsible. Whoever it was, they could wait.

Only, of course she couldn't ignore the message. How could she settle to sleep on the floor of her niece's bedroom knowing that there was a message on her phone she hadn't read, a message that had come in at 3 a.m.?

Mila put the bedding back onto her bed and picked up the phone.

The message was from Catherine Perry.

Mila could still hear the creaking of the rope from her dream. She could still see the body of Professor Perry turning slowly in the shade of the great tree. Her hand was trembling as she picked up the phone and read the message.

Tim still not home. He transferred £20k out of his account on Saturday.

_____

37

TUESDAY, 16 AUGUST

Dawn came at last, starting with a pallor seeping into the darkness of the sky, then ash-coloured light slowly filling the rooms inside the sea house.

The file Mila had created for Professor Perry was open on the computer screen in front of her and the picture of gentle-eyed, floppy-haired Tomas lay on the tabletop beside the professor's business card. She was listening once again to the song she'd recorded from Gosia's CD wondering if it really was Tomas's voice she was hearing; if his hands were strumming the guitar.

Mila had hardly slept. Catherine Perry's text had taken away any chance there might have been for her to settle. She'd been half-hoping for a second notification, a message that would tell her the professor had come home in the early hours. She'd hoped, but in her heart she'd known that no such message would come. If Sophie had been here, she would have taken her tarot cards from their box in the cabinet in the dining room and she'd have asked the cards to check to see if Timor Perry was alive or dead. But Sophie wasn't here, and Mila didn't know how to read the cards, and the dream that the professor had hanged himself tormented her.

She sipped her cooling coffee and listened to the birds singing beyond the window.

It was only a dream, she told herself. To believe the message in a dream was as irrational as believing that walking under a ladder would bring bad luck.

But why couldn't she have dreamed something positive? Something hopeful? Something good?

And there had been something else in the dream, something that she could not bring herself to think about. The man in Luke's bed: Carter Jackson. Jesus, what kind of fuck-up was she for her subconscious to have slipped that particular detail in there?

What was wrong with her?

The washing machine in the laundry room rattled to a halt. It contained mainly Ani's clothes. Setting the machine going had felt, small act that it was, like a tiny step in the direction of preparing Ani for boarding school. Mila would hang the clothes out – they wouldn't take long to dry; she could hear the breeze shaking the leaves at the tops of the trees outside. According to the weather forecast, this was supposed to be the last day in the stretch of fine weather that had lasted through most of July and August. A beautiful summer, people were saying, record-breaking, as if that were a good thing and not an indicator that the world was heating up.

Mila finished her coffee and went to the laundry room. She tumbled Ani's clothes into a plastic basket and hefted it onto her hip, carried it through the door out into the soft air, gulls wheeling. She put the basket on the ground and pegged out the clothes, one by one, gaining a quiet satisfaction from the work. Sophie would have made fun of her; she had never enjoyed domestic tasks. When Mila used to come to visit her stepsister here at the sea house, the little laundry room beyond the kitchen always used to be full of clothes, towels and bedding, Charlie, Sophie and Ani's things twisted together in a giant bundle. Mila would be itching to sort it out, to restore some order. 'Please let me help, I'd enjoy doing it,' she said to Sophie, and Sophie knew that it was true, that sorting out the chaos of the linen would bring satisfaction and even pleasure to Mila, but she always said: 'No'.

'It's our mess,' she used to say. 'We'll sort it out when we're ready.'

By 'we' she meant 'Charlie'.

When Charlie ran out of underwear, then he would he tackle the family's laundry, doing wash after wash, shoving coloureds in with whites, woollens in with synthetics, drying the clothes and linen over the branches of the apple trees when the line was full, laying towels over the backs of the garden chairs lined up to catch the sun. Chaos never bothered Sophie or Charlie. They thrived on it. Mess accumulated around them. It wasn't that they didn't care, nor even that they couldn't be bothered, more that order wasn't important to them. Plants were always dying because neither Sophie nor Charlie remembered to water them, food had to be thrown away because nobody had thought to cook it while it was fresh, they forgot to return borrowed items, or broke them; Ani missed appointments for vaccinations and to have her teeth checked. If Berthaud hadn't been able to supplement her diet with the small rodents she caught around the sea house, she would probably have starved to death.

Yet, despite their apparent uselessness, the Cooper family muddled through. They always seemed happy. They had survived, hadn't they, right up until last year?

Mila shook out the last item in the basket: a T-shirt of Ani's depicting a zebra on a sequinned background. Mila really loved that T-shirt. She'd wanted one the same. Ani told her that Sophie had found it in a vintage clothes shop in Bloemel. Mila had looked online, but she hadn't been able to find anything similar.

She hung the zebra T-shirt on the line next to the other clothes and used the prop to raise the line to its full height. And then she stepped on something. Because it hadn't rained for so long, whatever it was pressed into the side of her bare foot.

She leaned down to pick it up.

It was a laminated plastic card. On the front was the outline of a running antelope. Printed over the top of this were three words:

Kyern Dig: PASS.

...

38

_____

At exactly seven o'clock, Mila called Catherine Perry. Emily answered.

'Mum's in the bath,' she said. 'She didn't sleep last night because she was waiting for Daddy to come home and now she keeps crying. I thought a bath might be a good idea. I lit the candles for her and made her a cup of tea.'

'That's very thoughtful,' said Mila, thinking privately that Emily was almost too good to be true. No wonder poor Jake floundered by comparison. 'Have you heard from your grandmother?'

'She's arrived in Saint-Malo. She'll be here in a few hours.'

'You just hang in there for a little longer, Emily; you're doing a great job.'

'Do you think so?'

Emily sounded scared. Mila reminded herself that she was only a young teenager, and that she was having to go through this experience without the support of her friends back home.

'I really do. So,' Mila ventured more carefully, 'have there been any messages from your father? Any phone calls?'

'No.'

Mila asked a question she couldn't ask Catherine Perry directly.

'Do you know if your mum has tried to call your brother to see if he's heard from your dad?'

'She hasn't got his number. But even if she had, she wouldn't speak to him. He's dead to her.'

'Of course he is.'

'I spoke to Granny and she said she's sure Daddy'll turn up soon, and he'll be cross because we've all got ourselves in a twist and he'll be wondering what all the fuss was about.'

'Let's hope she's right,' said Mila. 'Have you been pestered by any more journalists?'

'The same lady as yesterday knocked on the door last night but we ignored her. And Daddy's students brought us a cassoulet and a bottle of wine for Mum. They said they're going to go house-to-house to try to find Dad this morning.'

'That's kind,' said Mila. 'They obviously think a great deal of your father.'

'Yep. He's the best.'

'Fingers crossed they find him.' A pause. 'Emily, while I've got you on the phone, you mentioned yesterday that Anaïs, my niece, gets picked on at school.'

'I didn't mean to say that.'

'But you did. Can you tell me who picks on her, and why?'

There was a long silence.

'Is it girls or boys who are responsible?' Mila prompted.

'It's some of the girls in our year.'

'Do they hurt her?'

'They just say stuff.'

'What kind of stuff?'

'I don't know.'

'Why do they pick on Ani?'

'It's not just Ani; they're mean to loads of people.'

'Okay,' said Mila. 'Could you give me their names?'

There was a long pause and then Emily said, 'I don't know their names.'

'They're not friends of yours, then?'

'Not exactly.'

Mila said, 'You know, don't you, Emily, that being unkind to other people is a horrible thing to do, often as bad or *worse* than hurting them physically?'

'Yes,' Emily said carefully.

'Sometimes bullying affects people for their whole lives,' Mila continued, to ram the point home. 'Not just the people who are bullied, but the bullies too. It taints their characters.'

Silence.

'So, if you ever see it happening again, even if the people doing the bullying *are* friends, you must tell someone with the power to intervene. A teacher, perhaps.'

'Yes.'

Mila waited another moment to let her words sink in.

Look at me, Sophie, she thought. *Look how carefully I handled that. You're definitely getting better at parenting.*

'Anyway, Emily,' she said more brightly. 'Please would you ask your mum to ring me when she has a chance.'

'Okay.'

'And like I said before, you're doing really well, looking after your mum and passing on all these messages. I know your dad would be really proud of you.'

Mila finished the call.

She tried to be positive, but the previous night's nightmare wouldn't leave her alone. It was tapping at her shoulders and whispering in her ears. The cemetery, the creaking rope. The man in the bed.

And on top of this was concern for Ani. Mila remembered from her own schooldays how creative and manipulative school bullies could be. There were girls who seemed to have been born with an instinctive knack for knowing how to make other children's lives a misery, girls who enjoyed needling at weak spots and vulnerabilities, girls who understood how to hurt and humiliate. Ani had never mentioned a word about any problems at school to Mila; Mila had had no idea it had been going on, but then, as she kept reminding herself, she hadn't been looking for it. She'd thought Ani was more resilient than she had been at that age, thought she would be okay. In fact, this was another example of Mila letting her niece down; one of the biggest failures on her part so far.

Ani wouldn't be going back to the international school, but Mila would speak to the staff anyway. And she'd make a point of asking the teachers at the Swiss school to keep an eye out for any signs of trouble going forward. Ani was never going to be bullied again, not on Mila's watch.

A headache niggled at Mila's temples and her eyes were dry. She'd drunk too much gin last night. Perhaps that was why she felt so bleak.

She scooped a handful of raspberries from the little bowl inside the fridge and ate them. She put the kettle on to make coffee. She looked again at the Kyern pass she'd found in the garden, turned it over between her fingers. There was no clue as to who it might belong to. It wasn't going to help her.

Mila went back to her computer, opened the file she'd made for Professor Perry and read what she'd written the previous night.

Timor Rupert Perry. Born 21 November 1973, Oxford, England.

Mother: Evelyn Amanda Perry (36), art historian.

Father: Philip Edward Perry (53), Professor of Classical Studies, University of Oxford.

School: Magdalen College School, Oxford (independent).

Timor was an exceptionally gifted student who excelled in history and languages.

At 17 years old he was offered a place at Cambridge University to read Ancient History. Tutors were #1, the world-renowned historian, Malgorzata Kowalczyk, and #2, author of the best-selling book All Our Fathers, Joseph Novak, who supervised TP's PhD & encouraged TP to get involved with the famous 'lost world' dig on the island of Sark. TP's work on this, and other digs, resulted in the publication of two books, one academic and one for popular consumption, both focusing on the transitioning aspects of Mesolithic peoples from hunter-gatherers to farming communities.

Spouse: Catherine Amanda Perry (née Stevenson, b: 1975, Southend, Essex.)

Children: Jake, aged 20 (recently dropped out of Liverpool University where he was studying computer sciences) and Emily, 14.

Current position: TP is employed as Professor at the School of Archaeology and Ancient History, Cambridge University. Lead archaeologist and director of Kyern, Brittany project.

Published work: (Link to articles, books etc. too numerous to list.)

No social media in his own name but he is active on various ancient history/archaeology chat boards. Checked these & found no evidence of controversy. Popular with students, who admire his enthusiasm and wealth of knowledge.

No convictions, bankruptcies or evidence of court cases that I can find.

£20k transferred out of his bank account on Saturday evening to unknown recipient.

Supports wildlife charities including the RSPB and WWF. Also

UNICEF and the charity supporting disadvantaged youth set up
by the Perrys' local church.

Mila read the notes again.

She couldn't see anything that didn't reflect the professor's
status as a pillar of the academic world – an example of a useful life
well lived.

But the money! Twenty thousand pounds. That was a big, red,
flashing light. Extortion of some kind seemed the most likely explanation for such a large sum to be moved, with not a word of explanation to his wife.

With prescience, the phone rang and it was Catherine Perry.

She sounded exhausted. She said she'd been up all night
worrying about her husband and then, when she saw that the
money had gone, she'd been worrying about that too.

'I phoned the bank,' she said, 'but they can't tell me anything.
Tim went through all the security procedures and used his card
reader to make the payment so there's no sign of any wrongdoing.'

'Do you know if Tim's paid out anything like this amount
before?'

'Not that I know of. No, he can't have done. We're not wealthy
people, that's why I was so cross when he gave that money to the
traveller woman.'

'Does he normally have that kind of money in his account?'

'He'd moved everything we had from our savings account into
his own.'

'He didn't mention that to you?'

'No. And I wouldn't have noticed if I hadn't gone looking. It was
money we were saving for Emily's future, for when she goes to
university; we kept it safe in an account we never touch.'

'Okay,' said Mila. 'So perhaps he was – *is* – planning to put it back. Perhaps he was hoping to replace it before you noticed it was missing.'

Or perhaps he was desperate, she thought.

'It doesn't make sense,' Catherine Perry said. 'Why didn't he talk to me?'

'We'll get to the bottom of it sooner or later,' said Mila. 'Try not to worry.'

She finished the call feeling more concerned than ever.

She looked at the photographs that she'd 'borrowed' from Mrs Perry's social media pages and copied onto her file.

There was Tim Perry as a youngish, bearded father, holding baby Jake in his arms with that expression of pride and surprise that new fathers so often seemed to adopt. Here he was on holiday in Mallorca with his wife and children. Emily was only small, four or five, chubby in leggings and a white smock with shoestring straps biting into the tanned flesh of her shoulders. Jake, standing slightly apart from the others, must have been about eleven. He had a grungy, pudding-basin haircut with a fringe that covered his eyes, round cheeks and a cute smile. From the age of about sixteen, Jake disappeared from the photographs. That must have been when he started to fall out with his mother.

Mila had taken other images of Tim Perry from archaeological websites showing him at work. He seemed happiest when he was out on site, with a trowel in his hand. Although he was obviously a shy man, he was perfectly at ease standing in front of a packed lecture hall with a spotlight shining down on him, discussing the life and times of ancient man, burial rites, art and artistry, indeed any aspect of how people used to live, and the detailed work carried out at various excavations around Europe.

There was absolutely nothing that she could see that might explain why anyone would dislike Professor Tim Perry so much that they'd go to such lengths to discredit him so cruelly.

She stared into the man's face. She'd spent so long looking into Tim Perry's pale grey eyes that she almost felt as if she knew him, as if he was a friend or relative. She detected kindness in his face, integrity, a touch of humour.

On an impulse, she went to YouTube, where she found a clip of the professor giving a talk to a group of disadvantaged children. He was on a stage, clowning around, clearly enjoying himself as he described what life would have been like for those same children if they'd been born eight thousand years earlier. Mila put her chin on her hand and smiled as he made a joke about a couple carbon-dating, a joke so corny that the children slapped their foreheads and groaned. She thought of the man she'd almost bumped into at the dig site a few days earlier, the flustered, anxious man, and she wondered what had changed in his life so much.

What had happened to Tim Perry since he'd arrived in Morannez?

39

It was still early. Mila decided to cycle to the boulangerie for fresh bread and croissants; she'd be back at the sea house before Ani was up and the fresh air would help clear her mind. If she was missing something, then perhaps exercise might make her realise what it was.

She went to Ani's room, opened the door a crack and looked in. Ani was asleep in the bed, one hand up close to her chin. She lay beneath the Shetland pony duvet she'd chosen to replace the previous *Moana* one after Sophie's death. The purple rabbit from the previous evening lay on the floor along with the patchwork bedcover. The old pink teddy that Sophie had bought for Ani when she was a tiny baby lay on the pillow beside her.

Mila crept in to check that Ani's phone was charged – it was. The room smelled sweet, a faint hint of nail polish, and the teenage girl smell of bubble-gum and sweat. Ani sighed and turned over. Mila withdrew.

It was cooler that morning, a blustery wind sending white and grey clouds racing across the blue backdrop of the sky, so Mila put on her jeans, a green jumper and her tennis shoes. She fastened her hair up and wriggled into the straps of her rucksack.

Before she left, she had a good look around, but nobody seemed to be in the vicinity of the sea house, only the washing danced on the line. Still, she made sure to lock the door before she went out.

She plugged in her earbuds, selected a playlist on her phone that started with the Jimmy Cliff version of 'I Can See Clearly Now' and set off on the bicycle.

After a short while, she reached the place where Gosia's van had been parked. There was little to show she'd ever been there now, only the faintest patch on the verge indicating where she'd lit her fire, and some indented wheel marks, all other traces of the old woman worn away.

'What is it, Gosia?' she asked the empty space. 'What connected you and Professor Perry? What is it that I need to figure out?'

The wind pushed the tops of the trees. They shook their branches and a few leaves spun to the ground.

Mila thought of all the questions she wanted to ask the traveller woman, all the questions she could so easily have asked her when she was alive.

Everything changed so quickly. You never knew when something that you'd assumed would be the same forever would change into something else. Nothing could be relied upon. Nothing could be taken for granted. If you didn't seize the moment, then it would disappear and it could never be brought back.

Mila thought of Sophie.

She thought of her dream, of the naked Carter Jackson in the bed. She closed her eyes in embarrassment, shuddered. Not that Carter, or anyone else in the world, would ever know.

I know, whispered Sophie.

You could have let me have him, Mila thought. *You didn't want him.*

But she knew that wasn't true. The heart wasn't like a gift that could be handed from person to person; it had its own desires. Even if Sophie had been honest with Carter about her own feelings, he would not have turned to Mila. He had been wiser, in retrospect, than she. He had been kinder.

She remembered that night in Paris when she'd offered herself to him like a consolation prize after Sophie had rejected him and she relived the humiliation of his dignified refusal and she wished there was some way she could rinse the memory altogether from her mind.

Thank God, she thought, *that I will soon be home.*

Back to Bristol, back to Luke – away from all this; these memories.

* * *

Mila cycled into Morannez. As she waited in the queue outside the boulangerie, someone behind her said 'Mila?' and she turned to see Carter Jackson in his jeans and boots. He wasn't wearing his leather jacket but a bulky red and white lumberjack-type affair.

Is he psychic? How come he keeps turning up every time you think of him? Sophie asked.

Morannez is just a very small town. And one which I'll be out of very soon.

'Hey,' said Carter.

'Good morning,' said Mila. 'You look awful.'

'Didn't sleep,' said Carter.

'Me neither. Were you worrying about the professor too?'

'Kinda. I've been in the office, going back through all the pictures I took of Professor Perry and the girl and enhancing the best ones, to get a clearer image of her face. Ceci's looking at them now,' he added, 'doing internet searches, hoping for an identification.'

'Ceci's in the office already?'

'She was there when I got in at daybreak.'

'She shouldn't have been. She's supposed to be taking care of herself after her heart attack.'

'She had a heart attack?'

'Last year. After Sophie died.'

Carter whistled. 'I didn't know.'

Bet he did, whispered Sophie. *Bet he knows everything.*

Mila turned back to the queue, feeling irritated and irritable. If she was honest with herself, though, it wasn't concern for Ceci's wellbeing that was niggling at her, nor frustration at having to explain the situation to Carter. No, it was the pull of insecurity, knowing that this man would be taking her place in Ceci's life – that from now on, it was he who would be sitting in the neighbouring office; he who would be following her instructions, answering her questions, basking in the glow of her approval; he who would be sent out to buy a pizza for lunch; he who would get to see autumn in Morannez and then winter, and then spring; he who would have to deal with the agency if Ceci were to fall ill again.

He was welcome to all of it: the responsibility, the ghosts, the memories, the sadness; let him take it all; let him deal with it.

You can start whispering into his ear now, Sophie, she thought.

How do you know I'm not already?

The interior of the bakery was warm and smelled of yeast and flour. Behind the counter, at the back, Monsieur Masud was heaving trays of baked rolls out of the ovens. His son, Mohammed, was replacing them with trays of unbaked dough. The girl behind the counter, a friendly red-head who sometimes used to babysit for Ani when she was small, was working fast, picking bread and pastries, packing them, handing them over, taking money. Her name was Sandrine.

The woman in front of Mila collected her bread and moved away.

'Bonjour, Mila!' Sandrine said cheerfully. 'Your usual?'

'Please.'

Sandrine put two croissants into a paper bag and a baguette into another and passed them to Mila. Mila tapped her card against the machine. A phone was ringing in the queue behind her. It was Carter's. He had given up his place to go outside to answer it. Mila followed him out of the shop and caught up with him in the bright square outside. A man outside the seafood restaurant was hosing down the terrace. A woman with three little Pomeranian dogs, each at the end of a brightly coloured lead, was talking to another woman unloading fresh flowers from the back of her van. Carter put the phone in his jacket pocket and turned to Mila.

'That was Ceci,' he said. 'She's identified the girl!'

40

Mila left her bike where it was and trotted after Carter as he strode through the narrow streets of Morannez, pressing himself against a wall every now and then to make way for a delivery van, raising a hand in greeting as he passed various people.

How come, Mila wondered, he'd made so many friends already? He'd only been in the town for five minutes. She'd been here almost a year and she didn't know as many people as Carter seemed to know. Perhaps they were people who remembered him from years back. Hardly anyone remembered her although that was hardly surprising because she had always existed in Sophie's shadow. Even now, sometimes, it felt as if that were the case.

Everyone seemed to like Carter though. And he liked them back.

'Is your daughter feeling better today?' he asked one woman.

'Give my regards to Amir!' he told another.

Mila wondered if she should have made more of an effort to fit in, although it had never seemed worth it, knowing she'd soon be gone. Even as that thought went through her mind, she was ashamed of it.

Wasn't all of life worth living to the full, even those stages that were destined to be temporary?

It's all temporary, Sophie reminded her. *Nothing lasts forever.*

She was out of breath by the time they reached the patisserie. Carter opened the door at the side and held it open for Mila to climb the stairs first.

Ceci was at the top, waiting for Carter.

'Mila!' she exclaimed. 'I wasn't expecting to see you here.'

'We bumped into one another at the boulangerie. Carter said you'd identified the girl!'

'Yes. Come and see, Carter. Mila, perhaps you'd put some coffee on.'

Mila ignored this and followed her stepmother into her office. Ceci had enlarged a photograph to take up the whole surface area on the screen of her Mac. It was one of Carter's images, taken at the dolmen. In the picture, Professor Perry and the girl had moved, so they were both standing in profile to the camera, and both were in bright sunlight. The girl had a small, sharply defined nose with a piercing in the crease of the right nostril, and her lips were full and shapely. Her chin was as sharp as her nose and an earring featuring a skull at the end of the chain was dangling from the lobe of her ear. Her hair was cut short at the sides.

'Look at the back of the ear,' said Ceci.

'What is it? I can't see exactly.'

'She's wearing a hearing aid.'

Ceci was right. It was a small device that hooked over the rim of the ear and nestled behind it, with a transparent plastic wire attached to a bud that went into the ear canal.

'Now look at this picture,' said Ceci.

She moved the mouse and a second image appeared on the screen. This wasn't such a sharp picture but it showed someone who looked like the same girl wearing the kind of clothes one would wear to a wedding: a blue, sleeveless dress with lace at the bodice, a shawl pulled over the shoulders. This time the girl's hair was longer and piled on top of her head into a bun, which was decorated with a large, fake flower. She was wearing different make-up: pink lipstick, and false eyelashes.

Her jewellery was silver and understated; tiny heart-shaped studs in her ears and nose.

'Is that her?' Carter asked.

'Look,' said Ceci.

She brought up a third image, a close-up of the same girl's face. She had her head turned to one side. She was holding a champagne flute to her lips. Ceci zoomed in on the girl's ear. Behind it was the same flesh-toned hearing aid. Then she superimposed the two images, one on top of the other. The features matched.

'It is her,' said Mila. 'You found her! Well done, Ceci!'

'Who is she?' asked Carter.

'She's a friend of the Perrys' son, Jake.'

'His girlfriend?'

'I don't think so. I've been back through the pictures and it seems they were in the same student flat in the same hall of residence right from their first day at university. I've looked through their social media, and as far as I can tell, it's a platonic friendship. They're more like brother and sister than girl and boyfriend.'

'Do you have a name for her?'

'Rhia Williams. She's from North Wales.'

'Is Jake Perry in some kind of trouble?' asked Mila. 'Is that why he dropped out of university?'

'That's the assumption I'm making,' said Ceci, 'that Jake has got himself into a mess of some kind, drugs, maybe? And Rhia travelled all the way to Brittany to ask Jake's papa to bail him out.'

'It's a long way to come to ask for help,' said Carter.

'Let's assume that Jake is in big trouble, then,' said Ceci.

'The money!' Mila said. 'Professor Perry transferred twenty thousand pounds out of the Perrys' joint back account into an account that Mrs Perry didn't recognise!' She glanced at Carter. 'I asked her to check the couple's finances last night, as you suggested.'

'But if that's the case, if the professor was simply talking to a friend of his son's, and bailing him out, why didn't he just tell his wife what was going on?' asked Carter. 'If the money was to get their son out of a hole, surely Mrs Perry would have understood.'

'Mrs Perry and Jake have fallen out big time,' said Mila. 'Tim Perry is in regular contact with the boy but she hasn't spoken to him in ages. She doesn't approve of Tim helping Jake out. She thinks he should learn to stand on his own two feet.'

'Harsh,' said Carter.

'But fair,' said Mila, not because she meant it but because *Harsh, but fair*, was a phrase that she and Sophie always used to play with.

'That explains why the girl was at the dig, but there's more to it than that,' said Ceci. 'There has to be. This doesn't explain fake Mrs Perry or the posters or why the professor has been humiliated in the way that he has.'

'Do you think this girl, Rhia, was blackmailing the professor? Threatening to ruin his reputation if he didn't give her the money?'

'It's possible, but she doesn't sound like the kind of person who'd do that. And anyway, he *had* transferred the money over the weekend. Why would she follow through with her threat once she'd got what she wanted?'

Ceci leaned forward, and flicked through various images, bringing them up on the screen of her computer. She'd harvested dozens from various social media accounts. There were pictures of student parties, Jake Perry and Rhia Williams standing with their arms around one another, both dressed as Ghostbusters, another of them raising glasses to the camera in a Mexican restaurant decorated for Christmas, the two of them, red-cheeked and wearing mittens, playing in the snow.

'They look like really good friends,' said Carter. 'Like they care for one another.'

'Can you find out why Jake Perry was in so much trouble, Ceci?' Mila asked.

'I can't get into his bank accounts or anything, but I think it's reasonable to assume he needed a lot of money quickly to pay off some kind of debt,' said Ceci. 'You're the expert. Does it look like drugs to you, Carter?'

Carter leaned forward and zoomed in on Jake Perry's face. He clicked back through the pictures.

'He's drunk here,' he said, showing them the Christmas restaurant image. 'Flushed cheeks, bloodshot eyes, and he's kinda off kilter.' He carried on studying the pictures. 'The rest of the time he seems sober. He doesn't look like a user.'

'He's not skinny,' said Ceci.

'Not all addicts are thin,' said Carter, 'but I'd put money on this kid not being an addict.'

'If it's not drugs, what could it be?'

'If it's not drugs,' said Carter, 'then nine times out of ten, it's gambling.'

'You both saw Professor Perry and Rhia Williams together, didn't you?' Ceci asked.

'Yes.'

'Did either of you get the impression that Rhia was acting a role? That she knew she was being photographed?'

'No,' Carter and Mila echoed one another.

'Let's say for now, then, that Rhia wasn't in on the framing-the-professor part of all this. She came to Brittany to hassle the professor for enough money to get Jake out of trouble. Mission accomplished, she checked the money had been transferred, and then went home.'

'So, she wouldn't have seen the posters, wouldn't even know about them?'

'No. In fact, she can't have seen them. If she had, then she'd have spotted our logo and don't you think we'd have heard from her by now?'

'I think,' said Ceci, 'that we're dealing with two separate issues here. The first is Jake Perry's gambling addiction, or whatever trouble he's got into. He's currently lying low, somewhere where the people to whom he owes the money can't find him. Rhia, bless her heart, comes along and puts pressure on the only source of money either of them can think of: Jake's father. She makes enough of a nuisance of herself for him to be thoroughly embarrassed and also, of course, he must be worried about his son. So, he pays the money and Rhia goes away.'

Carter nodded.

'And meanwhile, whoever it is who wants the professor off the dig sees an ideal opportunity to frame him. Gets us...' He caught Mila's glance and corrected himself. '... *me*, to take a mildly compromising picture of the professor with Rhia. Stick the picture all over town with a misleading caption and...'

'Voila!' said Ceci, with a flourish. 'Job done.'

Mila's phone buzzed. It was a text. She looked, hoping it would be one of the Perrys, but it was only Ani.

Where are you? I'll call you in a bit. I'm going out.

She put the phone back in her pocket.

'What now?' she asked.

'We still don't know the identity of fake Mrs Perry,' said Ceci. She looked at the computer. 'I think it's worth me keeping on searching online. I'll start with the Perrys' immediate family and then cast the net wider.'

'I was going to speak to Melodie Sohar about the Fendi suit,' said Mila. 'I never got round to it, but I could call in on the way back to the sea house.'

'And I'll work on Jake Perry and Rhia Williams,' said Carter. 'I'll check that our theory holds water and then I'll make contact and see if we're right.'

41

As she cycled out into the countryside, a million thoughts were circulating in Mila's mind. She was thinking about Rhia Williams, who had been prepared to go to such great lengths to help her friend, Jake Perry. She was thinking about Mrs Perry and how on earth she, Mila, was going to explain everything that she now knew about the Perry family's private business to the woman, when there was such a huge rift between her and her son. And obviously Professor Perry hadn't simply been trying to protect his wife by not telling her about the money, but he'd been trying to protect Jake too. She was thinking about Ani going off to boarding school, about the sea house standing empty, about the imminence of her departure.

She remembered that Ani would have woken once again to an empty house with no idea where her aunt was. Mila had only meant to be gone thirty minutes but already more than three times that amount of time had passed and she hadn't even taken back the pastries for breakfast.

She rode the bike off the road, stood close to a gate that opened into a field where Jersey cows were grazing amongst grass so lush and full of buttercups that it looked almost unreal, and she called her niece.

Ani didn't answer.

Her text said she was going out. She'd almost certainly go round to see Pernille. Mila was on her way to the Sohars' house anyway. Hopefully Ani would be there when she arrived.

The Sohars, Melodie and her husband Denis, both came from underprivileged backgrounds, and had been sweethearts at school; from the beginning they'd been part of the bande sauvage. In adult life, they'd done exceptionally well for themselves, their achievements culminating in the building of their villa on the side of one of the hills on the outskirts of Morannez. They'd started selling clothes from the back of a van, then opened a tiny boutique, eventually expanding to a chain of outlets that did great trade in the summer months selling unbleached linen tops and trousers, chunky necklaces and hammered bangles in the seaside resorts of northern France. The pandemic, according to Melodie, had done them a huge favour, because it forced them to get the online side of the business up to speed. Now they could sell all year round, all over the world. The results of their increased fortune were evident in the fact that both adult Sohars now drove Range Rovers and Pernille's father had recently upgraded his boat to something long, sleek and glamourous. Pernille had her own pony and JP rode a top-of-the-range moped.

Pernille was, and always had been, a loyal friend to Ani, and Ani liked spending time at Pernille's. As Mila cycled up the hill towards the villa, she understood why. The road snaked through a pretty forest, the kind one might see in an illustration for a book of fairy tales: gentle paths winding between green pine trees. At intervals, spectacular, modern villas were set back from the road. They'd all been constructed in the last few years; each was an individual, but most were boxy with wide verandas; the living rooms on the first floor had full-length windows that opened out to give views over the town and the sea. From time to time, Mila glimpsed the azure blue of a swimming pool in a garden full of shrubs, and flowers tumbling over walls and gazebos. The greens of the lawns were like a drink of water on a hot day.

It wasn't so hot today, though. Nobody was in the pools. The wind was still gusting, and the sound of it in the trees was invigorating. On the occasions when the view opened up and Mila had sight of the ocean, she saw that it was brilliantly blue, but broken up with white horses galloping in all directions over the water.

Ani wouldn't come up the road to get to Pernille's house; she'd follow the path through the woods. Mila tried not to worry about this. The girls had walked that path dozens of times together, and individually, and no harm had ever befallen either of them.

But what if whoever-it-was who had dropped the Kyern dig badge was still there, watching the house? What if they'd seen Mila go out on her own that morning and knew that Ani was there alone?

That was a stupid worry. Ani had messaged Mila. She hadn't hinted at any problem.

What if it wasn't Ani who sent those texts at all but some intruder who'd tied her up and taken her phone?

Stop it!

Then another thought assaulted Mila. A horrible thought.

She remembered her dream: Professor Perry's body swinging beneath a tree.

No, he wouldn't have... she told herself, but what if he had? What if Ani was right this moment walking up the path through the woods towards Pernille's house, earbuds in her ears, singing along quietly to herself and she suddenly saw a shadow on the path in front of her? Oh dear God, no!

Mila could hardly breathe with the exertion of pedalling the bike uphill. She stopped and gasped until she'd got her breath back and then she called Ani again. When there was no answer, she texted:

Ani, PLEASE tell me where you are.

After a moment and the reply came back:

At Pernille's.

Oh thank God.

You got there ok?

Yes!!!!!!

Mila was perhaps five minutes away from the Sohars' villa. There was no need to panic. For what felt like the thousandth time, Mila wondered how full-time parents coped with the stress of the constant anxiety about their children.

Soon enough, she reached the entrance to the Sohars' villa. She pressed the bell at the side of the gate and Melodie answered through the intercom.

'It's Mila,' Mila said. She heard herself sounding nervous, still feeling embarrassed about her surliness during the anniversary party/not-a-party conversation. 'I'm sorry to turn up out of the blue, but could I come in and have a quick word with you?'

'Of course! Come on in! I've been meaning to call you anyway.'

The gate clicked and then swung open. From the direction of the house, two sleek Dobermanns came bounding up the drive, barking. They looked frightening but Mila had met them several times before.

'Hey, Edith,' she said, crouching to embrace the larger of the pair. 'Hey, Marcel!'

Once she had paid the dogs the requisite amount of attention, she left the bike by the gate and walked the length of the drive, between immaculate borders, to the villa.

Melodie met her at the door, hair that was glossily ombré spilling over her shoulders. She was wearing a silky beach kimono in a pattern of gloriously coloured tropical birds over an expensive-looking swimsuit and jewelled flip-flops on her prettily manicured feet. She smelled, as always, divine, of sandalwood and jasmine.

The musical sound of female voices drifted up from beneath a set of marble stairs.

'I'd invited a couple of friends over to use the pool,' Melodie said, 'but it's really not the weather for it. So, we're sitting in the conservatory waiting for the jacuzzi to warm up. Would you like to join us? I could lend you a bikini.'

As if you'd fit in one of Melodie's bikinis! Sophie laughed.

'No, thanks. It's kind of you but I'm busy.' Mila smiled, feeling awkward and scruffy beside the perfectly groomed Melodie. Even if she, Mila, were to go to the trouble of exfoliating and fake-tanning and plucking and lightening her hair, she would never come close to achieving a fraction of Melodie Sohar's gloss.

She followed Melodie into a minimalist kitchen, all the surfaces so clean they were reflecting one another. No clutter anywhere. On the level below, on a terrace enclosed by a glass frame, she could see several of the clique Sophie used to call the Maman Mafia sitting around a big wooden table, with glasses of wine and the remains of a feast from the patisserie in evidence.

'I hope you won't mind me asking you this,' Mila said, 'but I couldn't think of anyone else who'd know. I need some fashion help.'

'I'll do my best.'

Mila took out her phone. She'd screenshotted the best picture of fake Mrs Perry; it clearly showed what she was wearing.

She showed the picture to Melodie who pursed her lips and blew out a stream of air. 'Nice suit!'

'It's Fendi,' said Mila. 'At least, Cecille thinks it's Fendi.'

'It certainly is,' said Melodie. 'Who's that, in the picture?'

'We don't know but we need to find her. We thought we might be able to narrow it down if we knew where she'd bought that suit. Presumably you couldn't get something like that locally?'

'No.' Melodie shook her head. 'You'd have to go to Paris – the Galeries Lafayette or Saint-Honoré. Of course, whoever she is could have been shopping online.' She took a bottle of wine out of one side of an enormous fridge and held it by the neck, gesturing towards Mila. 'Would you like a glass?' Mila shook her head.

'Do people really buy clothes like that over the internet?' Mila asked.

'People buy *everything* online these days. My sister knows someone who bought her wedding dress from a website.'

'Wow,' said Mila.

'How about some sparkling water?'

'Yes, please.'

Melodie filled a glass from a dispenser inside the fridge and passed it to Mila.

'I haven't been much help, have I?' said Melodie. 'But listen, while you're here, I wanted to ask if you and Ceci had had any further thoughts about Sophie's anniversary. Because a little group of us is thinking of having a quiet memorial get-together and I wanted to let you know. It would be awful if you heard about it afterwards, you know?'

Melodie's eyes were shining. Her sincerity was genuine. In the face of it, Mila, who had been trying so hard to avoid thinking about the approaching date, could not speak. She had a lump in her throat as if she'd swallowed a brick. When she was a child, she used to stammer when she was nervous, a response to her mother always barking at her to enunciate properly. Now, she struggled to make a sound but it was for a different reason. It was as if all the emotion she usually carried deep inside her had made its way up her windpipe.

Melodie continued, 'I'm sorry, I'm upsetting you... Would you rather we didn't? Only we're not talking about anything excessive. We thought we could go down to the beach, take a picnic... Mila, are you okay?'

Mila nodded, but she wasn't okay. She didn't want to let go of the weight of the thing in her throat; she was afraid that if she did, she would vomit it out; she imagined ugly pieces of grief strewn all over the walls and floor of Melodie Sohar's immaculate kitchen.

She said, 'Could I use your toilet?'

'Of course. That way. Second door on the left.'

Mila made it into Melodie's beautiful guest cloakroom. She ran both the taps at once so that the splashing of the water would disguise the sound of her tears.

'Sophie,' she sobbed, 'oh, Sophie, why did you have to go and leave us? Why?'

She listened as hard as she could for an answer, but Sophie, for once, would not come.

* * *

When Mila eventually, after several false starts, emerged from the cloakroom, Melodie was waiting in the kitchen. She must have heard everything.

'Here,' she said, passing a pot of face cream to Mila. It was cucumber-based, vegan, organic, probably hideously expensive, guaranteed to reinvigorate tired skin and reduce puffiness. 'I always use it when I've been crying,' Melodie said, in a matter-of-fact way. 'It's soothing.'

'Thanks,' said Mila. 'It smells delicious.'

She had seen her face in the cloakroom mirror. She had seen how it was swollen with crying, how her eyes were red and watery, how her edges seemed to have collapsed into a blur. Melodie's matter-of-factness in the face of her grief was reassuring.

She put a few dabs of cream on her face. It was blissfully cool and silky.

'Take some more,' said Melodie. 'Take the whole pot. I've got loads.'

Her kindness was almost unbearable.

'I can't take it.' Mila pushed the pot across the counter back towards Melodie.

'Of course you can.' Melodie pushed it back. 'Why won't you let anyone help you? Don't you understand that it would help us, if you'd let us help you?'

Mila couldn't speak.

'Grieving is hard, isn't it,' said Melodie.

Mila felt the lump begin to form in her throat again.

'It's not easy for anyone. It's not as if any of us is ever given lessons in how to let go of someone we love.'

Mila gave a small nod.

'That's why,' said Melodie, her voice as gentle as the face cream was cool, 'we need to make opportunities to show the children how to cope.'

Mila nodded again. 'Yes,' she croaked.

'So they don't find it as painful as we do.'

'No.'

Melodie put her hand on Mila's arm.

'We shared lots of good times, Sophie and me. I promise you we'll only do something she'd approve of. If you and Ceci are happy for me to go ahead, I'll ring round and organise something informal.'

'Would you mind?'

'I wouldn't have offered if I did. Will you and Ani and Ceci join us?'

'Probably. Not on the beach, though.'

'No?'

'Ani can't even bear to look at the sea.'

'Okay,' said Melodie. 'Not on the beach.'

She rubbed the top of Mila's arm gently. 'It'll be okay, you know. You'll get through this and so will Ani. She's got all her friends around her. And we're your friends as well as Sophie's, you know. We care about you too.'

'Thank you, Melodie. But you don't need to worry about me. I'll be back in England soon.'

'You're going back to England? For a break?'

'I'm going back for good. Didn't Ani tell you?'

'She hasn't said anything to me.'

'Well, maybe she told Pernille.'

'I'm certain she didn't; Pernille would have been distraught if she knew Ani was moving to Bristol.'

'Ani's not...' Mila began but couldn't bring herself to tell the truth.

She couldn't admit to this kind woman that her heartbroken niece was about to be packed off to boarding school in a different country altogether, a school where she didn't know anybody; where she'd be entirely alone.

The anxiety crashed back into her, and the shame. Melodie was watching her with concern. Perhaps she was waiting for Mila to offer up some reassuring words about how the two girls might stay in touch when Ani was in Bristol. Or maybe she thought Mila was about to provide an explanation about why she had decided to leave Morannez.

But why should she? She didn't need to make excuses: she had every right to return to her life! She had already done more than her duty! Sophie was the one at fault here, not Mila!

Mila took a moment to compose herself. Then she said:

'Can I have a quick word with Ani before I leave?'

She only intended to apologise for her absence that morning. She wanted to promise Ani that she'd do better going forward. She wanted to look into Ani's eyes and make sure that she was all right and then she'd reassure her that they would work through the next few weeks together. If Ani couldn't bring herself to tell her friends that she was leaving, Mila would help her come up with a plan to make it easier.

'Ani's not here,' said Melodie.

'Oh... I thought she was coming over. It was a spur-of-the-moment thing. Could you just check with Pernille?'

'Pernille isn't here either. She's gone on camp with her dance class and won't be back until after lunch on Friday. That's why I invited my girlfriends over! While the stroppy teenager's away...'

Mila shook her head as if she was an idiot for forgetting that Pernille was away.

'Of course. I've been so immersed in work lately that I'm forgetting everything. I'm sorry to have interrupted your get-together, Melodie. I'll be off now. Thanks anyway. Thanks for everything. Thank you!'

She headed out of the kitchen, towards the front door. The women's voices were becoming louder, almost rowdy. They were calling Melodie, saying they were ready for the hot tub.

Mila was feeling devastated, exhausted by the earlier grief and confused by the news about Ani. If she wasn't here, where was she? Why had she lied?

She was halfway down the drive, fingering the phone in her pocket, wondering what she would say to Ani when they spoke, when she heard her name called and turned to see Melodie running towards her, waving, the bright hues of her kimono making her appear for all the world like a giant, colourful bird. For a moment her heart lifted. Perhaps Melodie had got it wrong! Perhaps Ani was here after all!

'Mila!' Melodie called. 'I thought of somewhere else where that woman could have bought her Fendi suit!'

'Oh?'

'There's a vintage shop in Bloemel! I don't know why I didn't think of it before! It has some amazing second-hand clothes – Vivienne Westwood, Tom Ford, even Chanel! It's called Collette's and it's near the hotel! The woman who runs it, Collette – duh! – is a friend of mine. Tell her I sent you.'

Mila nodded.

'Collette. You've got that?'

'Collette.'

'That's right.' Melodie smiled. Then she leaned forward and kissed Mila lightly on both cheeks, the French way. 'Don't look so worried,' she said. 'Everything's going to be okay.'

42

Mila came out of the Sohars' drive and the electric gates closed seamlessly behind her.

She leaned against the wall and then slid down until she was sitting on the grass, with her forehead resting on her knees and her phone in her hand.

'Oh, Ani,' she whispered. 'Ani, Ani, Ani.'

In three weeks' time, the girl was going to fly to Switzerland to start a new chapter of her life in her new school. Yet she hadn't told anyone, not even her best friend. What was she thinking would happen? Was she simply going to disappear on September the eighth without telling anyone where she was going?

Did she think that if she didn't talk about a future away from Brittany, it might not happen? Was she burying her head in the sand to avoid facing the inevitable?

But there was no getting away from the fact that Ani had to go to boarding school. She couldn't stay in Morannez. There was nobody to look after her and, in any case, she needed to be in the care of experts. She'd have a fabulous time in Switzerland. She'd be away from the bullies at the international school; she'd be able to reinvent herself, if that was what she wanted to do; she'd be able to start again. A new chapter.

Even if Mila wanted to stay, which she didn't, Mila knew she was no good for Ani. She was a useless carer. She'd never wanted to be a parent; she'd had parenthood (of a sort) thrust upon her and truthfully, it had only accentuated how it was not for her. Ani wasn't stupid. In her heart, she must know that all of this was true and that going to Switzerland would be the best thing for her. It would be the making of her!

But where was Ani now?

Mila's first instinct was to call Ani, but the chances were that the girl wouldn't answer, and if she did answer, Mila's voice would give away the distress she was feeling. Mila's feelings were not Ani's responsibility; Ani was having enough trouble dealing with her own.

Mila put her head back against the wall and stared up at the sky, the clouds racing beyond the bending boughs of the trees.

She heard her father's voice suddenly. Patrick Shepherd was a playboy, a liar, a seducer, a heartbreaker. But – presumably because he'd instigated so many of his own – he had always been good in a crisis. Mila remembered him once saying that dealing with teenagers was like playing a never-ending game of chess, where the adult player was constantly being forced to re-strategise in response to some outrageous and unpredictable move on behalf of the teenager.

One thing at a time, Mila, she heard him say. *Deal with one thing at a time. Focus on your immediate priority.*

The immediate priority was finding Ani and making sure she was safe.

If Mila told Ani that she knew Ani wasn't at the Sohars' house, Ani would know she'd been caught out in a lie and would either go on the offensive or defensive. Instead, Mila gave her some wriggle room.

She texted:

I'm on my way round to the Sohars' place to talk to Melodie. I'll see you there in five minutes.

The response came back almost instantaneously.

I'm not there.

Where are you then?

Followed by a sweet emoji and a heart emoji.

A long pause during which the blue dots indicated Ani had started writing something several times, and then stopped.

Eventually the message came.

At the crazy golf with friends.

Thank God, thought Mila. *Thank God, thank God, thank God!*
She texted back:

Let me know when you're finished & I'll come to meet you xxx

No sooner had she sent the text than Catherine Perry called her.
'Hi, Mrs Perry. Have you heard from your husband?'
'No, but I wanted to ask you a favour,' said Mrs Perry. 'Would you pop down to the dig site and fetch Emily? I was having a nap and my mother told her she could go down there. I don't know why Mum said it was all right when I'd specifically told her that I wanted Emily to stay here.' The last two sentences were spoken in a

sarcastic tone of voice and nearby Mila heard Mrs Stephenson mutter something about fresh air and exercise. 'Anyway, she's with one of her teachers, Monsieur Hugo. He called to let me know she was safe but he can't leave the site. I don't want her cycling back on her own and I don't want to leave the house in case Tim turns up. Mum doesn't know the way, she has mobility issues, doesn't speak French and she doesn't know anyone so I can't send her.'

'It's no problem. I'm on my way to meet Ani in Morannez anyway.'

'I'll text her to tell her to look out for you. I don't want her hanging about down there on her own. People will be talking about her father. She might overhear something that she shouldn't.'

'Of course. I'll let you know when I've found her.'

'Thank you, Mila. You're a lifesaver.'

Mila was both relieved to have a reason to see Mrs Perry again, and apprehensive. When she took Emily back to her mother, she'd have to talk to her about her son and Rhia Williams and that wasn't a conversation she was looking forward to at all.

43

Mila took the turning for Kyern and cycled uphill, standing on the pedals, until she reached the car park at the top. There were a number of vehicles there, mostly the familiar old cars that looked as if they belonged to the dig people.

She left her bike behind the trees in the picnic area where she'd left it before and followed the path down through the woods. The weather was worsening. Dark grey clouds were thickening behind the lively white ones. There was a spit of rain in the air and Mila thought she heard distant thunder, although she could not be sure. The wind was gusting intermittently and there was a strange, ghostly singing noise. It took Mila a while to realise that it was caused by the vibrating of the ropes holding up the main marquee at the dig site and the wind catching in the throats of the poles.

It was less than a week since she'd been here before, and bumped into Professor Perry. She wished she could turn the clock back, tell the professor not to meet Rhia Williams by the dolmen, or else stop Carter taking his photographs. She could have done any one of a thousand small things that would have changed the course of events and prevented things unfolding as they had. But that was hindsight: no use for anything except exacerbating regret.

Superficially, looking down on it, everything about the dig looked pretty much as it had done before.

The marquees and tents were still in place; the kiosk selling food was open and the smells of fried onions and coffee were occasionally gusted towards Mila by the wind. A few people were milling about, although nowhere near as many as before, and the trenches were empty. Mila could see Carter Jackson standing talking to a couple of people. The pink-haired woman she'd spoken to before was also there, cleaning digging implements beside a tap attached to a huge plastic water tank. In the field behind, a large piece of agricultural machinery was cutting the tall corn stalks and processing them, shooting the resultant mass of husk and stalk, leaf and seed into a trailer being pulled by a tractor that was driving parallel with the first vehicle. The two between them were kicking up a cloud of dust that the wind sucked and punched this way and that. Mila assumed they were trying to get the corn harvested before the heavy rain came.

She followed the path down, looking for Emily Perry and Monsieur Hugo. The Kyern burial chamber was ahead. When the sun went in, the dolmen assumed a brooding, threatening character. The great cap-stone balancing, apparently precariously, on the tips of the three supporting stones weighed seventy-five tonnes; Luke had looked up that fact in a guidebook and she'd never forgotten it. Seventy-five tonnes! How did the ancient people lift it? How did they make that magnificent structure? Those men and women had laid their loved ones to rest beneath that stone. They'd believed their bodies would be there forever, but hardly any time passed – in the scheme of things – before the graves were opened up and robbed, by thieves and archaeologists.

Everything changed so quickly. You couldn't rely on anything except the moment in which you were living right now.

A curtain of rain blew across the valley. The corn-harvesting machine and the tractor reached the end of another row and turned with perfect synchronicity. Sparrows chattered in the trees and insects were busy about the undergrowth. Mila pulled the sleeves of her jacket down and wrapped her arms about herself. Autumn was in the air, the hint of green-fading-to-yellow in the leaves on the trees and the busyness of a pair of squirrels leaping crazily from branch to branch above her, harvesting hazelnuts.

She stopped close to the bottom of the hill to watch the machines working in the field. She looked again for Emily at the dig site, couldn't see either her or the teacher. The flock of gulls that had been following the farm machines settled on the disturbed earth left in great ridges where the corn had been cut. The two machines were coming towards Mila now, the corn disappearing before them. Mila suddenly felt light-headed. She brushed away a fly, saw sunlight glinting from the machines. It flashed on the windscreen of the tractor and the next moment the sun disappeared behind a cloud and the temperature dropped a few degrees.

And suddenly, almost as if she had written the script, Mila knew what was going to happen. She knew the corn-cutting machine was going to stop an instant before it did stop. She knew there would be a warning shout from the driver, and there was, and the tractor suddenly veered to the left before stopping too. Once the noises of their engines had been cut, an awful silence descended over the cornfield at Kyern. The silence lasted for perhaps ten seconds, and then the shouting started again. The drivers were some distance away, but Mila could hear the shape of their words; she could hear the panic in their voices:

'*Au secours!*'

'Help! Call the gendarmes, there's a man in the corn!'

'Il est mort!'

He's dead.

44

The professor's body was not found hanging from a rope as foreseen in Mila's dream, but instead slumped in a field in a windy, westerly corner of France, his trousers stained with blood, and blood soaked into the ground around him. A swarm of flies had gathered on and around the body. They buzzed away when the wind blew and the deceased professor's clothes and hair moved, and settled again when the wind was still.

Mila did not need to see the dead man but she went to look because she wanted to form her own opinion as to what had happened to him. She had the same feeling of obligation towards him as she had towards Gosia. She had known, deep down, that he was dead and now she wanted to know why. Who was behind this? Why had they, whoever 'they' were, punished the professor and his family in this way? And what was it that connected Professor Perry with Gosia?

She walked towards the place where the machines had stopped. She did not have to go through the dig site; it was quicker for her to go straight down the hill and through the ranks of corn until she reached the spot. She arrived at almost exactly the same moment as Carter Jackson.

They stared at one another over the body of Professor Perry, the sunburned dome of his head flecked with moles.

The canvas hat was nowhere to be seen.

'I've called the cops,' Carter said. 'They're on the way.'

He looked as shocked as Mila felt – shocked, but not surprised. The two farmhands had stepped away; Carter and Mila had the immediate area to themselves. Carter went closer; he crouched down although there was no need to check that the professor was dead – it was obvious; he'd been dead for some time.

'Your boots,' Mila said croakily. Carter looked up at her.

'Your boots,' she said, 'are trampling all over the crime scene.'

'We don't know it's a crime scene,' Carter said. 'It looks to me like a suicide. Guy cut his wrists.'

No, Mila thought, *no he didn't.*

It came to her as clear as day that the professor had no more died of suicide than Gosia had died of natural causes.

'Please,' Mila said, 'please come away from him. If there are other footprints, you're obscuring them.'

'I'm not. I'm taking care. I know what I'm doing.'

She could hear Luke's voice in her ear, complaining about the importance of securing a scene at the earliest possible opportunity. Still Carter Jackson moved around, circling the corpse, taking pictures with his phone. Mila felt weary of Carter, as she might have felt weary of a rambunctious child who wasn't related to her, but for whom she was responsible.

'Please,' she said again. 'Please leave him alone.'

'Nearly done,' he said.

Mila tried to concentrate on the scene, tried to memorise it. She would not take photographs. She did not want pictures of this tragedy on her phone nor would she betray the Perry family in that way. She noticed that the professor's phone was face down on the soil beside him. And his laptop was there too, its lid open, its keyboard horribly blackened with dried blood.

The two farmhands were standing nearby, but at a respectful distance. The younger, a good-looking, muscular young man, was drinking water from a plastic bottle he was holding in one hand, whilst texting on his phone with the other. The older man looked shocked and pale. Mila felt sorry for him: one moment driving into ranks of dry stalks, the next almost ploughing into the corpse of a sandy-haired, balding, inconspicuous and thoroughly decent man who appeared to have hidden himself away in the corn to kill himself out of shame at having been outed as a sex pest.

But Professor Perry had had no reason to kill himself! If they were right in their assumptions that he'd given his son the money to pay off his debtors. He could easily have proved the truth about the girl in the poster. Rhia Williams herself could easily have vindicated him.

How long before the police and ambulance arrived? Ten minutes, perhaps? Fifteen?

The older farmhand took a packet of cigarettes from the back pocket of his overalls, shook one out of the packet, put it between his lips and lit it. The faint smell of smoke made Mila feel slightly nauseous.

Carter Jackson at last stepped away from the professor and came to stand beside her.

The sun emerged from behind its cloud and Mila noticed for the first time the glint of a glass bottle tipped on its side close to the professor's body.

If she, or anyone, was asked to guess what had taken place in the moments preceding Tim Perry's death from the position of the body and the objects that surrounded it, Mila would have said it was a definite suicide. It looked as if the professor had come to this spot knowing he was unlikely to be disturbed as he committed his final act, and that his remains were unlikely to be discovered by his children or students but also that he would be found within a few days of his disappearance. The laptop was a means of conveying one final message to the people he loved. The police would check it and Mila was certain they'd find a carefully drafted and heartfelt suicide note saved unsent on the desktop. He had anaesthetised his body and numbed his mind with alcohol – he might well have taken some kind of sedative too – before he cut into his wrists. The professor was dressed in a short-sleeved beige shirt with the antelope logo embroidered over the left breast, and a pair of beige cotton trousers. He was wearing the same Jesus sandals on his feet as before, and grey socks that were speckled with blood and flies. Mila could see no other obvious injury beside the cuts to his wrists. The position of the professor, the items around him, everything made it appear as if he had organised his death with the thoughtfulness and conscientiousness with which he organised his life.

It was exactly what one would expect from a man like him.

She could hear sirens approaching now; it sounded as if they'd turned off the Kyern lane and were coming along the lower road, the road that led to the holiday park. They'd be able to get the vehicles closer that way. Carter heard them too. He suddenly said, 'Oh, fuck it.'

He jumped forward and, picking up a fragment of corn stalk, he pressed a button on the laptop with the stalk.

'It's still working,' he called to Mila.

'Carter, you *can't!*'

'I just did. There's no password. There's a half-written email on here, to Catherine...'

'His wife. What do you mean, no password?'

'I was straight in. He's sorry he let her down, sorry about the scandal, can't live with himself knowing that everyone thinks he's a pervert...'

'He didn't write that,' said Mila.

Carter took a picture of the laptop screen with his phone, then backed away.

Mila watched, horrified.

'*Carter!* We're going to end up in prison. They saw you! The farmhands saw you doing that!'

Carter raised his hand and waved at the two men. The older one put his cigarette in his mouth and held up a hand in acknowledgement in return.

'What are you doing?' Mila cried again.

'It's okay,' Carter replied. 'I know that guy. We used to play football together when we were kids.'

45

Mila turned and began to walk back the way she'd come, between the ranks of corn. The dry sheaves rustled and whispered. She stumbled over the stony ground. Carter's voice behind her called 'Mila! Wait!' but she ignored him and continued walking, hidden from view by the tall corn, startling a rabbit. She needed to find Emily Perry; she needed to get the girl home. She needed to talk to Ani. She needed the time and space to get her head straight.

But something was nagging at Mila, something urgent. It was a case Luke had told her about some months earlier that the media had dubbed 'the red dress murder'. The body of a woman had been found in an expensive flat in an exclusive development on the Bristol dockside. The flat belonged to a man in his forties who worked for a company importing food, specifically noodles. This man, 'the noodle man' as Luke called him, had met the red dress woman on a dating app some weeks previously; he claimed that they'd enjoyed a few evenings out together, but that he hadn't wanted to take the relationship any further. The woman, he said, had refused to accept that what they had was 'casual' and had begun to stalk him, hanging around the offices where he worked and surprising him at the entrance to his apartment block. She wrote him love letters, he said, plied him with presents. He asked his friends for advice and they told him that brutal honesty was the only way forward so, he told the police, he had had a 'no-holds-barred' chat with the woman, telling her in no uncertain terms to leave him alone, and that if she didn't, he'd contact a solicitor with a view to applying for a restraining order.

Two days later, the man said, he'd returned to his flat and found the woman dead from an overdose in his bed. Photographs showed the woman spread across the bed, arms and legs akimbo, one shoe off, one on. She was wearing make-up and a tightly fitting red dress. To all intents and purposes, it had looked like a suicide. But Luke had had his suspicions.

It soon transpired that the woman's closest-knit group of friends had been worried about her for some time. They said their late friend had changed her phone number, stopped walking home alone. She'd lost her confidence. From her behaviour, it would appear that she was the one who was afraid she was being followed. It didn't take long for the police to prove that the suicide had been staged and for the man to be charged with murder.

Mila reached the edge of the field and turned towards the dig site. She needed to be absolutely sure that Emily Perry wasn't there. The soles of her trainers skittered on the chalky gravel.

As she walked, she called Luke and he answered at once. She could hear that he was in a car.

'Can you talk? Are you driving?'

'Yes, I can talk if you're quick, and no, I'm not driving.'

'The red dress murder case, do you remember?'

'Of course.'

'You said from the beginning that you didn't believe it was a suicide, didn't you?'

'Yep.'

'Why?'

'Why didn't I believe it was suicide?'

There was a pause, while Luke thought back, treating the question with his traditional, meticulous consideration.

'The deathbed was too staged,' he said at last. 'It looked like a scene from a TV drama, even down to the fact that the victim's fingers were still holding a vodka glass, tipped to one side, with a lipstick print on the rim and a little vodka in the bottom of the glass. I know that can happen; it *does* happen, but it didn't feel natural. It felt choreographed.'

'*Choreographed*,' Mila echoed. 'That's it exactly. That's what this scene looks like.'

'What scene?'

'I'll tell you later. Thanks, Luke. Bye.'

Mila disconnected the call and stopped to look behind her. The land where she was standing was slightly higher than the cornfield and she could look down over the field and the ranks of caravans at the holiday park, and then the expanse of sea behind that, some patches glittering in the sunlight, others disappearing beneath swathes of rain falling in sheaves from the heavy grey clouds.

The gendarmes' cars and an ambulance had already arrived at the edge of the field. She could see flashing lights, officers striding forward. The two farmhands were standing separately. Mila narrowed her eyes. Carter had disappeared.

She was distracted by the sound of raised voices coming from the dig site. She quickened her pace, came around the marquee and saw Alban Hugo standing square, holding on to the shoulders of Emily Perry to prevent her going any closer to the end of the dig site and out onto the field where her father lay dead. She must have heard the sirens and it was fortunate that Monsieur Hugo had been quick enough to prevent her running towards the tragedy.

Monsieur Hugo had lost some of his composure. Dark sweat

stains were making half-moons beneath each armpit. Mila rushed forward, trying to smile and be casual.

'Hi, Emily,' she said. 'Your mum asked me to come and collect you.'

Emily blinked the raindrops from her eyes.

'Why are the police in the cornfield? Is it my dad? Have they found my dad?'

'I've explained to Emily that she can't go into the field just now,' said Monsieur Hugo. 'The gendarmes need everyone out of the way so they can do their work. It's none of our business.'

'It is my business if it's to do with my dad! Let go of me, Monsieur Hugo!'

The man glanced at Mila, who gave the smallest nod and he released his hands slowly, and took a step backwards, still blocking the path. Emily shook her shoulders and glared at him from beneath her fringe. She was pale, dark shadows beneath her eyes and she had a bruised, fragile look to her as if she had not slept.

Poor kid, thought Mila, pitying her for the fear she felt now and the pain she would soon have to endure.

'I know you're trying to help your family,' Mila said, 'but honestly, Emily, the best way to do that right now is to stay out of the way of the investigators so they can concentrate on their work. Your mum said you cycled here. Is that right?'

The girl nodded.

'Well, how about you follow me back into Morannez and...'

'What have they found in the field? Is it my dad? Is he okay?'

'We need to let the police get on with their job, Emily. Ani's at the crazy golf. Maybe we could stop and get some pizza and meet her there.'

It wasn't as if a few slices of delicious margherita pizza would do anything to alleviate the awful truth that Emily was going to have to face, but it would delay the inevitable for a short while and that was the best Mila could do. The girl looked dejected, and very young. She was wearing dungaree shorts with a cartoon unicorn embroidered on the breast panel. One of the shoulder straps had slipped down over her arm. Mila had to fight an urge to reach out and take hold of her hand.

Instead, she patted Emily's shoulder.

'Come on, Emily,' she said. 'Let's go and call your mum.'

46

Mila called Mrs Perry and told her that she was with Emily, and that the two of them were going into Morannez to meet Ani.

'I'll keep Emily with me for a few hours,' Mila said. 'I'll make sure she has something to eat.'

'That's very kind,' said Mrs Perry. 'It will do her good to be with other people. Take her mind off things.'

'I hope so.'

Morally, Mila thought, she should tell Mrs Perry that her husband's body had been found. But it would be cruel to convey information like that over the phone and how could Mila answer Mrs Perry's inevitable questions? No, it was better to leave that task to the gendarmes – better, she felt instinctively, to keep Emily out of the way.

They stopped at the pizzeria and, while they waited for their pizzas to cook, sat at the bench seat outside, Emily drinking Pepsi through a paper straw. When the pizzas were ready, they collected the boxes and made their way to the crazy golf.

'There they are!' Emily said.

Mila followed her finger. A group of teenagers, two boys and four girls, were playing together. Mila didn't recognise Ani at first. She was wearing her flares and her tank top, but her hair had been plaited. She was also, Mila realised with a shock, wearing make-up: mascara and eyeshadow, lip gloss. Ani was the smallest and quietest of the group but like this, dressed up and made up, she looked older than she was.

She looked unusual and exquisite, and the effect of her altered face on Mila was profoundly unsettling.

Yet she and Sophie used to experiment with make-up at that age, so why did she expect Ani to be any different?

One of the boys was JP; the other was slightly built but seemed older and more confident. He was dark-skinned and good-looking. Mila suspected from the way he was teasing Ani that he liked her, and from the way she smiled and didn't recoil from his teasing that she liked him back.

'Do you know who that boy is?' Mila asked Emily. 'The one in the baggy shorts?'

'That's JP's best friend.'

'What's his name?'

'Romeo.'

Romeo! For fuck's sake! said Sophie.

Mila watched for a little while and became certain that her initial observation was correct. 'He's sweet on Ani, isn't he?'

'I don't know what that means.'

'It means that he likes her. Romeo likes Ani.'

Emily shrugged.

Her cheeks were pink and her expression, now, was surly.

In a flash Mila realised that Emily liked this boy who liked Ani. She dug her fingernails into her hand. History was repeating itself. She was flooded with renewed pity for Emily, although soon Romeo would be the least of her troubles.

Ani hit the ball into the hole and Romeo cheered and did a

victory dance on her behalf. Ani smiled shyly as Romeo retrieved the ball and returned it to her with a little bow. Ani took it, and turned away, smiling. She twirled the end of one of her plaits between her fingers.

Another reason why Ani won't want to go to Switzerland, whispered Sophie.

* * *

After the eighteenth hole, the two boys went off together and the girls dispersed. Ani came over to Mila. When she saw Emily, the smile faded from her lips.

'Hi,' said Emily grumpily.

'Hi.' Ani looked embarrassed; perhaps she knew how Emily felt about Romeo.

'We have pizza,' Mila said, holding up the boxes. 'One margherita and one spicy chicken!'

She jollied the pair of them, neither speaking to the other, all the way back to the sea house.

* * *

By the time they reached home, big, fat drops of rain were starting to fall.

Mila put the pizza boxes on the kitchen table. She didn't bother laying the table, simply got out some plates and told the girls to help themselves.

'And close the lid when you've taken a piece because otherwise Berthaud will walk all over the pizza,' she said.

Emily giggled. 'Our dog, Buffy, wouldn't walk on it; she'd steal it off the table and eat it,' she said.

'I wish I had a dog,' said Ani.

'You can come and meet Buffy if you like.'

The ice wasn't breaking exactly, but a hairline fracture had appeared.

While the girls were eating, Mila went outside to fetch the washing in. The wind was gusting, roaring through the trees and she could hear the sea, waves crashing in at the horseshoe beach.

The forecast was unsettled all week. Mila hoped there'd be some fine weather before she left Morannez; it would be good to get a few decent swims in. She'd miss the sea when she was back home, but there'd be compensations.

Mila loved autumn in Bristol. She loved how the trees changed colour in the Avon Gorge, turning yellow, gold and red and framed by the cliffs and the suspension bridge. She loved those bright, cold mornings when anything seemed possible, when it was impossible not to be glad to be alive.

The day she heard that Sophie and Charlie had disappeared had been one of those days.

Mila hadn't had any sense of foreboding. She'd been feeling – well, if not giddily happy, perfectly content. Optimistic. The previous evening, she and Luke had gone out to eat at the little tapas place above the New Cut and afterwards, walking home, Luke had put his arm around Mila's shoulders, which he hardly ever did.

'I think we should get married,' he'd said.

'What?'

'I think we should get married.'

'Why?'

'We're both knocking on a bit now. There are tax benefits. And it's crazy running two households when we could consolidate.'

Even as Luke spoke, Mila was imagining herself recounting the proposal to Sophie and Sophie roaring with laughter.

"Knocking on a bit", "tax benefits"... That was how he proposed to you?'

Mila had looked forward to talking to Sophie in the morning. She'd looked forward to Sophie finding the whole situation ridiculous and funny, and yet being pleased for Mila at the same time.

Mila and Luke had been walking up a steep hill and they paused to catch their breath and to look at the lights of the city spread out below them. Luke wasn't a touchy-feely man and the proprietorial weight of his hand on Mila's shoulder had felt pleasing.

Mila said, 'I know why you're asking now. You don't want to miss out if my book sells millions and I end up filthy rich. You're after a slice of my future money pie, aren't you!'

'Oh bollocks,' said Luke, 'you saw through my cunning plan.'

'Not that cunning, inspector. The average literary fiction novel sells less than 300 copies in its first year.'

'Seriously?'

'Yep. But you know what,' said Mila, 'it's nice to be with a man who has confidence in my writing potential.'

They'd gone back to her house and kissed in the darkness of the tiny hallway, Mila pressed back against the coats hooked on their pegs. It had been a sweet, affectionate embrace. Luke's hand had gone inside her coat, found the waistband of her skirt, his fingers cold on the skin of her hip. She held on to him and then he pulled away and wiped his lips with the back of his hand. He reached behind him and turned on the light. Mila squinted. Luke unbuttoned his coat.

'Before we go up to bed, would you confirm if you actually answered "yes" to my proposal?' he asked, hanging the coat on a hanger. Luke liked nice clothes and he was particular about looking after them.

'I'm not going to take your name,' Mila said. 'I don't want to be Mrs Hogg.'

'Fair enough.'

'And I don't want a meringue dress or bridesmaids or a hen party,' she said as Luke went into the kitchen to put the kettle on. He liked a cup of tea before bed. 'I'm not going to stagger down Whiteladies Road holding an inflatable pink penis on the end of a length of string.'

'Your choice.'

'I don't want a first dance to some soppy song or confetti or a video. I'm not having my nails done.'

'God, you're so demanding.'

'And after we're married, I'd like us to adopt at least a couple of rescue dogs. Including Reggie.'

In their spare time, Mila and Luke were volunteer dog walkers at the local rescue centre. Reggie was a Jack Russell with so many behavioural problems that Mila was pretty certain nobody else would ever take him.

'Whatever you want, Ms Shepherd,' Luke had said.

The next evening, Mila had answered the phone to Ceci and found out that Sophie and Charlie had gone out sailing in *Moonfleet* and hadn't come back. She and Luke had never discussed marriage again.

In the garden of the sea house, Mila walked amongst the fruit trees, a few dried leaves already crunching underfoot. She wondered if the police had found their way to the Perrys' house yet and if they were breaking the awful news to Mrs Perry. She heard Emily and Ani laughing and her heart ached for them both.

* * *

A little later, Emily's grandmother turned up at the sea house in Tim Perry's Volvo to pick up her granddaughter. When Emily saw the maroon-coloured car pulling up, she called, 'My dad's here!' and ran outside.

'It's me, sweetie,' said Mrs Perry's mother, heaving herself out of the car. She was a large, short-haired woman wearing a mauve velour tracksuit with a silvery sheen and white deck shoes and although her face was pinched with stress, she had put on make-up: mascara and a touch of lipstick. It was clear to Mila that the woman knew the truth, and was putting on a brave face for Emily's sake. Mila respected her fortitude.

47

Mila went upstairs and into the main bedroom, Sophie and Charlie's old room.

Normally, she only went in there every other week to vacuum the rug, sweep the floorboards, dust and polish and get rid of any spiderwebs and dead flies that had found their way in and to open the windows to give the room an airing. Mostly, she let it be. But that evening, she went into the bedroom and knelt down and reached under the bed. Along with a suitcase and a bag containing Sophie's wedding dress and various pieces of musical paraphernalia belonging to Charlie, two large boot boxes made of heavy card helped fill the dark cavity beneath the mattress.

These were where Sophie kept her photographs.

The anniversary of the accident was in eight days' time. Mila couldn't put off addressing it with Ani any longer.

Sophie had many faults, but she could not be accused of not taking plenty of pictures. She was also good at remembering to have pictures printed so they wouldn't get lost when a phone was irreparably damaged or a digital camera dropped in the brackish water of the sea.

Mila brought the boxes downstairs one at a time because they were so heavy.

The weather had gradually worsened as the day went on and a storm was raging now. Berthaud, fortunately, had come in early and Mila hadn't only closed and locked the doors and window, but the cat flap too. She'd lit the fire in the living room grate, even though it was August, and she'd put lighted tealights and candles all around the room, so that if the power went off, as it sometimes did in bad weather, the room wouldn't be plunged into complete darkness.

Ani looked at the boxes suspiciously.

'What are you doing?'

'It's time we started sorting things out,' Mila said.

'Why now?'

'Because almost a year has gone by since we lost Sophie and Charlie, your maman and papa and we have to start talking about them sometime. I'm ready now,' Mila said. 'Are you ready, Ani?'

Ani was silent.

The make-up she'd been wearing earlier was smudged around her eyes. She looked both older than fourteen, and younger too.

'I thought we could start with these two boxes,' Mila said. 'We'll sort out the pictures we like into one box, and those we don't like will go in the other box, and that box, when we're finished, can go up in the loft and ta-da! Just like that we've cleared away half the boot boxes under Sophie and Charlie's bed!'

'Okay,' Ani said.

'And once we've done that, we'll sort out one of the wardrobes, maybe, or if that feels too much, the kitchen drawers or the cupboard in the dining room. Anything. As long as we do something.'

'Okay,' Ani said again.

'Okay,' said Mila.

She and Ani tipped out all the photographs, which weren't

arranged in any order, into one huge great heap of pictures. They extracted individual images, putting those they liked into one box, and those that were out of focus, or sun-damaged, or marked with a circle where someone had put a cup of coffee on top, in the other. Really damaged pictures went into the fire. Pictures of anyone neither Mila nor Ani recognised but who Ceci might know also went into the second box. There was some discussion over images of each other.

'What's wrong with that one?' Mila said, fishing the top picture from the rejects box. 'It's a lovely picture!'

'It's gross! I was such a fat baby, I could hardly open my eyes.' Ani puffed out her cheeks and made herself go cross-eyed.

'You weren't fat, you were perfect and your eyes were like that because you were always laughing. You were such a gorgeous, happy baby! Sorry, Ani, this photo is not going in box two.'

'You promised I could put whatever pictures I didn't like in that box.'

'Subject to my approval.'

'You never said that!'

'I thought it!'

'Doesn't count.'

'It does, because... Oh!'

The power had gone off.

'It's okay,' Mila said. 'We knew that was going to happen.'

She put another log on the fire. Their eyes adjusted to the softer light of the candles.

The pile of photographs was now greatly diminished, most of them being sorted into the boxes or the fire.

'Ani,' Mila said, 'next, we need to choose our favourite pictures of Sophie and Charlie for the anniversary next week.'

'Why?'

'Because Melodie and Pernille and other people we know are

going to be getting together to mark the occasion. Whether we go or not, we can put together an album for people to look at to bring back memories. How about this one?'

It was a picture of Charlie and Sophie in the garden, Charlie sitting on a collapsible picnic chair with one leg crossed over the other, an ankle resting on a knee, and Sophie making rabbit ears with her fingers behind his head. 'Do you remember when this was taken? I guess you must have been holding the camera.'

'I don't remember,' said Ani. She spread some of the photographs out on the rug and picked up another one. 'I remember this one, though. This was the day we went to Pointe du Raz and me and Papa went climbing on the rocks and first Maman lost her flip-flop down a crack in between the rocks and then her shawl blew off and while she was chasing after that, her hat lifted off and she was jumping up and down trying to catch it but it flew into the sea!'

She laughed at the memory and Mila, watching her, smiled too.

'And this is their wedding!' Ani said. 'Look how cute I am!'

'Did Sophie ever tell you the only reason she got married was because she wanted professional photographs of you wearing that dress?'

Ani looked up and smiled. It was such a Sophie thing to say.

'She kept the dress, you know,' Mila said. 'It's upstairs somewhere in an old shoe bag. We could find it tomorrow.'

'Maman showed me once,' said Ani. 'It had a stain down the front.'

'Oh yes, that's right! You fell asleep on Charlie's lap after the wedding and he spilled red wine all over you and never even noticed!'

Ani wrapped her arms about herself and chuckled with laughter as Mila picked up another picture.

Talking with Ani about Sophie and Charlie had seemed such an enormous thing to do, an insurmountable task.

Yet, as it turned out, remembering together wasn't so difficult after all.

* * *

When Ani was ready for bed, Mila said, 'Ani, earlier today, when you said you were at Pernille's, why did you lie? Why not tell me straight away that you were at the crazy golf? You know I wouldn't have minded.'

Ani looked sheepish, but she didn't leap to the default position of defensive.

'We weren't there to start with. We were just hanging around. If I'd texted that I was hanging around with JP and his friend, you'd have been worried.'

Mila thought about this for a moment and conceded that Ani was probably right.

'You're so busy all the time,' Ani continued. 'I didn't want you being worried about me when there were more important things you needed to do.'

'*Nothing* is more important than you, Ani.'

Ani was quiet for a moment and then said, 'Your book is.'

'No, no, Ani, it's not.'

How does she even know about the book?

Because you go on about it all the time. You don't think you do, but you do.

'But that's why you're going back to England, isn't it?' Ani asked. 'To finish writing the book?'

'It's part of the reason, but mainly I'm going back because my life is in England.'

'If your life is in England, what have you been doing here all this time? Not living?'

Mila was silent. She couldn't think of an answer.

'It's not your fault,' said Ani. 'You never wanted to have to look after me.'

'Oh, Ani, no! Hang on a minute, I *did* want to look after you. Obviously, I didn't want the circumstances to be as they were, but you, you're amazing. Of course I wanted to be with you as much as I could. I still do. You're my favourite, number one niece. You know that.'

Ani, in her leopard-print onesie, looked down at her feet, slender and long-toed.

'Why are you...' she began and then she tailed off. Mila knew what she had been about to ask. *Why are you sending me to boarding school then?*

Mila took Ani's hands in hers.

'Listen, sweetheart, it's late and it's been a long day. We'll talk about this tomorrow.'

Ani gave a small, disbelieving nod.

''Kay,' she said. 'Night then.'

She withdrew her hand and disappeared through the door that opened onto the stairs and climbed up, using her phone as a torch. The creak of the boards beneath her feet sounded so lonely that Mila could hardly bear it.

48

Four weeks ago, Mila Shepherd had never seen a dead body. Now she'd seen two, and the only obvious thing they had in common was that neither death seemed suspicious at first glance.

But it couldn't be coincidence that the professor and the traveller knew one another. Every instinct in Mila was telling her that the deaths were connected, that neither was what it seemed.

She kept thinking back to the word Luke had used to describe the position of the woman in the Bristol case: *choreographed.*

Gosia's death-bed scene had contained everything necessary for the doctor to be nudged into deciding that her death was due to natural causes, no need for an inquest. And all the unpleasantness of the last days leading to the apparent suicide of the professor, all that had been – or at least it had the appearance of having been – carefully organised too.

If Mila was right then someone was acting the role of choreographer, someone connected to the two dead people, someone with a reason to kill.

The power came back on. She checked her messages. There was an email from Carter. He had been in touch with Rhia Williams, and had managed to convince her to confirm their suspicions that she had come to Morannez to persuade Professor Perry to give her twenty thousand pounds to help Jake. She wouldn't say anything else, had been afraid of making a bad situation worse, but at least they knew they'd been right.

Mila considered this new information for a while, then she called Luke.

'Hey,' he said cheerfully, sounding a little drunk, 'it's 11 p.m. Are you calling for phone sex?'

'I don't know what that is,' said Mila, 'and I suspect you don't either.'

'We could try Google.'

'Actually, I need to tap into your police brain.'

Luke sighed. 'Okay, how can I help?'

Mila ran through the significant events of the last weeks, starting with the evening that Ani fell off her bike, and ending with the body in the cornfield. She told Luke everything that she thought was relevant, including putting the appeal for information about Gosia on the community internet forum, and the finding of the pass on the lawn in the back garden. Luke listened, and at the end of it he said, 'I think you're right. This isn't two separate cases, it's one case.' He fell silent again and then he said, 'This prowler, or whatever you want to call him, the time you saw him outside the sea house, that was after you'd put up the appeal for information about Gosia, right?'

'Right.'

'And you think he – or she – subsequently broke into the sea house and put some kind of subliminal flashcard onto your laptop.'

'A picture of Gosia's dead body, yes.'

'So, to have that picture, they must have been in the horsebox the night Gosia died.'

'Yes.'

'Hmm,' said Luke. 'Whoever "they" are knew you were interested in Gosia, so they broke into your house, not to steal, but to look at your laptop, to see what you knew already.'

'Which wasn't... still isn't much.'

'And they put something on there, some little worm or virus that would show you that picture when you opened the machine.'

'Yes. It felt like...'

'Like what?'

'Like a warning. As if they were trying to say: "If it can happen to Gosia, it can happen to you."' Even as she spoke the words, Mila remembered something Catherine Perry had said to her. 'The professor was threatened too, or at least he was worried that something might happen to him.'

'They're trying to frighten you away from looking any deeper into Gosia's background.'

'Yes, that's what I think,' said Mila, suddenly feeling very isolated and alone. Berthaud was curled up on her lap and she stroked the cat's soft body.

'Have you been to the police?'

'I don't know that I have anything specific to tell them.'

'You have information that they don't. You know that the professor was set up. You have fake Mrs Perry on video and they should be able to check out the phone number she gave you.'

'Okay.'

'Promise me you'll go and talk to them tomorrow?'

'Yes.'

'Mila, you need to be careful,' Luke said.

'I know.'

'Once you've been to the police, back away from this. You're coming home soon. There's no need for you to be involved in anything dangerous.'

'I want to find out who's behind this,' Mila said. 'I owe it to

Gosia, and we, the agency I mean, were partially responsible for what happened to the professor. Also, Luke, if we're right about this, and those two people were killed, that means there's a murderer here in Morannez. While they're at large, then everyone's at risk. Even when I come back to England, Ceci will still be here, and Ani when she's home for the school holidays and other people I care about.'

Luke sighed. Mila imagined him rubbing his forehead with his fingers.

'Mila...'

'What do I do next?' Mila asked.

'You're not going to let this go?'

'No.'

'Then go back over everything you have and examine the detail,' said Luke. 'Look at the things you've already dismissed as irrelevant. Delve into the backgrounds of the people on the periphery. Turn over every insignificant little stone. What you're looking for will be there, somewhere, and you'll recognise it when you find it.'

'Thank you, Luke.'

'And be careful.'

'Obviously.'

'Be careful about what you say and who you say it to.'

'Okay.'

Luke was quiet for a moment, then he said: 'I'm looking forward to you coming home and things being normal again.'

'Me too,' said Mila.

It was odd, though; as she spoke the words, doubt crept into her mind.

Until now, she had been counting down the minutes until she could pick up the pieces of her old life. Now, she wondered, for the first time, if that really was what she wanted to do.

49

Mila had next to no information on Gosia but she already had a good amount on the professor.

She went back to the biography that she'd curated and did as Luke had told her. She took out her virtual microscope, and she examined every detail forensically.

She started with Catherine Perry. She went back to Mrs Perry's social media accounts and trawled through them. She looked at the people in the backgrounds of the photographs, hoping to spot someone she recognised, and read online conversations between Mrs Perry and other self-employed crafters about the merits or otherwise of different kinds of glitter glue.

She couldn't find anything.

Emily was almost certainly too young to be significant to the case, and Mila could find no red flags associated with her. Jake was in the north-west of England, a long way from Brittany, hopefully feeling under a great deal less pressure now that his father had bailed him out. She wriggled deep into Jake's online persona and found some quirky TikTok videos he'd made. The boy, for all his problems, had a good sense of humour and, in Mila's opinion, a not inconsiderable talent.

He didn't seem to have any connection with potential criminals in France.

Who else was there?

Timor Perry's parents, Evelyn and Philip.

Mila did searches on both of them. Philip had passed away four years previously at a ripe old age and Evelyn was currently living in a crofter's cottage in the Highlands of Scotland close to her daughter, Tim's sister, Karen, who Mila had somehow missed off the family tree first time round. She metaphorically kicked herself; this was one of those slipped-through-the-net details that Luke was always complaining about, the kind of mistake that could cause all kinds of trouble later on.

Karen turned out to be a colourful character; she'd been an animal rights activist since her teenage years and had been in trouble with the police several times for illegal, but in Mila's opinion thoroughly laudable, activities, which included rescuing beagle puppies from laboratories, the liberation of battery-farmed hens and undercover filming to reveal the suffering of other factory-farmed animals. Mila was impressed to see that Karen Perry had been one of the writers of the script of the film that she and Sophie had watched as fourteen-year-olds about the processing of veal calves, the film that had made them both turn instantly vegetarian, much to Cecille's chagrin.

These days, Karen was less involved in activism but worked for an animal rescue charity and managed its fund-raising activities from home. Mila zoomed in on a picture of Karen, short-haired and doughty and wearing a fisherman's sweater and farmer's overalls, leaning on a fence surrounding a paddock where an assortment of elderly ponies were seeing out their days in the equine equivalent of a luxury retirement home.

There was no doubt that Karen Perry would have made plenty of enemies over the years, but Mila had a feeling that her brother would have approved of her work, and there was nothing about it that Mila could see that could have caused him any problems in Brittany.

The next name on the CV was that of Tim Perry's tutor at Cambridge, the 'world-renowned historian' Malgorzata Kowalczyk.

Mila copied and pasted the name into the search bar and Google came up with hundreds of hits. Mila opened the first one.

By the time she was in her mid-twenties, Polish-born historian Malgorzata Kowalczyk had already gained an international reputation for her exciting and innovative work into the lives of hunter-gather women during the so-called 'interim' period of pre-history. The Mesolithic period is sandwiched between the Upper Palaeolithic and the Neolithic periods. Malgorzata 'Gosia' Kowalczyk was the first academic of her generation to consider in depth the day-to-day lives of the females of this period.

Mila read this and stopped.
She read it again.

Malgorzata 'Gosia' Kowalczyk

She put down her drink and stared at the words.
Then she began to search the internet furiously.

Malgorzata Kowalczyk had come to work on secondment at Cambridge University in 1985, undertaking an official temporary job swap with a British colleague. By that time she was married to a Bosnian Muslim man, Ademir Orić. The couple had a ten-year-old son called Tomas.

Mila got up and went into the kitchen. The photograph that had been found in Gosia's van was there, held on to the front of the fridge by a magnet with a picture of two 1950s women embracing and the words *Friends: cheaper than psychiatrists*. Mila took the picture down.

'Is this you, Tomas?' she asked the floppy-haired young man looking out at her. 'Have I found you?'

Tomas was almost exactly the same age as Tim Perry.

Mila took the photograph back into the living room, together with a bottle of wine tucked under one arm. She topped up her glass, put the bottle on the fireplace where it could not be accidentally knocked over, added another log to the flames, and continued to read, piecing together bits of information from various different sites: an academic biography of Malgorzata Orić, an interview in the university's student magazine.

Ademir and Malgorzata bought a house on the outskirts of a town close to Srebrenica, in Bosnia and Herzegovina. It was a picture-postcard pretty place, surrounded by trees and mountains. People holidayed there. There were ski resorts, green meltwater rivers, places to walk, to enjoy nature, to paint, to relax. It was the perfect environment for a young couple to bring up their son. Ademir was a director of one of the area's renowned salt mines.

In 1991, Malgorzata Orić was present at a ceremony at Cambridge University in which the undergraduate student, Timor Perry, was awarded a prize for excellence for research work he'd carried out under Malgorzata's tutorage. There was a photograph of the two of them standing together in some leafy courtyard, their heads tilted towards one another, their mutual affection obvious. Tim Perry looked like a young version of himself but it was almost impossible for Mila to see the woman in middle-age who stood beside her star pupil as the shuffling old woman from the horsebox. This woman had shortish, black hair set in gentle waves around a pretty, elfin face. She was slender and neat; she wore her unassuming black dress and low-heeled shoes well. She was laughing. She had straight white teeth and although her eyes were almost closed because her head was slightly tipped back, Mila could see that she was a woman who took trouble over her appearance. Her eyebrows had been neatly plucked into arches; her fingernails were shaped and tidy.

'Oh, Gosia,' whispered Mila. 'What happened to you?'

In 1992, war broke out in the Balkans. Malgorzata left Cambridge to be at home, with her family, but she and Tim Perry stayed in touch. Mila knew this because they continued to write and publish articles together, articles that were on the list Mila had already linked to in her previous research. She hadn't bothered to read the titles or author notes in any detail; if she had, she'd have almost certainly spotted the connection straight away. Another mistake.

Mila read an open letter written and signed by a number of European academics, including Malgorzata Orić, in 1993, urging the rest of the world to wake up to what was going on in the Balkans, to the 'terrible things' that were happening to innocent people: the so-called ethnic cleansing; massacres, rapes and genocides; the cold-blooded murder of families sheltering in the basements of their own homes.

She found reference to Tomas Orić, a promising young musician, in an *Observer* article about talent emerging from war zones. Tomas told the interviewer that music was his soul-food, but that animals were his passion. He hoped, when the war was over, to be able to go to university and ultimately become a vet.

She listened to a song called 'Speakeasy' by a band called Zagreb. She couldn't find anything recorded by Tomas Orić.

She read about Serbian men, inspired by ruthless murderers like Radovan Karadžić, who had taken the war into their own hands, who were using war as an excuse for the fulfilling of sadistic

fantasies. She read that such atrocities were an inevitable conse-
quence of war. They were horribly predictable. Ademir Orić was
murdered in the Srebrenica genocide of 1995.

Lastly, she watched a video that she found by searching for the
name of the remote, picturesque town where Malgorzata and her
little family lived. The video, according to the accompanying
caption which the internet obligingly translated into English, had
been filmed by a schoolboy from the town. Initially it seemed
innocent-ish. A group of young men, boys really, Mila counted ten
of them, were being shepherded into a wooded area by a smaller
group of seven different boys. The group doing the shepherding
were holding pistols, which looked like toy guns. The young men
were self-conscious, as if they were playing at being soldiers and
captives for the benefit of the camera. Those being herded into
the woods were wearing the same Western-style clothes as the
other boys. They weren't bloodied or bruised; their hands weren't
tied. They looked like ordinary kids you'd find in any European
town or city. Both sets of boys were talking amongst themselves
and to those in the other group, joking around. The ones with the
pistols seemed more nervous than those they were controlling.
They were jumpy, jittery. The boy at the back kept looking over
his shoulder as if to check they weren't being followed. At one
point, just before they went into a rocky area, one of the group
being herded turned to look at the person holding the camera. He
smiled, and held up his hand in greeting. He and whoever was
holding the camera exchanged words; it sounded like friendly
banter.

The smiling young man was Tomas. Definitely Gosia's Tomas.
On video he was even more personable than in the still photograph. His smile was so warm and genuine that Mila, across all the
years and miles and everything that divided them, smiled back
at him.

The young man walking behind Tomas gave him a friendly push, and Tomas turned so that his back was to the camera again.

The camera followed all the young men into the rocky area. It was an open cave in the woodland, like a small quarry. The ground was flat. The walls were made of rock and beyond those were trees, tall trees that climbed up the side of the mountain.

One of the boys holding a gun said something to the unarmed group that sounded like a command. The other boys looked at him, then they looked at one another and grinned, scratched their heads, embarrassed. The leader of the controlling boys, a sturdy young man with curly blonde hair, shouted the command again, louder this time, sounding as if he meant it. He waved his gun around, pointed it at the ground. He must have said 'Lie down on your stomachs,' because the others began to get down, still laughing, but a little anxious now, not knowing what was going on.

It still looked like a game.

Or, perhaps, a practical joke.

The boys without guns lay down on their stomachs, face down, and those still standing pushed them with the toes of their trainers and made them wriggle until they were lying in a line, side by side, all ten of them, these ordinary young men in jeans and T-shirts and trainers.

And then the pistol boys lined up behind them and shot them in the back of their heads.

Bang bang bang bang bang bang bang bang bang bang.

The bodies jumped with the shock of the bullets; blood spurted from the wounds.

Tomas was third from the end.

50

Dragan Brđanin
Zoran Ačar
Suavi Bobetko
Janko Jelisić
Goran Kordić
Dario Petković
Milivoj Vasiljković

These were the seven names listed in the comments beneath the video.

Mila assumed that because there were seven names, not ten, that these were the murderers, rather than the victims. She stayed up into the early hours searching each name, one by one, and found that she was right.

Milivoj had been living in Perth, Australia and working as a golf instructor under the name Mike Adams. Twelve years ago, he'd been outed and convicted by the International Criminal Tribunal for the former Yugoslavia. There was no mention of who had found him and revealed his true identity, but in a news photo taken at the time of his extradition and published in the *Western Australia News*, Mila spotted a small, dark-haired woman watching from the back of the crowd.

Zoran had been in Argentina where he'd married a wealthy woman and was working the land. Dario had been in California, the manager of a jewellery store.

These three had been tracked down first, their true identities and the crimes they had committed revealed. The others had still been in Europe. One by one, six of the seven had been found and brought to justice. They'd all, every one of them, changed their names, adopting something suitable for the country in which they'd settled and each had created a new background and identity for himself. It couldn't have been easy to find them, because they hadn't wanted to be found. They'd become apparently respectable men, who were settled in their communities. They'd had families. They'd taught their children to respect others, to share, to be gentle, to be kind.

They hadn't been young men, either, by the time Gosia found them.

There was a film of Janko testifying: heavy, middle-aged. He had broken down and wept in court. He told how he had been plagued by nightmares and flashbacks to that day when he'd been 'coerced' into helping round up his schoolfriends and making them go into the forest.

Malgorzata had testified too. She said she and her husband, Ademir, hadn't known what had happened to their beloved son, Tomas. He wasn't the only boy in the town to be missing. Ten, altogether, had vanished, all at the same time.

The families and friends of the missing boys searched high and low but they didn't find any bodies because their killers had dragged them out of the quarry, one by one, and thrown them into a deep ravine.

Malgorzata didn't find out what had happened to Tomas until the video one of his schoolfriends had made of his murder began circulating online in the early 2000s.

She recognised the boys with guns, of course. She knew their mothers. Some had even been round to her house. As children they'd played on their bikes with Tomas; they'd built dens together; Ademir had taught Janko to play chess.

'I didn't want to do it,' Janko said, his lovely Danish wife watching stony-eyed from the observation gallery in the courtroom. 'I held the gun but I never fired a shot. I didn't kill anyone! If I'd refused to go along with what Dragan wanted, they'd have killed me too.'

'But you never told anyone what had happened. You saw the mothers of the murdered boys, their sisters and brothers, their grandparents brought down by grief, and you said nothing?'

Janko, a director of a multi-billion-dollar shipping insurance company, had clasped his hands in front of him, broken by shame; shame, Mila noted cynically, that didn't appear to have affected him until he was outed.

The judge had quoted the philosopher, Edmund Burke: 'All that is necessary for the triumph of evil is that good men do nothing.'

Goran was suffering from early onset dementia by the time he was found and had forgotten he was ever involved.

Suavi gave himself up when he heard about the others.

Mila topped up her wine glass. She imagined Gosia dedicating the last years of her life to searching for and finding the young men who had killed her son, and the other boys, in cold blood. The eccentric old traveller woman living in the back of a converted horsebox, collecting newspaper cuttings and photographs, filling her corkboard.

Writing the story down, meticulously, in her journal.

In 2017, a German journalist had written an article about Gosia's work after hearing her talk to the families of some of the murder victims outside the court where Suavi had been sentenced to thirty years in prison.

'I did not set out to humiliate these men,' Gosia had explained, 'but rather to make them acknowledge the truth about what they had done. Suavi has been hiding from his crime all his adult life, but there is no hiding. A man can pretend to be someone else, but even if he fools the rest of the world, his heart knows the truth.'

Six of the seven had been exposed; only the seventh remained at large.

The curly-haired blonde former waiter. Dragan Brđanin.

Was he here? Mila wondered.

Was that why Gosia had travelled hundreds of miles across Europe in her clapped-out, old converted horsebox? To reveal the truth about Dragan Brđanin, whoever he was, whatever he called himself now?

51

WEDNESDAY, 17 AUGUST

It was three o'clock in the morning.

Mila had gone past being tired. She was wide awake and she was exhilarated – not in a good way, in a nervy, anxious way, but at least now she understood.

Everything was clear. Her instincts had been right. Gosia, Malgorzata, *had* been murdered. Her book, her life's work had been stolen. She'd been killed by the seventh murderer, Dragan Brđanin, a man living under an assumed identity; someone who'd had everything to lose were she to remain alive. Professor Perry had been murdered too, both murders staged to look like something they were not. Mila was as sure as she could be that the professor had been killed for the same reason as Gosia, although she didn't yet fully understand how he was involved, nor how Professor Tim Perry and Malgorzata Orić had ended up simultaneously in this small town in Brittany.

Mila was desperate to talk to somebody about what she knew, to try to figure out the missing pieces of the puzzle. But it was too late for some, too early for others. She couldn't call Ceci; she couldn't call Luke. She toyed with the idea of calling Carter, but at this time of night it would seem weird, certainly it wouldn't appear professional. He might question her motives – God forbid he might think she was making a play for him. She couldn't risk it.

She remembered him moving around Tim Perry's body, potentially contaminating the scene and taking pictures, which was wrong in so many ways, although he behaved as if he knew more about such matters than she did, acting like he was Clint Eastwood.

'I know what I'm doing,' she said, in Carter's Canadian voice. 'Ah know what ah'm doin'.'

To be honest, that sounded more Texan than Canadian.

What a dick, said Sophie.

Me or him?

Both of you.

Mila picked up the wine bottle and emptied the dregs into her glass.

Fuck it, she thought.

She called Carter.

* * *

Mila woke the next morning to the sound of rain on the window. She was lying on the sofa with her head on the cushions and she was covered over with several of Sophie's brightly coloured throws. The door to the kitchen was open and someone was in there, opening and closing cupboard doors, making a noise. It was too early for Ani.

Two glasses were on the wooden table beside the settee, next to Mila's laptop. Also on the table was a different laptop. A large, clunky, industrial-type machine with a fancy blue, red and gold sticker on the back of the lid that said *Toronto Police*.

In the corner of the room, a leather jacket was folded over a motorcycle helmet.

Merde!

Carter came into the living room with a mug of coffee in each hand. He looked annoyingly bright-eyed, although his expression was wary.

'Hi,' he said.

'Hi.'

'Made you coffee.'

'Thanks.'

She took a mug from him. It was real coffee, black as tar.

'You said you didn't mind me crashing out here for a couple of hours,' Carter prompted.

'It's fine,' said Mila, hoping her face looked as if it remembered a conversation of which she had absolutely no recollection.

'You were falling asleep on the couch,' said Carter.

'Yes, yes, I know.'

'I took a few cushions and camped out on the floor in the dining room.'

'Good.'

The coffee smelled strong. Mila yearned for her usual instant variety.

'Do you mind if I...?' Carter indicated the rocking chair.

'No, of course not. Sit down.'

Carter sat on the edge of the chair with his knees wide apart.

Manspreading, said Sophie. Mila ignored her.

'While you were sleeping, I thought about what we discussed,' Carter said, 'and I think we were right. I don't see how it can be anything else.'

Berthaud jumped up onto his lap, turned round several times, paddled at the top of his jeans with her tiny paws and then curled up on one thigh, purring like an engine.

Mila had a vague recollection of the two of them, in the early hours, piecing the puzzle of Tim Perry and Malgorzata Orić together.

They'd come to the conclusion that the pair must have stayed closely in touch throughout Tim's career. She had been his mentor and his role model and it was obvious from their academic collaborations that they were friends as well as colleagues. He would certainly have let her know he'd been awarded the directorship of the Kyern dig.

When he arrived in Morannez, Carter had suggested Professor Perry had met someone who he'd recognised, or at least had his suspicions about: someone who might be Dragan Brđanin. He probably carried out some kind of investigation of his own to double-check his theory, and when he was certain, he had alerted Gosia. She'd then driven across Europe to finish her life's work, to expose the seventh murderer, show the people around him what kind of monster he was and make him pay for his crimes.

She must have made contact with Brđanin. And when he realised he was at risk of losing everything, he had killed her and taken everything that could have connected him with the original crime from the horsebox; the book, the phone, the pictures pinned to the corkboard. He had staged the death scene; putting prescription medication at the side of Gosia's bed, so the doctor and police would be convinced the death was natural. He knew that nobody would pay much attention to the loss of an eccentric vagrant.

Unfortunately for the murderer, Gosia wasn't the only person who knew the truth: Professor Perry knew too.

It was likely the murderer only discovered the connection between Gosia and Tim Perry when he looked in Gosia's book after her death. And then what? Did he tell Tim Perry that he'd hurt his family if the professor went to the police? Did he remind the professor that all the evidence pertaining to the case was gone? Or did he vow to destroy the professor's life piece by piece? Mild-mannered Tim Perry wouldn't have had a clue how to deal with the situation. And while all this was going on, the poor man was also being badgered by Rhia Williams for money to pay off his son's debts.

'It was so cruel what he did to Professor Perry,' said Mila, 'destroying the reputation he'd spent a lifetime building.' She sipped the coffee. It was bitter and strong.

Carter absentmindedly rubbed Berthaud's neck with the back of his finger.

'Giving a man who's lived a blameless life a compelling reason to kill himself so that people would believe he had killed himself took some doing.'

'Maybe,' said Mila quietly, 'the professor *did* kill himself. Maybe he'd been told it was the only way to protect his family.'

There was a noise from upstairs. Footsteps padded across the landing to the bathroom.

Carter drained his coffee. 'I'll get out of your way.'

He put the cat gently on the floor, stood up and collected his jacket, laptop and helmet when his eye was caught by a photograph of Sophie on top of the pile of pictures in the old boot box.

'Do you mind?' he asked, reaching for the photograph.

He picked it up without waiting for a response and stared at the image of Sophie: the woman he had loved, the woman who had never loved him back.

Perhaps, thought Mila, he didn't know that. Perhaps, even now, he believed he was a victim of circumstance, and not merely someone Sophie used to make Charlie jealous; to convince him to propose to her.

'She was so fucking beautiful,' he said.

Put the photo down, Mila begged him silently. *Please, put it down.*

Carter replaced the picture in the box. Mila pushed back her hair with her fingers. She heard water draining from the upstairs bathroom.

Now, get out before Ani comes down. Go away. You don't belong here. I should never have called you. I should never have let you in.

She followed Carter out of the room, into the hallway.

'So,' he said, 'you're going to go into Bloemel-sur-Mer and ask the woman in the vintage shop if she's sold a white designer suit to anyone lately.'

'Yes,' said Mila. 'Yes, I'll do that today.'

'And I'm going to go to the office and see if I can hack into the professor's documents and emails.'

'Right.'

'And with a fair wind behind us,' said Carter Jackson, 'in the next few hours, we'll find out who this seventh man is.'

52

Mila had breakfast laid out on the table when Ani came downstairs.

'I thought we could go into Bloemel this morning and have a look around the shops,' said Mila. She immediately felt bad about framing something she wanted to do as a treat for Ani. 'I need to go and have a quick chat with someone while we're there. But apart from that we can go into whatever shops you like.' She took a deep breath. 'We really ought to buy you some new things for when you go to your new school.'

Ani did not react at all to the school comment apart from leaning forward so her hair covered her face and Mila could no longer see her eyes.

'We don't have to spend long looking at school clothes,' Mila said gently, 'if there are other shops you'd rather visit.'

Ani stared at the cheese and sliced peach on her plate.

'Anyway, I'm going to have a quick shower and then we'll—'

'Who was here last night?' Ani asked.

'Oh, Carter, he came over in the early hours. It was work.'

'The motorbike man?'

'Yes.'

'You were drunk.'

'I wasn't drunk.'

'I could hear you. You were talking carefully like you always do when you're drunk.'

'I wasn't.'

Ani banged her hand on the table. '*You were!* Why are you lying to me? You said you'd never lie and you get mad when I tell little lies but you, you lie all the time, whenever you feel like it, about everything!'

They were both surprised by this outburst and stared at one another in shock.

Mila spoke first. 'I had had a few drinks, you're right. I called Carter and asked him to come over to help me with something to do with work.'

'But he stayed over.'

'Only because it was very late and he'd had some wine too. It wouldn't have been safe for him to get on the bike.'

'Do you like him?'

Mila hesitated. 'I've known him a long time.'

'That's not what I asked.'

'All right. As a colleague, yes, he's okay, I like him. Not in any other way.'

'But you still invited him over in the night when you were drunk. Does Luke know?'

Mila put a hand to her head. 'Ani, nothing untoward happened, okay? I don't have to ask Luke's permission to ask someone I work with to come and help me with a case.'

'So, you're not going to tell Luke?'

Mila had had enough of it now.

'Eat your breakfast, Ani,' she said. 'I'm going to shower and then we'll go into Bloemel. We can go in that lovely bookshop and have a look in the market. It's going to be fun.'

Ani scowled. 'You always say that.'

'And occasionally, you have to admit, I'm right.'

* * *

A little later they went to the bus stop, waited for, and caught, the wobbly old bus that bumped through the country lanes to Morannez's bigger and smarter neighbouring town while the bus driver, the same man as always, grumbled about being put upon by his employers, his customers, other road users, his wife and his neighbours. 'You know me,' he said, 'I'm not one to complain, but...'

The rain had given the streets and the countryside a wash and, looking through the window, Mila thought that the grass already looked greener and the flowers fresher. The sky was grey and there were puddles on the pavements and the roads. The other people on the bus were holidaymakers, campers, Mila guessed, wearing waterproofs and looking desperate. They'd obviously decided to spend the day out of the fresh air as much as possible. The family sitting immediately behind were discussing which film they were going to watch at the cinema.

It was a twenty-minute drive to Bloemel, known for its fancy hotel, now owned by the Girard family – a hotel with famously pretty grounds created by its original owner. There was a shell grotto with a fountain and a rose garden. This was where a British model and her French fiancé had married a few years back, propelling the hotel into the international limelight and making it an Instagram favourite location. Since then, its prices had become so inflated that it was inaccessible to local people. Even the British cream teas, for which there was a waiting list of several months, cost more than the average prix fixe three-course-lunch in a good local restaurant. The hotel took pride of place on the promenade and was surrounded by other grand, but not quite *as* grand, buildings with the features of classical architecture: lines of well-proportioned windows, balconies and pleasant courtyard areas protected from the weather by awnings.

The bus travelled along the seafront, giving the tourists the opportunity to admire the public gardens and remark on how much grander Bloemel was than Morannez, before turning in to the town centre and stopping at the bus station. Mila and Ani got off with the holidaymakers. Mila looked at the maps app on her phone. Collette's vintage shop was on the other side of the shopping area.

'Shall we look at the market first?' she asked.

Ani, who was still in a mood, scowled and said, 'Whatever.'

Mila, despite her tiredness, had to struggle not to laugh, so intense was her niece's sulk.

53

The market was large and noisy. Mila was overwhelmed. There were too many people, too many stalls, too much choice. She couldn't decide whether or not to buy a quarter watermelon – it looked delicious but she'd have to carry it – or olives, which came in a little pot but what if the lid was loose and the oil spilled all over the books that she might buy in the bookshop?

She looked at the racks of clothes, far cheaper than those available from the shops in Morannez, but if the zip didn't work on a dress, or it was the wrong size, it would be a lot of hassle to bring it back. Ani sloped along behind, only brightening when they came to a very noisy stall selling old vinyl records and CDs. The teenage lad who was in charge of the stall watched Ani and asked her questions about her musical tastes. Mila couldn't decide if he was being friendly or he was flirting. Things seemed to be moving fast with Ani on the growing-up front. She stood protectively by her niece, feeling old and irrelevant. Ani's replies to the boy were monosyllabic and eventually he moved away. Then Ani spent some time flicking through the racks before deciding there was no point buying anything because there was nothing back at the sea house on which to play either records or CDs.

They eventually emerged at the far side of the market with no purchases at all. Mila found and then followed the directions to Collette's through the back streets. Soon she and Ani were in an upmarket part of the town. Mila caught sight of the older Girard brother, Arnaud, standing beside a sleek, dark-coloured car, talking to a large, bearded man outside the Guidage Peche Finistère agency that organised sea-fishing tours. Arnaud was wearing a suit and sunglasses and Mila didn't think he had recognised her, or even noticed her.

Collette's was a small shop in a very old building. In the window was a single vintage silver Prada puffer jacket hanging on a coat hanger, with two small spotlights artfully illuminating it and a pair of Jimmy Choo stilettos beneath, one standing upright, its partner lying on its side.

'This is it,' Mila said cheerfully.

Ani brightened a little. The shop was definitely interesting.

Collette herself was a friendly woman a little older than Mila. She asked if they were looking for anything in particular and Ani asked if she had any vintage dresses that might fit her. She and Collette disappeared into the depths of the racks at the back of the shop while Mila browsed, admiring some of the beautiful clothes, knowing that she could never wear them. Most of them seemed to have been made for tiny women.

While Ani was trying clothes on, Collette returned to talk to Mila and she turned out to be both chatty, interesting and quite happy to divulge gossip once Mila had told her that she was a friend of Melodie Sohar's. The online side of her business was what kept Collette going: she'd bought and sold clothes all over the world. She had even once purchased a consignment from a British lady who, it turned out, was selling the items on behalf of one of the royals!

'No!' said Mila. 'Which one?'

Collette tapped the side of her nose. 'I couldn't possibly say.' And then she leaned forward and whispered the name of a royal princess into Mila's ear.

Ani came out of the changing rooms modelling a fir-green dress with a tight bodice and a tutu skirt.

'Hmm,' said Collette, hand on her chin. 'That's not really *you*, darling. Try on the Stella!'

Ani, who would have gone into a huff if Mila had made a similar comment, disappeared happily back behind the curtain.

Mila took the opportunity to ask Collette about the Fendi suit.

'I haven't had a suit lately,' said Collette, 'but I did sell a pencil skirt and a gorgeous woollen jacket with a Fendi buckle that I displayed as a suit.'

Ani took her phone out and showed her the picture of fake Mrs Perry.

'These pieces?'

'Yes, that's them!' Collette clapped her hands together. 'Oh, Joséphine looks great, doesn't she! But she's changed her hair.' She took the phone and zoomed in. 'Or is that a wig?'

'It's a wig,' said Mila.

'Is she a friend of yours too?' Collette asked.

'Kind of,' said Mila.

There was a swish from the curtain of the changing room and Ani came out.

'What about this?'

'Oh, *mon Dieu*,' said Collette. 'Oh! Wow!'

Ani was wearing a dayglo sweatshirt with a smiley face emoji on the front and a coordinated, splashy red tie-dye-style skirt. It was a fun and funky outfit, not too grown up.

'Stella McCartney suits you!' Collette said.

Ani twirled. She was smiling from ear to ear.

'Can I have these clothes?' Ani asked Mila. 'Please, *please*, can I have them?'

Mila tried not to think about what she was about to do.

'Sure,' she said. 'Why not.'

Ani went back into the changing room; Mila turned to Collette.

'Actually, I wanted to get a little gift for Joséphine. Do you have anything not too pricey that she might like?'

'That's so thoughtful! I'm sure I can find something! Hold on!'

Collette went to a rack where vintage accessories were displayed. 'What about this?' she asked, holding up a slim handbag compact. 'It's Chanel.'

'Perfect,' said Mila. 'She'll love it!'

She waited until Ani had emerged from the changing rooms and Collette was wrapping the compact in white tissue paper before she said, 'Collette, I'd like to drop this off for Joséphine today, but I just realised, I don't actually know where she works.'

'Saint Jeanne d'Arc's,' said Collette. 'The mental health facility on the way to Vannes.'

'Oh yes,' said Mila, 'of course!'

'I could drop it off if you like. I have to go past on the way to visit my mother.'

'No, no, it's fine. I'll take it myself. Thank you, though.'

Collette tied a slender black ribbon around the compact and made a bow.

'That looks beautiful,' said Mila.

Collette passed the little parcel to Mila.

'When you see Joséphine, give her my regards.'

Mila had her fingers crossed to counteract the lie, as she promised that she would.

54

'Can I wear my new clothes tonight?' Ani asked on the bus back to Morannez.

'Hmm?' Mila was distracted, looking at her phone. She was on the Saint Jeanne d'Arc website, trying to find a list of personnel.

'My new clothes, can I wear them tonight?'

'What's happening tonight?'

'The sleepout.'

'The sleepout?'

'Yes!'

Ani spoke in the exasperated way of someone who had mentioned something at least a dozen times to someone else who hadn't been listening. Mila, however, was absolutely certain that Ani hadn't said anything about the sleepout to her before. She'd only ever heard about it from Emily Perry.

'I didn't think you'd want to go,' Mila said. She'd found a *Meet Our Staff* page. There were thumbnail pictures of doctors, nurses and other employees of the facility.

'Everyone's going.'

There she was! Dr Joséphine Hugo BSc PhD, Consultant Psychiatrist.

Hugo?

'Sorry, Ani, what did you say?'

'That everyone's going to the sleepout so why wouldn't I want to go?'

'Pernille's away for a start.'

Mila didn't add, *I'm amazed you'd even consider going without Pernille*, because she didn't want Ani to feel she couldn't do things on her own. But she *was* amazed. Not to mention that the sleepout was on the beach and Ani had avoided the beach assiduously for the past year.

The bus lurched as the driver slowed behind a tourist family riding bicycles. He muttered abuse as he waited to pass.

While they were crawling behind the cyclists, a low-slung, dark-coloured car sailed past the bus; Mila looked down on the face of the driver, Arnaud Girard. He was staring straight ahead, oblivious to her.

She thought it strange how when they were all teenagers, playing football together on the beach, their backgrounds and family histories hadn't mattered. Arnaud and his brother, Gillaume, had been as much part of the group as the shy Mila, lively Sophie, boisterous Carter Jackson and Melodie Valette, as she was then, whose alcoholic mother lived in a tiny flat above the fishmongers' and who was rumoured to be a prostitute. But now they were adults they moved in their own different circles, their lives occasionally overlapping but their relationships with each other far less intense. Mila touched her left wrist; imagining a ghost tattoo.

The bus shuddered and finally managed to pass the tourists on their bikes.

Hugo?

'Hugo?' Mila said aloud.

'What?'

'Is "Hugo" a common French surname, Ani?'

'How would I know? I only know Monsieur Hugo from school.'

And Dr Joséphine Hugo would be about the right age to be his wife. Mila felt a sudden, almost joyous thrill. What was it Luke had said? Something about how, when things fell into place, you just *knew*.

'So can I wear my new things to the sleepout?' Ani persisted.

'I think we ought to ask Ceci if it's all right for you to go,' Mila said, clicking on the photograph of Joséphine Hugo to enlarge it.

'Why? What's it even got to do with her?'

'I don't feel qualified to make a decision about something like this.'

'Everyone else is going.'

'You keep saying that, but everyone else is not the point.' Mila paused to find the link to Dr Hugo's biography. She clicked on it. 'Is Romeo going?'

Ani flushed. 'Yes. Obviously. Everyone is. I told you!'

So that's why you're so keen to be there!

'What exactly goes on at these sleepouts?' Mila asked. The biography had opened but was difficult to read. The text was small, it was in French and the bus journey back was as bumpy as the journey out.

'Well, nobody sleeps,' said Ani.

Mila searched for a button to translate the text.

'Why aren't they called stay-awake-outs then?'

Ani ignored this. 'There's music and people light fires and stuff.'

And stuff. Mila imagined Sophie rolling her eyes at this although it was exactly the kind of thing that Sophie would have said.

Of course, Ani hadn't been to a sleepout before. She couldn't really know what to expect.

There was no translation option. She copied and pasted Joséphine Hugo's biography into a French-to-English language app.

'Romeo says it's fun,' said Ani.

Aha! said Sophie. *You were right, ma chère! She wants to get off with Romeo.*

She's too young to get off with anyone.

I had my first kiss at fourteen.

Shut up, Sophie. You're not being helpful.

Joséphine Hugo had studied psychiatry at Stanford University. It was where she had met her husband, Alban, who was born in Texas and who was training to become a teacher. So she *was* Monsieur Hugo's wife!

Mila suddenly felt light-headed.

Alban Hugo's wife, Joséphine, was fake Mrs Perry. She'd dressed up and come into the agency and persuaded Ceci and Carter to follow Professor Perry and take the photograph that would be used to compromise him. Mila had thought long and hard about why they had gone to so much trouble over this, and concluded that the agency logo on the posters was the key; it added authenticity to the image.

But if Joséphine had been put up to this by her husband, did that mean that he was the man they were looking for? The man Gosia had identified as the seventh killer. If Carter and Mila's theory was correct, Alban Hugo had not been born in Texas, but in the little salt-mining town in Bosnia. His name was not Alban Hugo but Dragan Brđanin. Did Joséphine *know* the truth about her husband? Had she any idea? If not, then how had he persuaded her to go along with the plan of being fake Mrs Perry? Did she know that Professor Perry was now dead?

'... if I promise, *swear* that I'll leave my phone switched on and I'll text you at least once an hour!' Ani said.

Mila looked at her. 'I didn't hear all of that.'

'You *never* listen to me.'

The other day, at the dig site, Monsieur Hugo had been with Emily Perry. He'd stopped her going into the field. How had he known to stop her? Had he known her father was dead?

Was it because he'd killed him?

'Mila!'

'Sorry?'

'You're *still* not listening!'

'I am.'

'What did I just say then?'

Mila sighed.

'Okay, Ani, here's what we'll do. We'll go round to Mamie's when we're back and we'll ask her what she thinks. And if she says it's okay for you to go to the sleepout, well, then it's okay with me if you do as you said, and leave your phone on and check in regularly.'

Alban Hugo had had his hands on Emily's shoulders. Were they the same hands that had murdered the professor?

'Good,' said Ani, knowing full well that Ceci would agree to anything.

Mila needed to tell someone about what she'd learned. Now. It was too much for her to process by herself.

They had arrived in Morannez town centre. They queued to get off the bus. It had stopped raining and the day was brightening. Ani jumped up on a low wall and, arms outstretched, balanced her way along it, pretending she was stepping along a catwalk. Mila called Carter Jackson. She told him she needed to see him as soon as possible.

So keen was she to share the news, that her voice tripped over the words as she told him she knew the name of the seventh killer.

55

They convened at the Toussaint's office. Ani couldn't wait to show Ceci her new second-hand clothes – Ceci approved on all fronts, and said she'd like to take her beautiful granddaughter out and treat her to a late lunch so that she could interrogate her about the sleepout. This left Carter and Mila free to 'catch up', as Ceci put it.

In the time it took Ceci and Ani to walk to the end of the route de Rosnuel, Carter had already carried out a sweeping internet search on Alban Hugo. If he *was* Dragan Brđanin, he'd done a superb job of burying his former identity. Alban Hugo had a birth certificate, school records, even a medical record of having his tonsils removed when he was eight years old. Everything appeared genuine, from his driving licence to his education and employment history.

'It has to be him, though, doesn't it?' asked Mila.

'It all fits,' said Carter. 'But we have no proof.'

'We know that his wife bought the Fendi suit she wore to trick Ceci.'

'She bought *a* Fendi suit. We'd never be able to prove it was the exact one. We need concrete evidence that Alban Hugo is Dragan Brđanin. We need Gosia's book.'

'If we're right, Hugo took it from the horsebox after he murdered Gosia. He'll have got rid of it by now.'

'Got rid of it how?' Carter asked.

'I don't know. Burned it?'

'You can't burn household waste outdoors in France.'

'The man who took Gosia's horsebox had a fire at his small-holding.'

'Yeah, but the Hugos live on a modern estate,' said Carter, nodding at his computer. 'There's nowhere he could have had a fire without drawing attention to himself.'

'Torn out the pages and burned then on an inside fire, then.'

'It's an eco-estate. No fireplaces. And he wouldn't risk dumping it because anyone could have found it. For the same reason, I doubt he'd have put it in a bin or taken it to a recycling centre.'

'Do you think he might still have it, then?'

'I think there's a good chance,' said Carter. 'If you were Alban-Hugo-slash-Dragan-Brđanin, where would you hide a big old book full of stuff that could ruin your life while you waited for an oppor-tunity to dispose of it?'

Mila thought about this for a little while. 'Who else is at home with Hugo? Just Joséphine?'

'Two daughters, the older daughter's boyfriend and two small grandchildren.'

'I wouldn't hide it at home, in that case.'

'Me neither. The dig site?'

'It wouldn't be safe. There might be lockers but they wouldn't be that big or that secure.'

'The school,' said Carter. 'It's closed for the holidays. Monsieur Hugo's bound to have his own office. And nobody would think it odd if he was coming and going because he's managing the educational side of the Kyern dig.'

56

The International School was housed inside a concrete, brutalist building five kilometres out of Morannez town, off one of the bigger roads that, after the school, opened into a retail park with an adjoining entertainment complex.

Mila had been there before for open evenings but had not paid much attention to her surroundings.

She had certainly never before arrived riding pillion on a Harley-Davidson WLA motorbike.

'It's lucky we can sneak up like this,' she said, dismounting the bike and pulling the stupidly tight helmet off her head. 'Nobody must ever hear you coming.'

'Funny,' said Carter.

Mila shook out her hair. She didn't want to admit that she had enjoyed the ride, but actually, once she'd overcome the anxiety she felt both at being on a motorbike and sitting so close to Carter, it had been thrilling. 'Just relax into the corners,' Carter had told her, as she gripped the handles on the back of the seat to avoid having to put her arms around him. 'Don't think about what's happening, just go with the bike,' which was exactly what she'd done and it had been gloriously exhilarating. Now they were here at the school which was undergoing a summer refurbishment. Contractors' vans were dotted about the car park; doors and windows were open, and there was a bustling atmosphere; the sound of hammering and sawing mixed with songs coming from radios.

'It's good that all these people are about,' said Carter. 'We won't stand out so much getting into the school. Act confident.'

They walked across the car park towards the main entrance, hidden amongst scaffolding poles and went inside without being challenged.

'Where now?' asked Carter.

'I don't know.'

Eventually they found themselves in a corridor where the teachers had their offices, each door marked with a small plaque with the occupant's name.

'They're locked,' Mila said, surreptitiously trying a handle as they went past.

'Not a problem,' said Carter.

'You know how to open locked doors?'

'It's obligatory in my former line of work.'

'There,' whispered Mila. They walked past a door labelled *Monsieur Hugo, A.*

'Keep going.'

They continued until they reached the far end of the corridor, when they stopped and looked back.

'No security cameras,' said Carter.

'So how do we do this?'

'I'll deal with the lock; you stand behind me. Cough if anyone comes.'

They walked slowly back to the door to Monsieur Hugo's office. Carter reached for the handle but before he could open it the door swung open. Alban Hugo was standing on the other side.

'Hello,' he said. 'Were you looking for me?'

* * *

'I thought I was going to have a heart attack,' Mila told Luke later, on the phone.

'What did you say to Hugo?'

'That I wanted to thank him for helping me with Emily at the dig site.'

'Did he buy that?'

'I think so.'

'So, you didn't get into his office?'

'No. But we waited outside until he came out. He didn't have the book with him, so if it was in the office, it's still there.'

'Hopefully the police will have opened an investigation then they can go in and search the place.'

'Yes,' said Mila quietly.

'You did go and talk to the police today, didn't you?' asked Luke. 'Like you promised you would.'

There hadn't been time. Mila fumbled for an excuse but at that moment Ani came downstairs wearing her new clothes. She did a little dance for Mila. Mila tucked the phone between her chin and shoulder and clapped her hands.

'Luke, I've got to go. I'm going to walk into town with Ani. She's going to a stay-awake-out.'

'A what?'

'I'll explain later.'

57

Mila and Ani arrived at the end of the wooden pier just after 9 p.m. Already a dozen or so of Ani's classmates were gathered around, chatting noisily. Mila wished with all her heart that Pernille was there, Pernille who exuded confidence, who had perfected the art of the withering look, who was an unstintingly loyal friend to Ani. But she wasn't and Ani was determined to do this and Mila was proud of her. Ani looked around but there was no sign of Romeo or JP – yet.

Ani had brought a rucksack with a sleeping bag rolled up beneath it. Inside the rucksack was a sweater, a waterproof cagoule and a pair of cashmere socks that Mila had found in the bottom of Sophie's wardrobe. Mila didn't want Ani to feel cold. She'd also packed a cheese and pickle roll, two chocolate bars, a banana and chunks of cheese and olives in a small pot.

Ani hadn't brought a towel or a costume. She would not be joining her classmates for a midnight swim and had promised Mila she wouldn't feel pressured to do so.

'Nobody could make me go in the sea,' she said. 'Ever. You *know* that. So, stop worrying.'

Some of the fathers had come up to the beach earlier and set up a line of pagoda tents with blankets spread over the sand, battery-operated lights, bottles of water and bowls of snacks. A music system was playing at a volume a fraction too low to annoy the townspeople. One of the dads had even lit a small fire in a portable fire pit and was offering the kids the opportunity to grill sausages or toast marshmallows over the flames if they wanted to do so. It reminded Mila of an informal Scout camp and she was relieved by the level of parental supervision.

A couple of the girls, who Mila recognised, came up to Ani and started chatting to her in French. There was giggling and whispering, admiration of Ani's new clothes.

'Shall we put your bag in one of the pagodas, Ani?' Mila asked.

Ani turned to her aunt and smiled, and, in the firelight, it was such a happy smile that Mila wanted to hold Ani and tell her how proud she was. Ani looked like any other teenager. Young, yes, and vulnerable, but brimming with potential. Her life lay ahead of her; the trauma of the last year would gradually become a smaller and smaller part of her life. In that moment, Mila knew that, so long as she and Ceci took great care of Ani, the girl would be okay.

'I'll be fine now, Mila,' Ani said. 'You can go.'

'Okay,' Mila said.

She didn't go very far. She walked to the bar across the road, went inside and ordered a coffee and a glass of water. She hadn't had much sleep the night before; she'd need as much caffeine as she could consume to keep her going now.

There were only a few seats left. She asked if she might join a couple of women at a table outside and they made space for her. They were both in their early forties and although she didn't recognise them, she soon realised they were parents of sleepouters too, doing what she was doing, observing the goings-on on the beach. It was noisy in the bar and she was weary and worrying about Carter going back to the International School on his own to break in and search for Gosia's book. Something was niggling at her, something she should have taken into account but hadn't. She was thinking about this when a third woman joined the two already at the table and said clearly in French, 'That poor little orphan girl is down there on the beach.'

Mila was slouched inside a hoodie, her hair hiding her face. She hunched a little lower.

'Really? I didn't think she was allowed out of her aunt's sight!'

Mila sat very still, with the rim of her glass of water touching her lips.

'Apparently the aunt is packing the poor child off to boarding school any day now,' the first woman continued. 'It's not even local. It's in Switzerland!'

'It's so hard on her! First, she loses her parents, then everything else is taken from her too!'

Mila stood up and walked out of the bar, her head held high and her cheeks burning.

* * *

The night wore on, painfully slowly. Mila walked up and down the seafront, her arms crossed over her chest, watching from a distance. For a long time, Ani remained in the company of the two girls who'd first come to talk to her. Mila saw them, arms linked, crossing the road and looking in through the window of the gelateria. Some of the boys got a little rowdy at one point, pushing one another into the water off the shallow end of the pier, but the firepit father was there in moments, good-humouredly putting a stop to the trouble.

At midnight there were fireworks and a group of the youngsters stripped down to their swimsuits, held hands, and ran into the sea, the bolder ones diving into the black water.

Mila, standing on the seafront in the shadows, watched and envied those kids their innocence, and their joy.

There was still no sign of JP or Romeo, but Ani was down there with her classmates and they all seemed to be having fun. Poor Emily Perry, who had been looking forward to the sleepout, must be at home with her grieving mother and her grandmother, no doubt trying to make sense of a world that had imploded.

Mila thought of Alban Hugo: war criminal turned pillar of the community. Malgorzata Orić and Tim Perry weren't the only victims of this tragedy.

Had they known one another, Tim Perry and Dragan Brđanin, back in the old days, before the Balkan War? While she was teaching at Cambridge, Malgorzata might well have invited her star student back to her home, to see the beautiful place where she lived, to meet her husband and son, to get a taste of the culture. If Tim recognised Dragan, then, almost certainly, Dragan would have recognised Tim. It was unlikely either would have directly addressed the subject of Alban Hugo's previous identity. Probably Tim Perry had got in touch with Malgorzata on the quiet, and Alban Hugo had hoped for the best. But when Gosia had turned up in her horsebox, he must have known he'd been outed. Had she underestimated the seventh killer? Had she assumed she was safe because Tim knew the truth, never realising that the truth, rather than protecting them, had placed them both in danger?

It didn't matter now. Alban Hugo's lies would soon be exposed. As soon as Carter had the book safe, he was going to call Mila. They would look at it together to make sure their theory was correct and deliver it to the police in the morning. She looked forward to this, and also to telling Luke that she'd done as he'd said.

Mila yawned. She walked down onto the beach and found a lounger on its side. She tipped it upright, put it against the wall, and lay on it, staring at the stars in the sky above. She yawned again.

She closed her eyes, just for a second, and the second turned into a delicious minute and then she thought she'd let herself have a tiny sleep.

A teeny, tiny sleep while she was waiting for Carter to call.

58

Mila was woken by the vibrating of the phone beneath her cheek. She was so disorientated that it took her a moment to remember where she was and why. She fumbled for the phone, dropped it in the sand, picked it up, dusted it down and then answered.

'Hello?'

'It's me, Carter. I've been calling for ages.'

'Sorry, I fell asleep. Did you get the book?'

'Yep. It was in Hugo's office in an IKEA bag. I think he must've been planning to scoot back and pick it up tonight.'

Mila sat up and looked up and down the beach. A bundle of young teenagers were gathered in and around the pagodas. Some were sitting around the fire pit. She couldn't pick out Ani, or the two girls she'd been with.

'Did you look inside?'

'It's all there. Everything. It's not in English, but there are pictures of Hugo then and now – cuttings, diagrams, even sketches. Gosia was a thorough investigator.'

Mila stood up. She wandered towards the pagodas.

'Where are you?' Carter asked.

'On the beach. Supervising Ani. Except I can't see her. Where are you?'

'At the office. I thought the book would be safest here. We can copy the most important bits and pass the whole thing on to the police tomorrow.'

'I've got to go,' she said. 'Thanks, Carter, for getting the book.'

'Pleasure,' he replied.

Mila checked the time. It was gone 2 a.m. She had lost her shoes. She walked barefoot through the cool sand. She spotted JP and Romeo, naked except for swimming shorts, messing about in the shallow water. She trotted over to them and waved.

'JP! Hi! I'm looking for Ani! Have you seen her?'

'She was dancing with the other girls.'

'Where?'

'Over there!' He gestured to where the music system had been set up. Music was still playing but the volume was quieter now.

'Was she okay?'

'Yeah!'

Mila glanced at Romeo. He smiled his charming smile.

'All right, thanks.'

Mila walked to the firepit. The two girls Ani had been with earlier were there, huddled together like dormice, looking as if they'd rather be in bed.

She went up to them.

'Hi, I'm Ani's aunt. Do you know where she is?'

'She fell asleep,' said the taller of the girls.

'Where?'

'Over there.' The girl pointed in the general direction of the pier.

'Is she okay?'

The other girl looked sheepish. 'She might have had some cider.'

'Might have?'

'She might have been a bit sick too.'

'Shit,' said Mila.

'It's okay. One of the teachers is looking after her.'

Mila jogged back up the beach, cursing herself for falling asleep. She took out her phone and called Ani. The phone rang and rang but there was no answer.

'Ani!' she called.

She zig-zagged up and down the beach, checking every beach chair, every shadow to see if it was Ani sleeping, but she couldn't find her.

Oh God, what if she'd gone into the water?

She wouldn't go in the water.

What if she was drunk and she went into the water? What if she was sick on her new clothes and went into the sea to clean herself up and...

A teacher is looking after her! She's safe!

'Ani! *Ani!*'

She called Carter.

'Can you come down to the beach? I can't find Ani. Can you come now? Oh! Hold on, there's an incoming call! It's her phone, hold on, don't go away... Hello? Ani?'

'Ms Shepherd?' A man's voice.

Mila stopped running. She stood stock still. She felt as if her heart had stopped. There was a burning pain in her legs.

She remembered now what it was that she should have realised earlier: that whoever was responsible for Gosia's death had known that she was looking into it; that they had seen her post on the internet forum; that they had come to the sea house and looked on her laptop. That as soon as Monsieur Hugo opened the door to his office at the school earlier, and saw Mila standing outside it, he would have known she was onto him.

'Alban Hugo?' she asked.

'Spot on,' said the voice. 'No need to worry, Ms Shepherd. Ani is with me.'

59

'Is she all right?' Mila asked.

The hand holding the phone was trembling, but it was important to be calm, important to keep her voice normal.

'Is Ani all right, Monsieur Hugo?' she asked again.

'She's sleeping. She didn't realise how strong the local cider is. It's an easy mistake to make; a rite of passage for the Morannez kids.'

Mila had reached the beach end of the wooden pier. She stood with one hand on the closest upright and tried to untangle her panic from the rational part of her brain.

'Where are you?' she asked. 'Where's Ani?'

'At the far end of the pier.'

Mila looked to her left. She saw a blinking light a long way away.

She thought of the deep water.

She thought of Charlie down there somewhere in that water. She thought of Sophie's body washed ashore. She remembered how frightened Ani was of that water. She tried to stay calm.

'Ani is lying on the boards,' said Monsieur Hugo. 'She's deeply asleep. She'll be fine as long as she remains still.'

Mila had a flashback to the Bosnian video: the boys, face down, on the floor of the cave, the other boys prodding them with their feet. She remembered the callous eyes of the curly-haired leader of the killers. Anyone who had it in them to murder his friends in that way wouldn't think twice about pushing Ani into the sea.

'What do you want?' Mila asked. 'What do you want me to do?'

'I want the book back. And please, *please*, Ms Shepherd, don't play games with me. You know which book I mean, and I know you have it.'

'My colleague has it.'

'Then tell him to bring it to you, here at the pier. And then you bring it to me. Just you. I have a very good view of the pier from where I am. I'll know if anyone's with you.'

'Okay,' said Mila.

'Bring it now.'

'It'll take him a little time to get here.'

'Five minutes, then. Call me on this number when you're on your way.'

60

Carter was still holding on the line.

Mila went back to him.

'Hugo's here,' she said. 'He's at the end of the pier. He's got Ani. He wants the book back. You have to bring it here, Carter – now!'

'I haven't copied anything yet.'

'You can't. There isn't time. He'll push Ani in the water if we don't get the book back to him in minutes.'

Carter was silent for a moment.

'We know he'll do it,' Mila said. 'He doesn't care. He's killed two people over this book already. If Ani goes into the sea she'll drown and everyone will say she was drunk and it was another tragic accident. He's manipulated it so that it'll look like an accident. He's staged it all again!'

'Okay,' said Carter, 'I'm coming.'

'Bring the book,' she said. 'Don't try to trick him. It's only a book. I can't let Ani go into the water.' Her voice was high-pitched, almost hysterical.

'Okay,' said Carter, 'Mila, it's okay. You're right, it's only a book. I'm on my way.'

Mila walked along the beach towards the firepit. She turned and walked back. She strained her ears.

Please, please, hurry up.

She checked the time; turned and paced again.

God's sake, Carter, where are you?

At last – at first she couldn't be sure, but then she was – she heard the growling sound of the Harley-Davidson's engine disturbing the cooling night air.

She ran towards it, and there was the bike, pulling up on the seafront, its headlight illuminating swathes of beach as Carter found a space for it. He was carrying a large, blue IKEA bag on his lap. Mila had reached him before he'd taken off his helmet. She leaned over and took the bag. It was heavier than she'd expected. She looked inside, to be certain, and there was Gosia's book.

'Wait! Mila! I'll come with you,' said Carter.

'You can't,' said Mila. 'He said just me. He can see down the pier and he'll know if there's more than one person. I can't take any chances with Ani. *I can't!*'

'He's a psychopath. He might throw her in the water anyway.'

'Not until I get there, and if he does it when I'm there, I'll go in after her. I'm a good swimmer.'

The weight of the book in the bag pulled at her shoulders. She held it in her arms as if it were a large, heavy baby.

'You can't go on your own,' Carter said.

'I can. I'll be okay.'

'I'll wait here,' said Carter. 'Call me if...'

'Yeah,' said Mila.

She climbed over the barrier that said *Danger!* and began to walk, barefoot, along the wooden pier. After a little while, when she was far enough along to see only water when she looked down, she stopped and took the phone from her pocket and called Ani's number.

'It's Mila,' she said, when Alban Hugo answered. 'I'm on the pier. I'm on my own.'

'I can see you. Do you have the book?'

'Yes.'

'Come here then. Tread carefully. We don't want any accidents at this stage.'

It was an old pier and some of the wood was rotten. Planks had come loose and fallen into the sea, leaving gaps. There was no handrail, nothing to hold on to, only the light that spilled out from the seafront to guide Mila. It was difficult to balance, but she knew she mustn't fall. She mustn't drop the book into the sea. She mustn't put a foot wrong, not until she was with Ani and had brought the girl back to safety.

Slowly, slowly, Mila made progress along the pier. The wood still held residual heat from the day's sunshine. The sea moved gently around its legs, swelling and falling. It was some distance now back to the beach. She could no longer hear music, or any human sound at all; only the movement of the water. If Mila had to swim back with Ani, would she make it? She wasn't sure. Probably not. It was too far and the water too cold, and Ani would be heavy, dragged down by her new clothes. But at least they'd be together. At least Mila wouldn't have abandoned Ani; the girl wouldn't be on her own.

The board beneath her foot snapped and broke and there was a splash as the wood fell into the water below. Mila lost her balance, stumbled, almost dropped the bag, but held on to it.

She waited until her heart had resumed a bearable rhythm, then, tentatively, she took another step forward.

* * *

Alban Hugo, or Dragan Brđanin, was waiting at the end of the pier: a big, bulky silhouette against the sky. The moon had set a long time ago but the stars still shone and out to sea the lights of faraway ships pricked the darkness.

For a moment Mila thought Ani wasn't there, but then she saw her, a small figure lying, as the man had said she was, close to the end of the pier with nothing to stop her falling if she were to move another few centimetres to her right. She looked like a bundle of clothes. If she so much as rolled over, she would tumble from the pier and into the sea water.

'Good evening,' said Dragan Brđanin. Whatever essence of the teacher had been there before was gone now. The man in front of Mila exuded cruelty.

'Here's the book,' Mila said, placing the bag on the boards. Dragan opened the bag to peer inside, using the light from his phone to check it contained Gosia's book.

'Where's your phone?' he asked Mila.

She gave it to him and he tossed it into the water. It disappeared with the smallest splash.

'Where's your colleague? The lone ranger?'

'He's at the other end of the pier.'

'Good. Lie down.'

'What?'

'I said, *lie down*. Face down. On the boards.'

'No,' said Mila.

'No?'

The man pressed the toe of his foot against Ani's waist. She moved a fraction towards the water. It would take no effort at all to flip her over the edge. Mila knew then that he knew she had seen the video. He knew exactly what he was doing. He knew how to make her afraid.

'Lie down,' Monsieur Hugo said. 'I won't ask again.'

Mila dropped to her knees, and then she crawled forwards until she was flat on the boards. She wriggled sideways, so that her body was touching Ani's. She felt, through the skin of her arm, the warmth of Ani's arm. She could feel her niece's pulse. *If we die*, she thought, *we'll die together.*

'Put your hands behind your back.'

Mila did as he said. She thought of Tomas and the other boys in the quarry lying side by side. She felt oddly calm. She could hear the sea moving below her and feel Ani breathing beside her. She thought, *I did my best*, and Sophie whispered in her ear, *I know, ma chère, I know.*

He bound her hands together. Her cheek was pressed against the board; it smelled of dry wood and saltwater. She could feel her body doing its work: heart beating, blood pumping, lungs inflating. She could feel Ani beside her. The man moved around her. She felt the pier creak as he moved.

Sophie? she whispered.

It's okay, Mila, I'm here.

She closed her eyes and waited. Sophie and Ani, beside her, at the end of the pier, in the dark. She waited to die.

There was more creaking. A slight lurching of the boards.

Then the peace of the night was interrupted by the sound of an engine. Mila tried to raise her head. She saw a bright light, a disturbance in the sea. A speedboat pulled away from the end of the pier. Mila smelled the tang of fuel, heard the water sloshing against the legs of the pier in the boat's wake.

Ceci held a glass of water to Ani's mouth. Ani tried to drink but it was as if her tongue and her lips weren't working properly and most of the water spilled down her front.

'Sorry,' she murmured.

'Darling, you have nothing to be sorry for,' said Ceci, stroking the girl's hair. 'You've been so brave and we're all so proud of you.'

Mila nodded her agreement. She had a lump in her throat. She was struggling to believe that they'd actually made it back to Ceci's because she had thought she and Ani were going to die.

She'd been helpless at the end of the pier. She couldn't so much as roll over, couldn't hold onto Ani, couldn't pick her up, couldn't move her, was terrified the girl might wake and panic, roll into the sea and drown, or simply move in her sleep and fall into the water – that her death might, in the end, be caused by something so mundane as a trapped nerve. Mila, without the use of her arms, wouldn't have been able to help her.

But Carter had finally come. It had felt like hours, but it wasn't that long. He'd heard the boat pulling away from the end of the pier, and had come to find them. He'd sat beside Ani, between her and the pier edge, forming a protective barrier. He'd cut the tie that bound Mila's hands with the blade of the flick knife he kept in his pocket, and helped her to sit up, and then to stand. When he was confident that Mila was capable of making her own way back along the treacherous pier, he'd told her to follow him, to step where he trod. He had carried Ani in his arms. Mila, bracing herself to see him fall, had been amazed at the grace of the man, his strength and his calmness. Sophie had been with her, whispering encouragement at every step.

Back at the beach, Ani had begun to rouse. She'd been sick and they'd given her some water and then Carter had carried her again, all the way to Ceci's apartment. And here they were, in Ceci's beautiful living room, a ragged, careworn little group amongst the rugs and the silk-covered furniture; exhausted and wretched but alive.

And safe.

Dawn was breaking beyond the window.

Mila, wrapped in a blanket, sipped peppermint tea.

Ani was confused. She couldn't remember anything beyond being dropped off at the beach and chatting to her girlfriends.

Ceci persuaded Ani to go with her to the bathroom. She promised Ani that she'd feel better after a warm bath.

Carter and Mila went to stand on the balcony, to watch the dawn.

'Dragan Brđanin has got away,' Mila said. 'After all that effort, all those deaths, all those lives ruined, he's gone. And he's taken the evidence that would have convicted him.'

'Doesn't matter,' said Carter. 'Nothing really matters except that you and Ani are safe.'

But it had mattered to Gosia.

It had mattered to Professor Perry.

It had mattered to the families of the boys who were murdered.

It did matter.

It did.

62

WEDNESDAY, 24 AUGUST

Ani and Mila were in the kitchen. They were scanning the photographs of Sophie and Charlie that they'd picked out of the boot boxes. They were going to enlarge them and then print them, not for an album, but to stick up around the sea house ready for the party they were hosting to commemorate the lives of Ani's parents.

They'd decided to call it a party because that was what it was going to be: a celebration. They were going to have music and dancing and food and drink and lights in the garden. They were going to talk about Sophie and Charlie and raise a toast to them. Anyone who'd known them and cared about them was invited to come along and join in.

Mila had called her father, Patrick, and asked him to come. He'd been fond of Sophie; and she'd liked him; maybe even loved him. But Patrick was in South America, making a film with an up-and-coming Argentinian director and it was too short notice for him to change his schedule.

Mila was disappointed but she understood.

'Are you going to wear your Stella McCartney tonight, darling?' Mila asked Ani in a false, posh voice. She lifted a picture of Sophie from the printer. It was a close up of Sophie and Ani's faces, both of them cross-eyed, hamming it up for the camera.

'Yes, I think I might,' Ani answered in the same tone. 'How about you, darling?'

'Oh, I might throw on the Chanel,' said Mila. She smiled at Ani, then reached across the table, took hold of her hand, raised it to her lips and kissed it.

I love you, she thought.

Tell her! cried Sophie.

But Mila couldn't.

* * *

Because it was a day for remembering those who were gone, once they were ready for the party, but before anyone came, Ani and Mila, all dressed in their best clothes, picked some flowers from the garden and then got on their bicycles and cycled up to the place where Gosia's van had been parked.

'Where shall we scatter the flowers?' Mila asked.

'All around,' said Ani.

So that's what they did.

'Tell me about her and why she was here,' Ani said. 'The truth. You promised you'd always tell me the truth.'

Mila said, 'Oh, Ani, it's complicated.'

'Just tell me the important things.'

'There was a war,' said Mila, 'a horrible war. Some young men killed Gosia's son, Tomas, and other people's sons too and after the war, they ran away and hid. Gosia tracked the killers down. The last one was here in Morannez. It was Emily's father, Professor Perry, who tipped her off.'

'And the murderer was Monsieur Hugo?'

'Yes. Gosia had all the evidence she needed for him to be

convicted in that great big book of hers: like she told you, it was her work. But now the evidence has disappeared, and so has Monsieur Hugo.'

'What about the copies of the book?'

'Gosia might have made copies on her phone, but Monsieur Hugo stole the phone too.'

'No, he didn't.'

'He did, sweetheart. The phone wasn't in the van when the police came and searched it after Gosia's death.'

'That's because Gosia didn't keep it in the van,' said Ani.

'What?'

Ani spoke very slowly. 'Gosia didn't keep her phone in the van. Not while she was sleeping. She hid it in the hole in that tree over there in case anybody came along and robbed her during the night.'

'She hid her phone in the hole in the tree?' Mila repeated stupidly.

'Yes. She asked me to put it there the night I fell off my bike, before you came. She said: "It'll be one job less for me to do after you've gone home."'

Mila stared at Ani. 'Is the phone still there, Ani?'

Ani shrugged. 'How should I know?'

Mila exhaled slowly. 'Well, let's have a look.'

63

TUESDAY, 6 SEPTEMBER

In Morannez town, the boys packing up the fairground rides on the seafront whistled as they worked. The girl in the gelateria had her elbows on the counter and her chin in her hands. She hadn't sold a single ice cream all day and was staring out at the horizon, daydreaming. The Sohars' clothes shop was still open but the rails that usually stood outside, hung with linen shirts and hippy dresses, were empty. The revolving rack of old postcards had been moved from outside the gift shop, which was closed.

Mila Shepherd cycled through the back lanes, past the menhirs and dolmens, between the trees whose branches were hung with leaves in every shade of green and gold and yellow and brown, past fields of sunflowers, their heads still faithfully following the course of the sun even though the petals were withering and the seeds had become food for the finches.

On the lines that were strung between the telegraph poles, the swallows lined up like tiny sentinels, tweeting and chattering, building up to the moment when they would take to the air for the last time that year, fly up high and start their journey south to Africa.

Two weeks earlier, on 24 August, the anniversary of the accident in which Sophie Cooper died, Sophie's daughter, Ani, had stood on tiptoe and put her hand into the hole in the old oak tree where Malgorzata Orić hid her phone every night, and she extracted a plastic bag. The bag was grubby, but it had kept its integrity, and remained watertight. The phone, once it was charged, had sprung back to life.

Mila and Carter had contacted the International Criminal Tribunal for the former Yugoslavia and a representative had flown out to see them. She had examined the phone and found the evidence that Gosia had copied onto it.

Monsieur Hugo had been arrested in Amsterdam where he'd been trying to catch a flight out to Australia. His family hadn't known anything about his past. His wife, Joséphine, refused to believe any of it. She was convinced that her husband had been set up by shady figures who were members of a conspiratorial elite. This was why she'd agreed to wear the Fendi suit and act as fake Mrs Perry, in order to discredit Professor Perry, who she truly believed was a fantasist out to ruin her husband. After Hugo's arrest, Joséphine's daughters had persuaded their mother to go and stay with family friends in the Loire.

Mila stopped at the top of the hill and looked down over the valley. The afternoon light was painting the Kyern dolmen apricot-gold. A few late tourists were taking photographs of themselves with the stones as a backdrop.

The dig was finished, the tents and marquee gone. Two men in yellow jackets were standing in the middle of the field, close to the spot where Professor Perry's body had been found, consulting paper plans. Work on the new restaurant and leisure complex would soon begin.

The police were investigating Professor Perry's death as a murder, not a suicide. Mila hadn't spoken to Catherine Perry, but she'd sent a card and flowers to her home in England. Ani had messaged Emily. The two girls were planning a reunion. When the professor's body was eventually released back to the family, Ceci had suggested that they all go to England for the funeral.

A pair of buzzards was circling high in the sky above the holiday park. Beyond, the sea was green-blue and autumn-choppy. Mila pulled up her jacket collar and cycled on.

Luke was coming over this weekend, definitely.

His murder inquiry was finished so he was taking a few days' leave. Mila thought they could perhaps visit Morlaix, or Quimper, or Concarneau, or another of the region's exquisite little fishing ports. Perhaps they could eat out in one of the excellent seafront restaurants that were quiet now the summer holidaymakers were gone and afterwards they could wrap up warm, drink a glass of liqueur at a table on the cobbles and watch the moon rise over the sea. They could hold hands, kiss on stony beaches where the salt-water foam whipped against their faces. They could enjoy one another's company.

Mila hadn't explicitly said to Luke that she wasn't coming home to Bristol, but he knew. There was no need to explain. Mila didn't know where this left their relationship and, for now, it didn't matter. What was important was that Ani was where she needed to be, and that was here, in Morannez, in the sea house. Now Mila was no longer a full-time employee of Toussaint's Agency, she could concentrate on editing her book while Ani was at school – not the Swiss boarding school, but the international school on the outskirts of Morannez town where she'd always been a pupil. Mila had met with Ani's teacher and her head of year. They had put together a plan to make sure Ani was safe from bullying going forward. They had included Ani in the discussions and would be taking care to make sure she didn't suffer any more.

As for Carter, he had found a studio flat to rent close to the estate where the Perrys had lived. It wasn't great but it was better than the caravan and it was on a complex that had a shared pool and other facilities. His son, Harry, was due to come to stay for the first time next week. Carter had enlisted Ani's help in preparing Harry's room. It now resembled a Bedouin tent with a distinctive purple and black colour theme as designed by Ani. Carter said Harry would love it.

Carter and Mila hadn't talked about the past; not yet. But Carter had said something odd when he and Mila were moving one of the single beds out of the sea house, ready to take to Carter's apartment. They had been talking about Carter's decision to return to France and he'd said his mind had been made up when he heard about Sophie.

'But you didn't find out she had died until you came here,' Mila reminded him. 'That first day we saw one another again, at the restaurant, remember? Ceci told you.'

Carter had laughed it off. He said he'd meant to say 'Emmanuelle', not 'Sophie'. It was when he heard about Emmanuelle, his wife, moving back to France that he'd made up his mind to come was what he'd intended to say.

Mila hadn't thought too much about it at the time, but over the last few days she'd kept replaying the exchange in her mind. She knew it would have to be addressed at some point. She did not trust him.

And something else was bothering her too.

It was the memory of what Sophie had whispered to her that July evening last year in Morannez town. She had a secret, she'd said. *It's about someone we used to know.*

She had died before she'd divulged the secret and now it was plaguing Mila like a mosquito in a dark room.

Who had Sophie been talking about?

Who?

Mila turned in to the lane that led to the sea house. Fallen leaves swept the track ahead of her; a rabbit scooted into its burrow and the birds were calling. She could see the sheets blowing on the washing line in the garden; apples were ripening on the trees. Berthaud jumped up onto the green gate and stretched her body into an arch and the wind carried laughter from the woodland where Pernille, Ani and Romeo were collecting blackberries. Mila thought she glimpsed someone, a man, disappearing into the fringes of the forest, but it was probably only the wind shaking the bramble bushes.

It had happened a few times lately; she catching sight of someone who nobody else saw. Ceci, pragmatic as always, had suggested she go for an eye test. Whatever. There was no need to worry. Luke would be with her soon and Patrick had promised to visit as soon as he'd finished filming in La Rioja.

The wind blew cool. Mila pulled her jacket tight. She could feel the nights drawing in, the weather changing, the year turning.

'Summer's over,' she said to Sophie. 'It's gone.'

Sophie sighed and her breath was like the breeze whispering through the turning leaves.

It will come again, she said to Mila. *It always does.*

ACKNOWLEDGMENTS

With this book, I owe an even bigger-than-normal debt of gratitude to the team at Boldwood Books. I so appreciate your hard work and support, as well as your patience and kindness.

So firstly, a massive 'thank you' to my wonderful editor and lovely friend, Sarah Ritherdon. Also thank you to the truly brilliant Boldwood team, especially Nia and Claire, but *all of you.* Thank you to Becca Allen and Rose Fox for your amazing editorial work and for putting up with me changing everything, all the time. Thank you to Becky Glibbery for designing the beautiful cover. Thank you to the Boldwood authors, and all the other authors, most of whom I've never met in person, but all of whom I consider friends. Thank you to the teams responsible for making audio and print versions of the book. Thank you to the librarians, book bloggers, sellers, promoters, enthusiasts and influencers. Thank you to RNA. Thank you to every person who's read any of my books and to readers, everywhere. Thank you to everyone, involved in any way, with the publishing industry. Thank you to my friends in person, on Facebook and Twitter who help make writing fun.

And lastly, thank you to my incredible agent and friend, Marianne Gunn O'Connor. Even after ten books, I still can't quite believe my luck that you took me on. Thank you to the constantly kind and patient Pat Lynch, Vicki Satlow and all those involved in the associated agencies.

You are the best and I'm so lucky to have you in my life.

MORE FROM LOUISE DOUGLAS

We hope you enjoyed reading *The Lost Notebook*. If you did, please leave a review.

If you'd like to gift a copy, this book is also available as an ebook, digital audio download and audiobook CD.

Sign up to Louise Douglas' mailing list for news, competitions and updates on future books.

http://bit.ly/LouiseDouglasNewsletter

The House By The Sea another chilling and captivating novel from Louise Douglas is available now.

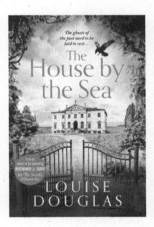

ABOUT THE AUTHOR

Louise Douglas is the bestselling and brilliantly reviewed author of 6 novels including *The Love of my Life* and *Missing You* - a RNA award winner. *The Secrets Between Us* was a Richard and Judy Book Club pick. She lives in the West Country.

Follow Louise on social media:

facebook.com/Louise-Douglas-Author-340228039335215
twitter.com/louisedouglas3
bookbub.com/authors/louise-douglas

Boldw∞d

Boldwood Books is an award-winning fiction publishing company seeking out the best stories from around the world.

Find out more at www.boldwoodbooks.com

Join our reader community for brilliant books, competitions and offers!

Follow us
@BoldwoodBooks
@BookandTonic

Sign up to our weekly deals newsletter

https://bit.ly/BoldwoodBNewsletter

Ingram Content Group UK Ltd.
Milton Keynes UK
UKHW040821270423
420808UK00003B/55

9 781838 892920